Big Timber
A Story Of The Northwest

By

Bertrand W. Sinclair

Double 9
BOOKS

Big Timber
A Story Of The Northwest
by Bertrand W. Sinclair

Copyright © 2024

All Rights reserved.

ISBN: 978-93-61155-25-3

Published by

DOUBLE 9 BOOKS

2/13-B, Ansari Road
Daryaganj, New Delhi – 110002
info@double9books.com
www.double9books.com
Tel. 011-40042856

ABOUT THE AUTHOR

Canadian novelist Bertrand William Sinclair is well-known for his tales and novels that are set in the untamed regions of the Canadian West. Sinclair, who was born in Edinburgh, Scotland, emigrated to Canada at an early age together with his family. He lived most of his life in the western provinces, and many of his creations reflect this local influence. Sinclair frequently addressed the environment, the hardships faced by those living in the woods, and the effects of industrial and economic activity on the terrain in his writing. His works portraying life in the forestry and wood business have gained him particular recognition, as they mirror his own experiences working in a variety of vocations before pursuing writing. His tales are renowned for their realism and realistic depiction of the difficulties people encounter in Canada's isolated and untamed regions. Even though Sinclair's readership declined in the second half of the 20th century, his writings are still worthwhile for fans of Western wilderness fiction and Canadian literature.

CONTENTS

CHAPTER I
GREEN FIELDS AND PASTURES NEW

The Imperial Limited lurched with a swing around the last hairpin curve of the Yale canyon. Ahead opened out a timbered valley,—narrow on its floor, flanked with bold mountains, but nevertheless a valley,—down which the rails lay straight and shining on an easy grade. The river that for a hundred miles had boiled and snarled parallel to the tracks, roaring through the granite sluice that cuts the Cascade Range, took a wider channel and a leisurely flow. The mad haste had fallen from it as haste falls from one who, with time to spare, sees his destination near at hand; and the turgid Fraser had time to spare, for now it was but threescore miles to tidewater. So the great river moved placidly—as an old man moves when all the headlong urge of youth is spent and his race near run.

On the river side of the first coach behind the diner, Estella Benton nursed her round chin in the palm of one hand, leaning her elbow on the window sill. It was a relief to look over a widening valley instead of a bare-walled gorge all scarred with slides, to see wooded heights lift green in place of barren cliffs, to watch banks of fern massed against the right of way where for a day and a night parched sagebrush, brown tumble-weed, and such scant growth as flourished in the arid uplands of interior British Columbia had streamed in barren monotony, hot and dry and still.

She was near the finish of her journey. Pensively she considered the end of the road. How would it be there? What manner of folk and country? Between her past mode of life and the new that she was hurrying toward lay the vast gulf of distance, of custom, of class even. It was bound to be crude, to be full of inconveniences and uncouthness. Her brother's letters had partly prepared her for that. Involuntarily she shrank from it, had been shrinking from it by fits and starts all the way, as flowers that thrive best in shady nooks shrink from hot sun and rude winds. Not that Estella Benton was particularly flower-like. On the contrary she was a healthy, vigorous-bodied young woman, scarcely to be described as beautiful, yet undeniably attractive. Obviously a daughter of the well-to-do, one of that American type which flourishes in families to which American politicians unctuously refer as the backbone of the nation. Outwardly, gazing riverward through the dusty pane, she bore herself with utmost serenity. Inwardly she was full of misgivings.

Four days of lonely travel across a continent, hearing the drumming clack of car wheels and rail joint ninety-six hours on end, acutely conscious that every hour of the ninety-six put its due quota of miles between the known and the unknown, may be either an adventure, a bore, or a calamity, depending altogether upon the individual point of view, upon conditioning circumstances and previous experience.

Estella Benton's experience along such lines was chiefly a blank and the conditioning circumstances of her present journey were somber enough to breed thought that verged upon the melancholy. Save for a natural buoyancy of spirit she might have wept her way across North America She had no tried standard by which to measure life's values for she had lived her twenty-two years wholly shielded from the human maelstrom, fed, clothed, taught, an untried product of home and schools. Her head was full of university lore, things she had read, a smattering of the arts and philosophy, liberal portions of academic knowledge, all tagged and sorted like parcels on a shelf to be reached when called for. Buried under these externalities the ego of her lay unaroused, an incalculable quantity.

All of which is merely by way of stating that Miss Estella Benton was a young woman who had grown up quite complacently in that station of life in which—to quote the Philistines—it had pleased God to place her, and that Chance had somehow, to her astonished dismay, contrived to thrust a spoke in the smooth-rolling wheels of destiny. Or was it Destiny? She had begun to think about that, to wonder if a lot that she had taken for granted as an ordered state of things was not, after all, wholly dependent upon Chance. She had danced and sung and played lightheartedly accepting a certain standard of living, a certain position in a certain set, a pleasantly ordered home life, as her birthright, a natural heritage. She had dwelt upon her ultimate destiny in her secret thoughts as foreshadowed by that of other girls she knew. The Prince would come, to put it in a nutshell. He would woo gracefully. They would wed. They would be delightfully happy. Except for the matter of being married, things would move along the same pleasant channels.

Just so. But a broken steering knuckle on a heavy touring car set things in a different light—many things. She learned then that death is no respecter of persons, that a big income may be lived to its limit with nothing left when the brain force which commanded it ceases to function. Her father produced perhaps fifteen to twenty thousand dollars a year in his brokerage business, and he had saved nothing. Thus at one stroke she was put on an equal footing with the stenographer in her father's office. Scarcely equal either, for the stenographer earned her bread and was technically equipped for the task, whereas Estella Benton had no training whatsoever, except in social usage. She did not yet fully realize just what had overtaken her. Things had happened so swiftly, to ruthlessly, that she still verged upon the incredulous. Habit clung fast. But she had begun to think, to try and establish some working relation between herself and things as she found them. She had discovered already that certain theories of human relations are not soundly established in fact.

She turned at last in her seat. The Limited's whistle had shrilled for a stop. At the next stop—she wondered what lay in store for her just beyond the next stop. While she dwelt mentally upon this, her hands were gathering up some few odds and ends of her belongings on the berth.

Across the aisle a large, smooth-faced young man watched her with covert admiration. When she had settled back with bag and suitcase locked and strapped on the opposite seat and was hatted and gloved, he leaned over and addressed her genially.

"Getting off at Hopyard? Happen to be going out to Roaring Springs?"

Miss Benton's gray eyes rested impersonally on the top of his head, traveled slowly down over the trim front of his blue serge to the polished tan Oxfords on his feet, and there was not in eyes or on countenance the slightest sign that she saw or heard him. The large young man flushed a vivid red.

Miss Benton was partly amused, partly provoked. The large young man had been her vis-à-vis at dinner the day before and at breakfast that morning. He had evinced a yearning for conversation each time, but it had been diplomatically confined to salt and other condiments, the weather and the scenery. Miss Benton had no objection to young men in general, quite the contrary. But she did not consider it quite the thing to countenance every amiable stranger.

Within a few minutes the porter came for her things, and the blast of the Limited's whistle warned her that it was time to leave the train. Ten minutes later the Limited was a vanishing object down an aisle slashed through a forest of great trees, and Miss Estella Benton stood on the plank platform of Hopyard station. Northward stretched a flat, unlovely vista of fire-blackened stumps. Southward, along track and siding, ranged a single row of buildings, a grocery store, a shanty with a huge sign proclaiming that it was a bank, dwelling, hotel and blacksmith shop whence arose the clang of hammered iron. A dirt road ran between town and station, with hitching posts at which farmers' nags stood dispiritedly in harness.

To the Westerner such spots are common enough; he sees them not as fixtures, but as places in a stage of transformation. By every side track and telegraph station on every transcontinental line they spring up, centers of productive activity, growing into orderly towns and finally attaining the dignity of cities. To her, fresh from trim farmsteads and rural communities that began setting their houses in order when Washington wintered at Valley Forge, Hopyard stood forth sordid and unkempt. And as happens to many a one in like case, a wave of sickening loneliness engulfed her, and she eyed the speeding Limited as one eyes a departing friend.

"How could one live in a place like this?" she asked herself.

But she had neither Slave of the Lamp at her beck, nor any Magic Carpet to transport her elsewhere. At any rate, she reflected, Hopyard was not her abiding-place. She hoped that her destination would prove more inviting.

Beside the platform were ranged two touring cars. Three or four of those who had alighted entered these. Their baggage was piled over the hoods, buckled on the running boards. The driver of one car approached her. "Hot Springs?" he inquired tersely.

She affirmed this, and he took her baggage, likewise her trunk check when she asked how that article would be transported to the lake. She had some idea of route and means, from her brother's written instruction, but she thought he might have been there to meet her. At least he would be at the Springs.

So she was whirled along a country road, jolted in the tonneau between a fat man from Calgary and a rheumatic dame on her way to take hot sulphur baths at St. Allwoods. She passed seedy farmhouses, primitive in construction, and big barns with moss plentifully clinging on roof and gable. The stretch of charred stumps was left far behind, but in every field of grain and vegetable and root great butts of fir and cedar rose amid the crops. Her first definitely agreeable impression of this land, which so far as she knew must be her home, was of those huge and numerous stumps contending with crops for possession of the fields. Agreeable, because it came to her forcibly that it must be a sturdy breed of men and women, possessed of brawn and fortitude and high courage, who made their homes here. Back in her country, once beyond suburban areas, the farms lay like the squares of a chess board, trim and orderly, tamely subdued to agriculture. Here, at first hand, she saw how man attacked the forest and conquered it. But the conquest was incomplete, for everywhere stood those stubborn roots, six and eight and ten feet across, contending with man for its primal heritage, the soil, perishing slowly as perish the proud remnants of a conquered race.

Then the cleared land came to a stop against heavy timber. The car whipped a curve and drove into what the fat man from Calgary facetiously remarked upon as the tall uncut. Miss Benton sighted up these noble columns to where a breeze droned in the tops, two hundred feet above. Through a gap in the timber she saw mountains, peaks that stood bold as the Rockies, capped with snow. For two days she had been groping for a word to define, to sum up the feeling which had grown upon her, had been growing upon her steadily, as the amazing scroll of that four-day journey unrolled. She found it now, a simple word, one of the simplest in our mother tongue— bigness. Bigness in its most ample sense,—that was the dominant note. Immensities of distance, vastness of rolling plain, sheer bulk of mountain, rivers that one crossed, and after a day's journey crossed again, still far from source or confluence. And now this unending sweep of colossal trees!

At first she had been overpowered with a sense of insignificance utterly foreign to her previous experience. But now she discovered with an agreeable sensation of surprise she could vibrate to such a keynote. And while she communed with this pleasant discovery the car sped down a straight stretch and around a corner and stopped short to unload sacks of mail at a weather-beaten yellow edifice, its windows displaying indiscriminately Indian baskets, groceries, and hardware. Northward opened a broad scope of lake level, girt about with tremendous peaks whose lower slopes were banked with thick forest.

Somewhere distant along that lake shore was to be her home. As the car rolled over the four hundred yards between store and white-and-green St. Allwoods, she wondered if Charlie would be there to meet her. She was weary of seeing strange faces, of being directed, of being hustled about.

But he was not there, and she recalled that he never had been notable for punctuality. Five years is a long time. She expected to find him changed— for the better, in certain directions. He had promised to be there; but, in this respect, time evidently had wrought no appreciable transformation.

She registered, was assigned a room, and ate luncheon to the melancholy accompaniment of a three-man orchestra struggling vainly with Bach in an alcove off the dining room. After that she began to make inquiries. Neither clerk nor manager knew aught of Charlie Benton. They were both in their first season there. They advised her to ask the storekeeper.

"MacDougal will know," they were agreed. "He knows everybody around here, and everything that goes on."

The storekeeper, a genial, round-bodied Scotchman, had the information she desired.

"Charlie Benton?" said he. "No, he'll be at his camp up the lake. He was in three or four days back. I mind now, he said he'd be down Thursday; that's to-day. But he isn't here yet, or his boat'd be by the wharf yonder."

"Are there any passenger boats that call there?" she asked.

MacDougal shook his head.

"Not reg'lar. There's a gas boat goes t' the head of the lake now an' then. She's away now. Ye might hire a launch. Jack Fyfe's camp tender's about to get under way. But ye wouldna care to go on her, I'm thinkin'. She'll be loaded wi' lumberjacks—every man drunk as a lord, most like. Maybe Benton'll be in before night."

She went back to the hotel. But St. Allwoods, in its dual capacity of health-and-pleasure resort, was a gilded shell, making a brave outward show, but capitalizing chiefly lake, mountains, and hot, mineral springs. Her room was a bare, cheerless place. She did not want to sit and ponder. Too much real grief hovered in the immediate background of her life. It is not always sufficient to be young and alive. To sit still and think—that way lay tears and despondency. So she went out and walked down the road and out upon the wharf which jutted two hundred yards into the lake.

It stood deserted save for a lone fisherman on the outer end, and an elderly couple that preceded her. Halfway out she passed a slip beside which lay moored a heavily built, fifty-foot boat, scarred with usage, a squat and powerful craft. Lakeward stretched a smooth, unrippled surface. Overhead patches of white cloud drifted lazily. Where the shadows from these lay, the lake spread gray and lifeless. Where the afternoon sun rested, it touched the water with gleams of gold and pale, delicate green. A white-winged yacht lay offshore, her sails in slack folds. A lump of an island lifted two miles beyond, all cliffs and little, wooded hills. And the mountains surrounding in a giant ring seemed to shut the place away from all the world. For sheer wild, rugged beauty, Roaring Lake surpassed any spot she had ever seen. Its quiet majesty, its air of unbroken peace soothed and comforted her, sick with hurry and swift-footed events.

She stood for a time at the outer wharf end, mildly interested when the fisherman drew up a two-pound trout, wondering a little at her own subtle changes of mood. Her surrounding played upon her like a virtuoso on his violin. And this was something that she did not recall as a trait in her own character. She had never inclined to the volatile—perhaps because until the motor accident snuffed out her father's life she had never dealt in anything but superficial emotions.

After a time she retraced her steps. Nearing the halfway slip, she saw that a wagon from which goods were being unloaded blocked the way. A dozen men were stringing in from the road, bearing bundles and bags and rolls of blankets. They were big, burly men, carrying themselves with a reckless swing, with trousers cut off midway between knee and ankle so that they reached just below the upper of their high-topped, heavy, laced boots. Two or three were singing. All appeared unduly happy, talking loudly, with deep laughter. One threw down his burden and executed a brief clog. Splinters flew where the sharp calks bit into the wharf planking, and his companions applauded.

It dawned upon Stella Benton that these might be Jack Fyfe's drunken loggers, and she withdrew until the way should be clear, vitally interested because her brother was a logging man, and wondering if these were the human tools he used in his business, if these were the sort of men with whom he associated. They were a rough lot—and some were very drunk. With the manifestations of liquor she had but the most shadowy acquaintance. But she would have been little less than a fool not to comprehend this.

Then they began filing down the gangway to the boat's deck. One slipped, and came near falling into the water, whereat his fellows howled gleefully. Precariously they negotiated the slanting passage. All but one: he sat him down at the slip-head on his bundle and began a quavering chant. The teamster imperturbably finished his unloading, two men meanwhile piling the goods aboard.

The wagon backed out, and the way was clear, save for the logger sitting on his blankets, wailing his lugubrious song. From below his fellows urged him to come along. A bell clanged in the pilot house. The exhaust of a gas engine began to sputter through the boat's side. From her after deck a man hailed the logger sharply, and when his call was unheeded, he ran lightly up the slip. A short, squarely-built man he was, light on his feet as a dancing master.

He spoke now with authority, impatiently.

"Hurry aboard, Mike; we're waiting."

The logger rose, waved his hand airily, and turned as if to retreat down the wharf. The other caught him by the arm and spun him face to the slip.

"Come on, Slater," he said evenly. "I have no time to fool around."

The logger drew back his fist. He was a fairly big man. But if he had in mind to deal a blow, it failed, for the other ducked and caught him with both arms around the middle. He lifted the logger clear of the wharf, hoisted him to the level of his breast, and heaved him down the slip as one would throw a sack of bran.

The man's body bounced on the incline, rolled, slid, tumbled, till at length he brought up against the boat's guard, and all that saved him a ducking was the prompt extension of several stout arms, which clutched and hauled him to the flush after deck. He sat on his haunches, blinking. Then he laughed. So did the man at the top of the slip and the lumberjacks clustered on the boat. Homeric laughter, as at some surpassing jest. But the roar of him who had taken that inglorious descent rose loudest of all, an explosive, "Har—har—har!"

He clambered unsteadily to his feet, his mouth expanded in an amiable grin.

"Hey, Jack," he shouted. "Maybe y' c'n throw m' blankets down too, while y'r at it."

The man at the slip-head caught up the roll, poised it high, and cast it from him with a quick twist of his body. The woolen missile flew like a well-put shot and caught its owner fair in the breast, tumbling him backwards on the deck—and the Homeric laughter rose in double strength. Then the boat began to swing, and the man ran down and leaped the widening space as she drew away from her mooring.

Stella Benton watched the craft gather way, a trifle shocked, her breath coming a little faster. The most deadly blows she had ever seen struck were delivered in a more subtle, less virile mode, a curl of the lip, an inflection of the voice. These were a different order of beings. This, she sensed was man in a more primitive aspect, man with the conventional bark stripped clean off him. And she scarcely knew whether to be amused or frightened when she reflected that among such her life would presently lie. Charlie had written that she would find things and people a trifle rougher than she was used to. She could well believe that. But—they were picturesque ruffians.

Her interested gaze followed the camp tender as it swung around the wharf-end, and so her roaming eyes were led to another craft drawing near. This might be her brother's vessel. She went back to the outer landing to see.

Two men manned this boat. As she ranged alongside the piles, one stood forward, and the other aft with lines to make fast. She cast a look at each. They were prototypes of the rude crew but now departed, brown-faced, flannel-shirted, shod with calked boots, unshaven for days, typical men of the woods. But as she turned to go, the man forward and almost directly below her looked her full in the face.

"Stell!"

She leaned over the rail.

"Charlie Benton—for Heaven's sake."

They stared at each other.

"Well," he laughed at last. "If it were not for your mouth and eyes, Stell, I wouldn't have known you. Why, you're all grown up."

He clambered to the wharf level and kissed her. The rough stubble of his beard pricked her tender skin and she drew back.

"My word, Charlie, you certainly ought to shave," she observed with sisterly frankness. "I didn't know you until you spoke. I'm awfully glad to see you, but you do need *some one* to look after you."

Benton laughed tolerantly.

"Perhaps. But, my dear girl, a fellow doesn't get anywhere on his appearance in this country. When a fellow's bucking big timber, he shucks off a lot of things he used to think were quite essential. By Jove, you're a picture, Stell. If I hadn't been expecting to see you, I wouldn't have known you."

"I doubt if I should have known you either," she returned drily.

CHAPTER II
MR. ABBEY ARRIVES

Stella accompanied her brother to the store, where he gave an order for sundry goods. Then they went to the hotel to see if her trunks had arrived. Within a few yards of the fence which enclosed the grounds of St. Allwoods a man hailed Benton, and drew him a few steps aside. Stella walked slowly on, and presently her brother joined her.

The baggage wagon had brought the trunks, and when she had paid her bill, they were delivered at the outer wharf-end, where also arrived at about the same time a miscellaneous assortment of supplies from the store and a Japanese with her two handbags. So far as Miss Estella Benton could see, she was about to embark on the last stage of her journey.

"How soon will you start?" she inquired, when the last of the stuff was stowed aboard the little steamer.

"Twenty minutes or so," Benton answered. "Say," he went on casually, "have you got any money, Stell? I owe a fellow thirty dollars, and I left the bank roll and my check book at camp."

Miss Benton drew the purse from her hand bag and gave it to him. He pocketed it and went off down the wharf, with the brief assurance that he would be gone only a minute or so.

The minute, however, lengthened to nearly an hour, and Sam Davis had his blow-off valve hissing, and Stella Benton was casting impatient glances shoreward before Charlie strolled leisurely back.

"You needn't fire up quite so strong, Sam," he called down. "We won't start for a couple of hours yet."

"Sufferin' Moses!" Davis poked his fiery thatch out from the engine room. "I might 'a' known better'n to sweat over firin' up. You generally manage to make about three false starts to one get-away."

Benton laughed good-naturedly and turned away.

"Do you usually allow your men to address you in that impertinent way?" Miss Benton desired to know.

Charlie looked blank for a second. Then he smiled, and linking his arm affectionately in hers, drew her off along the wharf, chuckling to himself.

"My dear girl," said he, "you'd better not let Sam Davis or any of Sam's kind hear you pass remarks like that. Sam would say exactly what he thought about such matters to his boss, or King George, or to the first lady of the land, regardless. Sabe? We're what you'll call primitive out here, yet. You want to forget that master and man business, the servant proposition, and proper respect, and all that rot. Outside the English colonies in one or two big towns, that attitude doesn't go in B.C. People in this neck of the woods stand pretty much on the same class footing, and you'll get in bad and get me in bad if you don't remember that. I've got ten loggers working for me in the woods. Whether they're impertinent or profane cuts no figure so long as they handle the job properly. They're men, you understand, not servants. None of them would hesitate to tell me what he thinks about me or anything I do. If I don't like it, I can fight him or fire him. They won't stand for the sort of airs you're accustomed to. They have the utmost respect for a woman, but a man is merely a two-legged male human like themselves, whether he wears mackinaws or broadcloth, has a barrel of money of none at all. This will seem odd to you at first, but you'll get used to it. You'll find things rather different out here."

"I suppose so," she agreed. "But it sounds queer. For instance, if one of papa's clerks or the chauffeur had spoken like that, he'd have been discharged on the spot."

"The logger's a different breed," Benton observed drily. "Or perhaps only the same breed manifesting under different conditions. He isn't servile. He doesn't have to be."

"Why the delay, though?" she reverted to the point. "I thought you were all ready to go."

"I am," Charlie enlightened. "But while I was at the store just now, Paul Abbey 'phoned from Vancouver to know if there was an up-lake boat in. His people are big lumber guns here, and it will accommodate him and won't hurt me to wait a couple of hours and drop him off at their camp. I've got more or less business dealings with them, and it doesn't hurt to be neighborly. He'd have to hire a gas-boat otherwise. Besides, Paul's a pretty good head."

This, of course, being strictly her brother's business, Stella forbore comment. She was weary of travel, tired with the tension of eternally being shunted across distances, anxious to experience once more that sense of restful finality which comes with a journey's end. But, in a measure her movements were no longer dependent upon her own volition.

They walked slowly along the broad roadway which bordered the lake until they came to a branchy maple, and here they seated themselves on the grassy turf in the shadow of the tree.

"Tell me about yourself," she said. "How do you like it here, and how are you getting on? Your letters home were always chiefly remarkable for their brevity."

"There isn't a great lot to tell," Benton responded. "I'm just beginning to get on my feet. A raw, untried youngster has a lot to learn and unlearn when he hits this tall timber. I've been out here five years, and I'm just beginning to realize what I'm equal to and what I'm not. I'm crawling over a hump now that would have been a lot easier if the governor hadn't come to grief the way he did. He was going to put in some money this fall. But I think I'll make it, anyway, though it will keep me digging and figuring. I have a contract for delivery of a million feet in September and another contract that I could take if I could see my way clear to finance the thing. I could clean up thirty thousand dollars net in two years if I had more cash to work on. As it is, I have to go slow, or I'd go broke. I'm holding two limits by the skin of my teeth. But I've got one good one practically for an annual pittance. If I make delivery on my contract according to schedule it's plain sailing. That about sizes up my prospects, Sis."

"You speak a language I don't understand," she smiled. "What does a million feet mean? And what's a limit?"

"A limit is one square mile—six hundred and forty acres more or less— of merchantable timber land," he explained. "We speak of timber as scaling so many board feet. A board foot is one inch thick by twelve inches square. Sound fir timber is worth around seven dollars per thousand board feet in the log, got out of the woods, and boomed in the water ready to tow to the mills. The first limit I got—from the government—will scale around ten million feet. The other two are nearly as good. But I got them from timber speculators, and it's costing me pretty high. They're a good spec if I can hang on to them, though."

"It sounds big," she commented.

"It *is* big," Charlie declared, "if I could go at it right. I've been trying ever since I got wise to this timber business to make the governor see what a chance there is in it. He was just getting properly impressed with the possibilities when the speed bug got him. He could have trimmed a little here and there at home and put the money to work. Ten thousand dollars would have done the trick, given me a working outfit along with what I've got that would have put us both on Easy Street. However, the poor old chap didn't get around to it. I suppose, like lots of other business men, when he stopped, everything ran down. According to Lander's figures, there won't be a thing left when all accounts are squared."

"Don't talk about it, Charlie," she begged. "It's too near, and I was through it all."

"I would have been there too," Benton said. "But, as I told you, I was out of reach of your wire, and by the time I got it, it was all over. I couldn't have done any good, anyway. There's no use mourning. One way and another we've all got to come to it some day."

Stella looked out over the placid, shimmering surface of Roaring Lake for a minute. Her grief was dimming with time and distance, and she had all her own young life before her. She found herself drifting from painful memories of her father's sudden death to a consideration of things present and personal. She found herself wondering critically if this strange, rude land would work as many changes in her as were patent in this bronzed and burly brother.

He had left home a slim, cocksure youngster, who had proved more than a handful for his family before he was half through college, which educational finishing process had come to an abrupt stop before it was complete. He had been a problem that her father and mother had discussed in guarded tones. Sending him West had been a hopeful experiment, and in the West that abounding spirit which manifested itself in one continual round of minor escapades appeared to have found a natural outlet. She recalled that latterly their father had taken to speaking of Charlie in accents of pride. He was developing the one ambition that Benton senior could thoroughly understand and properly appreciate, the desire to get on, to grasp opportunities, to achieve material success, to make money.

Just as her father, on the few occasions when he talked business before her, spoke in a big way of big things as the desirable ultimate, so now Charlie spoke, with plans and outlook to match his speech. In her father's point of view, and in Charlie's now, a man's personal life did not seem to matter in comparison with getting on and making money. And it was with that personal side of existence that Stella Benton was now chiefly concerned. She had never been required to adjust herself to an existence that was wholly taken up with getting on to the complete exclusion of everything else. Her work had been to play. She could scarce conceive of any one entirely excluding pleasure and diversion from his or her life. She wondered if Charlie had done so. And if not, what ameliorating circumstances, what social outlet, might be found to offset, for her, continued existence in this isolated region of towering woods. So far as her first impressions went,

Roaring Lake appeared to be mostly frequented by lumberjacks addicted to rude speech and strong drink.

"Are there many people living around this lake?" she inquired. "It is surely a beautiful spot. If we had this at home, there would be a summer cottage on every hundred yards of shore."

"Be a long time before we get to that stage here," Benton returned. "And scenery in B.C. is a drug on the market; we've got Europe backed off the map for tourist attractions, if they only knew it. No, about the only summer home in this locality is the Abbey place at Cottonwood Point. They come up here every summer for two or three months. Otherwise I don't know of any lilies of the field, barring the hotel people, and they, being purely transient, don't count. There's the Abbey-Monohan outfit with two big logging camps, my outfit, Jack Fyfe's, some hand loggers on the east shore, and the R.A.T. at the head of the lake. That's the population—and Roaring Lake is forty-two miles long and eight wide."

"Are there any nice girls around?" she asked.

Benton grinned widely.

"Girls?" said he. "Not so you could notice. Outside the Springs and the hatchery over the way, there isn't a white woman on the lake except Lefty Howe's wife,—Lefty's Jack Fyfe's foreman,—and she's fat and past forty. I told you it was a God-forsaken hole as far as society is concerned, Stell."

"I know," she said thoughtfully. "But one can scarcely realize such a— such a social blankness, until one actually experiences it. Anyway, I don't know but I'll appreciate utter quiet for awhile. But what do you do with yourself when you're not working?"

"There's seldom any such time," he answered. "I tell you, Stella, I've got a big job on my hands. I've got a definite mark to shoot at, and I'm going to make a bull's-eye in spite of hell and high water. I have no time to play, and there's no place to play if I had. I don't intend to muddle along making a pittance like a hand logger. I want a stake; and then it'll be time to make a splurge in a country where a man can get a run for his money."

"If that's the case," she observed, "I'm likely to be a handicap to you, am I not?"

"Lord, no," he smiled. "I'll put you to work too, when you get rested up from your trip. You stick with me, Sis, and you'll wear diamonds."

She laughed with him at this, and leaving the shady maple they walked up to the hotel, where Benton proposed that they get a canoe and paddle to where Roaring River flowed out of the lake half a mile westward, to kill the time that must elapse before the three-thirty train.

The St. Allwoods' car was rolling out to Hopyard when they came back. By the time Benton had turned the canoe over to the boathouse man and reached the wharf, the horn of the returning machine sounded down the road. They waited. The car came to a stop at the abutting wharf. The driver handed two suitcases off the burdened hood of his machine. From out the tonneau clambered a large, smooth-faced young man. He wore an expansive smile in addition to a blue serge suit, white Panama, and polished tan Oxfords, and he bestowed a hearty greeting upon Charlie Benton. But his smile suffered eclipse, and a faint flush rose in his round cheeks, when his eyes fell upon Benton's sister.

CHAPTER III
HALFWAY POINT

Miss Benton's cool, impersonal manner seemed rather to heighten the young man's embarrassment. Benton, apparently observing nothing amiss, introduced them in an offhand fashion.

"Mr. Abbey—my sister."

Mr. Abbey bowed and murmured something that passed for acknowledgment. The three turned up the wharf toward where Sam Davis had once more got up steam. As they walked, Mr. Abbey's habitual assurance returned, and he directed part of his genial flow of conversation to Miss Benton. To Stella's inner amusement, however, he did not make any reference to their having been fellow travelers for a day and a half.

Presently they were embarked and under way. Charlie fixed a seat for her on the after deck, and went forward to steer, whither he was straightway joined by Paul Abbey. Miss Benton was as well pleased to be alone. She was not sure she should approve of young men who made such crude efforts to scrape acquaintance with women on trains. She was accustomed to a certain amount of formality in such matters. It might perhaps be laid to the "breezy Western manner" of which she had heard, except that Paul Abbey did not impress her as a Westerner. He seemed more like a type of young man she had encountered frequently in her own circle. At any rate, she was relieved when he did not remain beside her to emit polite commonplaces. She was quite satisfied to sit by herself and look over the panorama of woods and lake—and wonder more than a little what Destiny had in store for her along those silent shores.

The Springs fell far behind, became a few white spots against the background of dusky green. Except for the ripples spread by their wake, the water laid oily smooth. Now, a little past four in the afternoon, she began to sense by comparison the great bulk of the western mountains,—locally, the Chehalis Range,—for the sun was dipping behind the ragged peaks already, and deep shadows stole out from the shore to port. Beneath her feet the screw throbbed, pulsing like an overdriven heart, and Sam Davis poked his sweaty face now and then through a window to catch a breath of cool air denied him in the small inferno where he stoked the fire box.

The *Chickamin* cleared Echo Island, and a greater sweep of lake opened out. Here the afternoon wind sprang up, shooting gustily through a gap between the Springs and Hopyard and ruffling the lake out of its noonday siesta. Ripples, chop, and a growing swell followed each other with that marvellous rapidity common to large bodies of fresh water. It broke the monotony of steady cleaving through dead calm. Stella was a good sailor, and she rather enjoyed it when the *Chickamin* began to lift and yaw off before the following seas that ran up under her fantail stern.

After about an hour's run, with the south wind beginning to whip the crests of the short seas into white foam, the boat bore in to a landing behind a low point. Here Abbey disembarked, after taking the trouble to come aft and shake hands with polite farewell. Standing on the float, hat in hand, he bowed his sleek blond head to Stella.

"I hope you'll like Roaring Lake, Miss Benton," he said, as Benton jingled the go-ahead bell. "I tried to persuade Charlie to stop over awhile, so you could meet my mother and sister, but he's in too big a hurry. Hope to have the pleasure of meeting you again soon."

Miss Benton parried courteously, a little at a loss to fathom this bland friendliness, and presently the widening space cut off their talk. As the boat drew offshore, she saw two women in white come down toward the float, meet Abbey, and turn back. And a little farther out through an opening in the woods, she saw a white and green bungalow, low and rambling, wide-verandahed, set on a hillock three hundred yards back from shore. There was an encircling area of smooth lawn, a place restfully inviting.

Watching that, seeing a figure or two moving about, she was smitten with a recurrence of that poignant loneliness which had assailed her fitfully in the last four days. And while the *Chickamin* was still plowing the inshore waters on an even keel, she walked the guard rail alongside and joined her brother in the pilot house.

"Isn't that a pretty place back there in the woods?" she remarked.

"Abbey's summer camp; spells money to me, that's all," Charlie grumbled. "It's a toy for their women,—up-to-date cottage, gardeners, tennis courts, afternoon tea on the lawn for the guests, and all that. But the Abbey-Monohan bunch has the money to do what they want to do. They've made it in timber, as I expect to make mine. You didn't particularly want to stay over and get acquainted, did you?"

"I? Of course not," she responded.

"Personally, I don't want to mix into their social game," Charlie drawled. "Or at least, I don't propose to make any tentative advances. The women put on lots of side, they say. If they want to hunt us up and cultivate you, all right. But I've got too much to do to butt into society. Anyway, I didn't want to run up against any critical females looking like I do right now."

Stella smiled.

"Under certain circumstances, appearances do count then, in this country," she remarked. "Has your Mr. Abbey got a young and be-yutiful sister?"

"He has, but that's got nothing to do with it," Charlie retorted. "Paul's all right himself. But their gait isn't mine—not yet. Here, you take the wheel a minute. I want to smoke. I don't suppose you ever helmed a forty-footer, but you'll never learn younger."

She took the wheel and Charlie stood by, directing her. In twenty minutes they were out where the run of the sea from the south had a fair sweep. The wind was whistling now. All the roughened surface was spotted with whitecaps. The *Chickamin* would hang on the crest of a wave and shoot forward like a racer, her wheel humming, and again the roller would run out from under her, and she would labor heavily in the trough.

It began to grow insufferably hot in the pilot house. The wind drove with them, pressing the heat from the boiler and fire box into the forward portion of the boat, where Stella stood at the wheel. There were puffs of smoke when Davis opened the fire box to ply it with fuel. All the sour smells that rose from an unclean bilge eddied about them. The heat and the smell and the surging motion began to nauseate Stella.

"I must get outside where I can breathe," she gasped, at length. "It's suffocating. I don't see how you stand it."

"It does get stuffy in here when we run with the wind," Benton admitted. "Cuts off our ventilation. I'm used to it. Crawl out the window and sit on the forward deck. Don't try to get aft. You might slip off, the way she's lurching."

Curled in the hollow of a faked-down hawser with the clean air fanning her, Stella recovered herself. The giddiness left her. She pitied Sam Davis back in that stinking hole beside the fire box. But she supposed he, like her brother, was "used to it." Apparently one could get used to anything, if she could judge by the amazing change in Charlie.

Far ahead loomed a ridge running down to the lake shore and cutting off in a bold promontory. That was Halfway Point, Charlie had told her, and under its shadow lay his camp. Without any previous knowledge of camps, she was approaching this one with less eager anticipation than when she began her long journey. She began to fear that it might be totally unlike anything she had been able to imagine, disagreeably so. Charlie, she decided, had grown hard and coarsened in the evolution of his ambition to get on, to make his pile. She was but four years younger than he, and she had always thought of herself as being older and wiser and steadier. She had conceived the idea that her presence would have a good influence on him, that they would pull together—now that there were but the two of them. But four hours in his company had dispelled that illusion. She had the wit to perceive that Charlie Benton had emerged from the chrysalis stage, that he had the will and the ability to mold his life after his elected fashion, and that her coming was a relatively unimportant incident.

In due course the *Chickamin* bore in under Halfway Point, opened out a sheltered bight where the watery commotion outside raised but a faint ripple, and drew in alongside a float.

The girl swept lake shore, bay, and sloping forest with a quickening eye. Here was no trim-painted cottage and velvet lawn. In the waters beside and lining the beach floated innumerable logs, confined by boomsticks, hundreds of trunks of fir, forty and sixty feet long, four and six feet across the butt, timber enough, when it had passed through the sawmills, to build four such towns as Hopyard. Just back from the shore, amid stumps and littered branches, rose the roofs of divers buildings. One was long and low. Hard by it stood another of like type but of lesser dimension. Two or three mere shanties lifted level with great stumps,—crude, unpainted buildings. Smoke issued from the pipe of the larger, and a white-aproned man stood in the doorway.

Somewhere in the screen of woods a whistle shrilled. Benton looked at his watch.

"We made good time, in spite of the little roll," said he. "That's the donkey blowing quitting time—six o'clock. Well, come on up to the shack, Sis. Sam, you get a wheelbarrow and run those trunks up after supper, will you?"

Away in the banked timber beyond the maples and alder which Stella now saw masked the bank of a small stream flowing by the cabins, a faint call rose, long-drawn:

"Tim-ber-r-r-r!"

They moved along a path beaten through fern and clawing blackberry vine toward the camp, Benton carrying the two grips. A loud, sharp crack split the stillness; then a mild swishing sound arose. Hard on the heels of that followed a rending, tearing crash, a thud that sent tremors through the solid earth under their feet. The girl started.

"Falling gang dropped a big fir," Charlie laughed. "You'll get used to that. You'll hear it a good many times a day here."

"Good Heavens, it sounded like the end of the world," she said.

"Well, you can't fell a stick of timber two hundred feet high and six or eight feet through without making a pretty considerable noise," her brother remarked complacently. "I like that sound myself. Every big tree that goes down means a bunch of money."

He led the way past the mess-house, from the doorway of which the aproned cook eyed her with frank curiosity, hailing his employer with nonchalant air, a cigarette resting in one corner of his mouth. Benton opened the door of the second building. Stella followed him in

It had the saving grace of cleanliness—according to logging-camp standards. But the bareness of it appalled her. There was a rusty box heater, littered with cigar and cigarette stubs, a desk fabricated of undressed boards, a homemade chair or two, sundry boxes standing about. The sole concession to comfort was a rug of cheap Axminster covering half the floor. The walls were decorated chiefly with miscellaneous clothing suspended from nails, a few maps and blue prints tacked up askew. Straight across from the entering door another stood ajar, and she could see further vistas of bare board wall, small, dusty window-panes, and a bed whereon gray blankets were tumbled as they fell when a waking sleeper cast them aside.

Benton crossed the room and threw open another door.

"Here's a nook I fixed up for you, Stella," he said briskly. "It isn't very fancy, but it's the best I could do just now."

She followed him in silently. He set her two bags on the floor and turned to go. Then some impulse moved him to turn back, and he put both hands on her shoulders and kissed her gently.

"You're home, anyway," he said. "That's something, if it isn't what you're used to. Try to overlook the crudities. We'll have supper as soon as you feel like it."

He went out, closing the door behind him.

Miss Estella Benton stood in the middle of the room fighting against a swift heart-sinking, a terrible depression that strove to master her.

"Good Lord in Heaven," she muttered at last. "What a place to be marooned in. It's—it's simply impossible."

Her gaze roved about the room. A square box, neither more nor less, fourteen by fourteen feet of bare board wall, unpainted and unpapered. There was an iron bed, a willow rocker, and a rude closet for clothes in one corner. A duplicate of the department-store bargain rug in the other room lay on the floor. On an upturned box stood an enamel pitcher and a tin washbasin. That was all.

She sat down on the bed and viewed it forlornly. A wave of sickening rebellion against everything swept over her. To herself she seemed as irrevocably alone as if she had been lost in the depths of the dark timber that rose on every hand. And sitting there she heard at length the voices of men. Looking out through a window curtained with cheesecloth she saw her brother's logging gang swing past, stout woodsmen all, big men, tall men, short-bodied men with thick necks and shoulders, sunburned, all grimy with the sweat of their labors, carrying themselves with a free and reckless swing, the doubles in type of that roistering crew she had seen embark on Jack Fyfe's boat.

In so far as she had taken note of those who labored with their hands in the region of her birth, she had seen few like these. The chauffeur, the footman, the street cleaner, the factory workers—they were all different. They lacked something,—perhaps nothing in the way of physical excellence; but these men betrayed in every movement a subtle difference that she could not define. Her nearest approximation and the first attempt she made at analysis was that they looked like pirates. They were bold men and strong; that was written in their faces and the swing of them as they walked. And they served the very excellent purpose of taking her mind off herself for the time being.

She watched them cluster by a bench before the cookhouse, dabble their faces and hands in washbasins, scrub themselves promiscuously on towels, sometimes one at each end of a single piece of cloth, hauling it back and forth in rude play.

All about that cookhouse dooryard spread a confusion of empty tin cans, gaudily labeled, containers of corn and peas and tomatoes. Dishwater and refuse, chips, scraps, all the refuse of the camp was scattered there in unlovely array.

But that made no more than a passing impression upon her. She was thinking, as she removed her hat and gloves, of what queer angles come now and then to the human mind. She wondered why she should be sufficiently interested in her brother's hired men to drive off a compelling attack of the blues in consideration of them as men. Nevertheless, she found herself unable to view them as she had viewed, say, the clerks in her father's office.

She began to brush her hair and to wonder what sort of food would be served for supper.

CHAPTER IV
A FORETASTE OF THINGS TO COME

Half an hour later she sat down with her brother at one end of a table that was but a long bench covered with oilcloth. Chairs there were none. A narrow movable bench on each side of the fixed table furnished seating capacity for twenty men, provided none objected to an occasional nudging from his neighbor's elbow. The dishes, different from any she had ever eaten from, were of enormously thick porcelain, dead white, variously chipped and cracked with fine seams. But the food, if plain, was of excellent quality, tastily cooked. She discovered herself with an appetite wholly independent of silver and cut glass and linen. The tin spoons and steel knives and forks harrowed her aesthetic sense without impairing her ability to satisfy hunger.

They had the dining room to themselves. Through a single shiplap partition rose a rumble of masculine talk, where the logging crew loafed in their bunkhouse. The cook served them without any ceremony, putting everything on the table at once,—soup, meat, vegetables, a bread pudding for dessert, coffee in a tall tin pot. Benton introduced him to his sister. He withdrew hastily to the kitchen, and they saw no more of him.

"Charlie," the girl said plaintively, when the man had closed the door behind him, "I don't quite fathom your social customs out here. Is one supposed to know everybody that one encounters?"

"Just about," he grinned. "Loggers, Siwashes, and the natives in general. Can't very well help it, Sis. There's so few people in this neck of the woods that nobody can afford to be exclusive,—at least, nobody who lives here any length of time. You can't tell when you may have to call on your neighbor or the fellow working for you in a matter of life and death almost. A man couldn't possibly maintain the same attitude toward a bunch of loggers working under him that would be considered proper back where we came from. Take me, for instance, and my case is no different from any man operating on a moderate scale out here. I'd get the reputation of being swell-headed, and they'd put me in the hole at every turn. They wouldn't care what they did or how it was done. Ten to one I couldn't keep a capable working crew three weeks on end. On the other hand, take a bunch of loggers on a pay roll working for a man that meets them on an equal footing—why, they'll go to hell and back again for him. They're as loyal as soldiers to the flag. They're a mighty self-sufficient, independent lot, these lumberjacks, and that goes for most everybody knocking about in this country,—loggers, prospectors, miners, settlers, and all. If you're what they term 'all right,' you can do anything, and they'll back you up. If you go to putting on airs and trying to assert yourself as a superior being, they'll go out of their way to hand you packages of trouble."

"I see," she observed thoughtfully. "One's compelled by circumstances to practice democracy."

"Something like that," he responded carelessly and went on eating his supper.

"Don't you think we could make this place a lot more homelike, Charlie?" she ventured, when they were back in their own quarters. "I suppose it suits a man who only uses it as a place to sleep, but it's bare as a barn."

"It takes money to make a place cosy," Benton returned. "And I haven't had it to spend on knickknacks."

"Fiddlesticks!" she laughed. "A comfortable chair or two and curtains and pictures aren't knickknacks, as you call them. The cost wouldn't amount to anything."

Benton stuffed the bowl of a pipe and lighted it before he essayed reply.

"Look here, Stella," he said earnestly. "This joint probably strikes you as about the limit, seeing that you've been used to pretty soft surroundings and getting pretty nearly anything you wanted whenever you expressed a wish for it. Things that you've grown into the way of considering necessities *are* luxuries. And they're out of the question for us at present. I got a pretty hard seasoning the first two years I was in this country, and when I set up this camp it was merely a place to live. I never thought anything about it as being comfortable or otherwise until you elected to come. I'm not in a position to go in for trimmings. Rough as this camp is, it will have to go as it stands this summer. I'm up against it for ready money. I've got none due until I make delivery of those logs in September, and I have to have that million feet in the water in order to make delivery. Every one of these men but the cook and the donkey engineer are working for me with their wages deferred until then. There are certain expenses that must be met with cash—and I've got all my funds figured down to nickels. If I get by on this contract, I'll have a few hundred to squander on house things. Until then, it's the simple life for us. You can camp for three or four months, can't you, without finding it completely unbearable?"

"Why, of course," she protested. "I wasn't complaining about the way things are. I merely voiced the idea that it would be nice to fix up a little cosier, make these rooms look a little homelike. I didn't know you were practically compelled to live like this as a matter of economy."

"Well, in a sense, I am," he replied. "And then again, making a place away out here homelike never struck me as being anything but an inconsequential detail. I'm not trying to make a home here. I'm after a bundle of money. A while ago, if you had been here and suggested it, you could have spent five or six hundred, and I wouldn't have missed it. But this contract came my way, and gave me a chance to clean up three thousand dollars clear profit in four months. I grabbed it, and I find it's some undertaking. I'm dealing with a hard business outfit, hard as nails. I might get the banks or some capitalist to finance me, because my timber holdings are worth money. But I'm shy of that. I've noticed that when a logger starts working on borrowed capital, he generally goes broke. The financiers generally devise some way to hook him. I prefer to sail as close to the wind as I can on what little I've got. I can get this timber out—but it wouldn't look nice, now, would it, for me to be buying furniture when I'm standing these boys off for their wages till September?"

"I should have been a man," Miss Estella Benton pensively remarked. "Then I could put on overalls and make myself useful, instead of being a drone. There doesn't seem to be anything here I can do. I could keep house— only you haven't any house to keep, therefore no need of a housekeeper. Why, who's that?"

Her ear had caught a low, throaty laugh, a woman's laugh, outside. She looked inquiringly at her brother. His expression remained absent, as of one concentrated upon his own problems. She repeated the question.

"That? Oh, Katy John, I suppose, or her mother," he answered. "Siwash bunch camping around the point. The girl does some washing for us now and then. I suppose she's after Matt for some bread or something."

Stella looked out. At the cookhouse door stood a short, plump-bodied girl, dark-skinned and black-haired. Otherwise she conformed to none of Miss Benton's preconceived ideas of the aboriginal inhabitant. If she had been pinned down, she would probably have admitted that she expected to behold an Indian maiden garbed in beaded buckskin and brass ornaments. Instead, Katy John wore a white sailor blouse, a brown pleated skirt, tan shoes, and a bow of baby blue ribbon in her hair.

"Why, she talks good English," Miss Benton exclaimed, as fragments of the girl's speech floated over to her.

"Sure. As good as anybody," Charlie drawled. "Why not?"

"Well—er—I suppose my notion of Indians is rather vague," Stella admitted. "Are they all civilized and educated?"

"Most of 'em," Benton replied. "The younger generation anyhow. Say, Stell, can you cook?"

"A little," Stella rejoined guardedly. "That Indian girl's really pretty, isn't she?"

"They nearly all are when they're young," he observed. "But they are old and tubby by the time they're thirty."

Katy John's teeth shone white between her parted lips at some sally from the cook. She stood by the door, swinging a straw hat in one hand. Presently Matt handed her a parcel done up in newspaper, and she walked away with a nod to some of the loggers sitting with their backs against the bunkhouse wall.

"Why were you asking if I could cook?" Stella inquired, when the girl vanished in the brush.

"Why, your wail about being a man and putting on overalls and digging in reminded me that if you liked you may have a chance to get on your apron and show us what you can do," he laughed. "Matt's about due to go on a tear. He's been on the water-wagon now about his limit. The first man that comes along with a bottle of whisky, Matt will get it and quit and head for town. I was wondering if you and Katy John could keep the gang from starving to death if that happened. The last time I had to get in and cook for two weeks myself. And I can't run a logging crew from the cook shanty very well."

"I daresay I could manage," Stella returned dubiously. "This seems to be a terrible place for drinking. Is it the accepted thing to get drunk at all times and in public?"

"It's about the only excitement there is," Benton smiled tolerantly. "I guess there is no more drinking out here than any other part of this North American continent. Only a man here gets drunk openly and riotously without any effort to hide it, and without it being considered anything but a natural lapse. That's one thing you'll have to get used to out here, Stell—I mean, that what vices men have are all on the surface. We don't get drunk secretly at the club and sneak home in a taxi. Oh, well, we'll cross the bridge when we come to it. Matt may not break out for weeks."

He yawned openly.

"Sleepy?" Stella inquired.

"I get up every morning between four and five," he replied. "And I can go to sleep any time after supper."

"I think I'll take a walk along the beach," she said abruptly.

"All right. Don't hike into the woods and get lost, though."

She circled the segment of bay, climbed a low, rocky point, and found herself a seat on a fallen tree. Outside the lake heaved uneasily, still dotted with whitecaps whipped up by the southerly gale. At her feet surge after surge hammered the gravelly shore. Far through the woods behind her the wind whistled and hummed among swaying tops of giant fir and cedar. There was a heady freshness in that rollicking wind, an odor resinous and pungent mingled with that elusive smell of green growing stuff along the shore. Beginning where she sat, tree trunks rose in immense brown pillars, running back in great forest naves, shadowy always, floored with green moss laid in a rich, soft carpet for the wood-sprites' feet. Far beyond the long gradual lower slope lifted a range of saw-backed mountains, the sanctuary of wild goat and bear, and across the rolling lake lifted other mountains sheer from the water's edge, peaks rising above timber-line in majestic contour, their pinnacle crests grazing the clouds that scudded before the south wind.

Beauty? Yes. A wild, imposing grandeur that stirred some responsive chord in her. If only one could live amid such surrounding with a contented mind, she thought, the wilderness would have compensations of its own. She had an uneasy feeling that isolation from everything that had played an important part in her life might be the least depressing factor in this new existence. She could not view the rough and ready standards of the woods with much equanimity—not as she had that day seen them set forth. These things were bound to be a part of her daily life, and all the brief span of her years had gone to forming habits of speech and thought and manner diametrically opposed to what she had so far encountered.

She nursed her chin in her hand and pondered this. She could not see how it was to be avoided. She was there, and perforce she must stay there. She had no friends to go elsewhere, or training in the harsh business of gaining a livelihood if she did go. For the first time she began dully to resent the manner of her upbringing. Once she had desired to enter hospital training, had been properly enthusiastic for a period of months over a career in this field of mercy. Then, as now, marriage, while accepted as the ultimate state, was only to be considered through a haze of idealism and romanticism. She cherished certain ideals of a possible lover and husband, but always with a false sense of shame. The really serious business of a woman's life was the one thing to which she made no attempt to apply practical consideration.

But her parents had had positive ideas on that subject, even if they were not openly expressed. Her yearnings after a useful "career" were skilfully discouraged,—by her mother because that worthy lady thought it was "scarcely the thing, Stella dear, and so unnecessary"; by her father because, as he bluntly put it, it would only be a waste of time and money, since the chances were she would get married before she was half through training, and anyway a girl's place was at home till she did get married. That was his only reference to the subject of her ultimate disposition that she could recall, but it was plain enough as far as it went.

It was too late to mourn over lost opportunities now, but she did wish there was some one thing she could do and do well, some service of value that would guarantee self-support. If she could only pound a typewriter or keep a set of books, or even make a passable attempt at sewing, she would have felt vastly more at ease in this rude logging camp, knowing that she could leave it if she desired.

So far as she could see things, she looked at them with measurable clearness, without any vain illusions concerning her ability to march triumphant over unknown fields of endeavor. Along practical lines she had everything to learn. Culture furnishes an excellent pair of wings wherewith to soar in skies of abstraction, but is a poor vehicle to carry one over rough roads. She might have remained in Philadelphia, a guest among friends. Pride forbade that. Incidentally, such an arrangement would have enabled her to stalk a husband, a moneyed husband, which did not occur to her at all. There remained only to join Charlie. If his fortunes mended, well and good. Perhaps she could even help in minor ways.

But it was all so radically different—brother and all—from what she had pictured that she was filled with dismay and not a little foreboding of the future. Sufficient, however, unto the day was the evil thereof, she told herself at last, and tried to make that assurance work a change of heart. She was very lonely and depressed and full of a futile wish that she were a man.

Over across the bay some one was playing an accordeon, and to its strains a stout-lunged lumberjack was roaring out a song, with all his fellows joining strong in the chorus:

"Oh, the Saginaw Kid was a cook in a camp, way up on the Ocon-to-o-o.
And the cook in a camp in them old days had a damn hard row to hoe-i-oh!
Had a damn hard row to hoe."

There was a fine, rollicking air to it. The careless note in their voices, the jovial lilt of their song, made her envious. They at least had their destiny, limited as it might be and cast along rude ways, largely under their own control.

Her wandering gaze at length came to rest on a tent top showing in the brush northward from the camp. She saw two canoes drawn up on the beach above the lash of the waves, two small figures playing on the gravel, and sundry dogs prowling alongshore. Smoke went eddying away in the wind. The Siwash camp where Katy John hailed from, Miss Benton supposed.

She had an impulse to skirt the bay and view the Indian camp at closer range, a notion born of curiosity. She debated this casually, and just as she was about to rise, her movement was arrested by a faint crackle in the woods behind. She looked away through the deepening shadow among the trees and saw nothing at first. But the sound was repeated at odd intervals. She sat still. Thoughts of forest animals slipped into her mind, without making her afraid. At last she caught sight of a man striding through the timber, soundlessly on the thick moss, coming almost straight toward her.

He was scarcely fifty yards away. Across his shoulders he bore a reddish-gray burden, and in his right hand was a gun. She did not move. Bowed slightly under the weight, the man passed within twenty feet of her, so close that she could see the sweat-beads glisten on that side of his face, and saw also that the load he carried was the carcass of a deer.

Gaining the beach and laying the animal across a boulder, he straightened himself up and drew a long breath. Then he wiped the sweat off his face. She recognized him as the man who had thrown the logger down the slip that day at noon,—presumably Jack Fyfe. A sturdily built man about thirty, of Saxon fairness, with a tinge of red in his hair and a liberal display of freckles across nose and cheek bones. He was no beauty, she decided, albeit he displayed a frank and pleasing countenance. That he was a remarkably strong and active man she had seen for herself, and if the firm round of his jaw counted for anything, an individual of considerable determination besides. Miss Benton conceived herself to be possessed of considerable skill at character analysis.

He put away his handkerchief, took up his rifle, settled his hat, and strode off toward the camp. Her attention now diverted from the Siwashes, she watched him, saw him go to her brother's quarters, stand in the door a minute, then go back to the beach accompanied by Charlie.

In a minute or so he came rowing across in a skiff, threw his deer aboard, and pulled away north along the shore.

She watched him lift and fall among the waves until he turned a point, rowing with strong, even strokes. Then she walked home. Benton was poring over some figures, but he pushed aside his pencil and paper when she entered.

"You had a visitor, I see," she remarked.

"Yes, Jack Fyfe. He picked up a deer on the ridge behind here and borrowed a boat to get home."

"I saw him come out of the woods," she said. "His camp can't be far from here, is it? He only left the Springs as you came in. Does he hunt deer for sport?"

"Hardly. Oh, well, I suppose it's sport for Jack, in a way. He's always piking around in the woods with a gun or a fishing rod," Benton returned. "But we kill 'em to eat mostly. It's good meat and cheap. I get one myself now and then. However, you want to keep that under your hat—about us fellows hunting—or we'll have game wardens nosing around here."

"Are you not allowed to hunt them?" she asked.

"Not in close season. Hunting season's from September to December."

"If it's unlawful, why break the law?" she ventured hesitatingly. "Isn't that rather—er—"

"Oh, bosh," Charlie derided. "A man in the woods is entitled to venison, if he's hunter enough to get it. The woods are full of deer, and a few more or less don't matter. We can't run forty miles to town and back and pay famine prices for beef every two or three days, when we can get it at home in the woods."

Stella digested this in silence, but it occurred to her that this mild sample of lawlessness was quite in keeping with the men and the environment. There was no policeman on the corner, no mechanism of law and order visible anywhere. The characteristic attitude of these woodsmen was of intolerance for restraint, of complete self-sufficiency. It had colored her brother's point of view. She perceived that whereas all her instinct was to know the rules of the game and abide by them, he, taking his cue from his environment, inclined to break rules that proved inconvenient, even to formulate new ones to apply.

"And suppose," said she, "that a game warden should catch you or Mr. Jack Fyfe killing deer out of season?"

"We'd be hauled up and fined a hundred dollars or so," he told her. "But they don't catch us."

He shrugged his shoulders, and smiling tolerantly upon her, proceeded to smoke.

Dusk was falling now, the long twilight of the northern seasons gradually deepening, as they sat in silence. Along the creek bank arose the evening chorus of the frogs. The air, now hushed and still, was riven every few minutes by the whir of wings as ducks in evening flight swept by above. All the boisterous laughter and talk in the bunkhouse had died. The woods ranged gloomy and impenetrable, save only in the northwest, where a patch of sky lighted by diffused pink and gray revealed one mountain higher than its fellows standing bald against the horizon.

"Well, I guess it's time to turn in." Benton muffled a yawn. "Pleasant dreams, Sis. Oh, here's your purse. I used part of the bank roll. You won't have much use for money up here, anyway."

He flipped the purse across to her and sauntered into his bedroom. Stella sat gazing thoughtfully at the vast bulk of Mount Douglas a few minutes longer. Then she too went into the box-like room, the bare discomfort of which chilled her merely to behold.

With a curious uncertainty, a feeling of reluctance for the proceeding almost, she examined the contents of her purse. For a little time she stood gazing into it, a queer curl to her full red lips. Then she flung it contemptuously on the bed and began to take down her hair.

"'A rich, rough, tough country, where it doesn't do to be finicky about anything,'" she murmured, quoting a line from one of Charlie Benton's letters. "It would appear to be rather unpleasantly true. Particularly the last clause."

In her purse, which had contained one hundred and ten dollars, there now reposed in solitary state a twenty-dollar bill.

CHAPTER V
THE TOLL OF BIG TIMBER

Day came again, in the natural sequence of events. Matt, the cook, roused all the camp at six o'clock with a tremendous banging on a piece of boiler plate hung by a wire. Long before that Stella heard her brother astir. She wondered sleepily at his sprightliness, for as she remembered him at home he had been a confirmed lie-abed. She herself responded none too quickly to the breakfast gong, as a result of which slowness the crew had filed away to the day's work, her brother striding in the lead, when she entered the mess-house.

She killed time with partial success till noon. Several times she was startled to momentary attention by the prolonged series of sharp cracks which heralded the thunderous crash of a falling tree. There were other sounds which betokened the loggers' activity in the near-by forest,— the ringing whine of saw blades, the dull stroke of the axe, voices calling distantly.

She tried to interest herself in the camp and the beach and ended up by sitting on a log in a shady spot, staring dreamily over the lake. She thought impatiently of that homely saw concerning Satan and idle hands, but she reflected also that in this isolation even mischief was comparatively impossible. There was not a soul to hold speech with except the cook, and he was too busy to talk, even if he had not been afflicted with a painful degree of diffidence when she addressed him. She could make no effort at settling down, at arranging things in what was to be her home. There was nothing to arrange, no odds and ends wherewith almost any woman can conjure up a homelike effect in the barest sort of place. She beheld the noon return of the crew much as a shipwrecked castaway on a desert shore might behold a rescuing sail, and she told Charlie that she intended to go into the woods that afternoon and watch them work.

"All right," said he. "Just so you don't get in the way of a falling tree."

A narrow fringe of brush and scrubby timber separated the camp from the actual work. From the water's edge to the donkey engine was barely four hundred yards. From donkey to a ten-foot jump-off on the lake shore in a straight line on a five per cent. gradient ran a curious roadway, made by placing two logs in the hollow scooped by tearing great timbers over the soft earth, and a bigger log on each side. Butt to butt and side to side, the outer sticks half their thickness above the inner, they formed a continuous trough the bottom and sides worn smooth with friction of sliding timbers. Stella had crossed it the previous evening and wondered what it was. Now, watching them at work, she saw. Also she saw why the great stumps that rose in every clearing in this land of massive trees were sawed six and eight feet above the ground. Always at the base the firs swelled sharply. Wherefore the falling gangs lifted themselves above the enlargement to make their cut.

Two sawyers attacked a tree. First, with their double-bitted axes, each drove a deep notch into the sapwood just wide enough to take the end of a two-by-six plank four or five feet long with a single grab-nail in the end, — the springboard of the Pacific coast logger, whose daily business lies among the biggest timber on God's footstool. Each then clambered up on his precarious perch, took hold of his end of the long, limber saw, and cut in to a depth of a foot or more, according to the size of the tree. Then jointly they chopped down to this sawed line, and there was the undercut complete, a deep notch on the side to which the tree would fall. That done, they swung the ends of their springboards, or if it were a thick trunk, made new holding notches on the other side, and the long saw would eat steadily through the heart of the tree toward that yellow, gashed undercut, stroke upon stroke, ringing with a thin, metallic twang. Presently there would arise an ominous cracking. High in the air the tall crest would dip slowly, as if it bowed with manifest reluctance to the inevitable. The sawyers would drop lightly from their springboards, crying:

"Tim-ber-r-r-r!"

The earthward swoop of the upper boughs would hasten till the air was full of a whistling, whishing sound. Then came the rending crash as the great tree smashed prone, crushing what small timber stood in its path, followed by the earth-quivering shock of its impact with the soil. The tree once down, the fallers went on to another. Immediately the swampers fell upon the prone trunk with axes, denuding it of limbs; the buckers followed them to saw it into lengths decreed by the boss logger. When the job was done, the brown fir was no longer a stately tree but saw-logs, each with the square butt that lay donkeyward, trimmed a trifle rounding with the axe.

Benton worked one falling gang. The falling gang raced to keep ahead of the buckers and swampers, and they in turn raced to keep ahead of the hook tender, rigging slinger, and donkey, which last trio moved the logs from woods to water, once they were down and trimmed. Terrible, devastating forces of destruction they seemed to Stella Benton, wholly unused as she was to any woodland save the well-kept parks and little areas of groomed forest in her native State. All about in the ravaged woods lay the big logs, scores of them. They had only begun to pull with the donkey a week earlier, Benton explained to her. With his size gang he could not keep a donkey engine working steadily. So they had felled and trimmed to a good start, and now the falling crew and the swampers and buckers were in a dingdong contest to see how long they could keep ahead of the puffing Seattle yarder.

Stella sat on a stump, watching. Over an area of many acres the ground was a litter of broken limbs, ragged tops, crushed and bent and broken younger growth, twisted awry by the big trees in their fall. Huge stumps upthrust like beacons in a ruffled harbor, grim, massive butts. From all the ravaged wood rose a pungent smell of pitch and sap, a resinous, pleasant smell. Radiating like the spokes of a wheel from the head of the chute ran deep, raw gashes in the earth, where the donkey had hauled up the Brobdingnagian logs on the end of an inch cable.

"This is no small boy's play, is it, Stell?" Charlie said to her once in passing.

And she agreed that it was not. Agreed more emphatically and with half-awed wonder when she saw the donkey puff and quiver on its anchor cable, as the hauling line spooled up on the drum. On the outer end of that line snaked a sixty-foot stick, five feet across the butt, but it came down to the chute head, brushing earth and brush and small trees aside as if they were naught. Once the big log caromed against a stump. The rearward end flipped ten feet in the air and thirty feet sidewise. But it came clear and slid with incredible swiftness to the head of the chute, flinging aside showers of dirt and small stones, and leaving one more deep furrow in the forest floor. Benton trotted behind it. Once it came to rest well in the chute, he unhooked the line, freed the choker (the short noosed loop of cable that slips over the log's end), and the haul-back cable hurried the main line back to another log. Benton followed, and again the donkey shuddered on its foundation skids till another log laid in the chute, with its end butted against that which lay before. One log after another was hauled down till half a dozen rested there, elongated peas in a wooden pod.

Then a last big stick came with a rush, bunted these others powerfully so that they began to slide with the momentum thus imparted, slowly at first then, gathering way and speed, they shot down to the lake and plunged to the water over the ten-foot jump-off like a school of breaching whales.

All this took time, vastly more time than it takes in the telling. The logs were ponderous masses. They had to be maneuvered sometimes between stumps and standing timber, jerked this way and that to bring them into the clear. By four o'clock Benton and his rigging-slinger had just finished bunting their second batch of logs down the chute. Stella watched these Titanic labors with a growing interest and a dawning vision of why these men walked the earth with that reckless swing of their shoulders. For they were palpably masters in their environment. They strove with woodsy giants and laid them low. Amid constant dangers they sweated at a task that shamed the seven labors of Hercules. Gladiators they were in a contest from which they did not always emerge victorious.

When Benton and his helper followed the haul-back line away to the domain of the falling gang the last time, Stella had so far unbent as to strike up conversation with the donkey engineer. That greasy individual finished stoking his fire box and replied to her first comment.

"Work? You bet," said he. "It's real graft, this is. I got the easy end of it, and mine's no snap. I miss a signal, big stick butts against something solid; biff! goes the line and maybe cuts a man plumb in two. You got to be wide awake when you run a loggin' donkey. These woods is no place for a man, anyway, if he ain't spry both in his head and feet."

"Do many men get hurt logging?" Stella asked. "It looks awfully dangerous, with these big trees falling and smashing everything. Look at that. Goodness!"

From the donkey they could see a shower of ragged splinters and broken limbs fly when a two-hundred-foot fir smashed a dead cedar that stood in the way of its downward swoop. They could hear the pieces strike against brush and trees like the patter of shot on a tin wall.

The donkey engineer gazed calmly enough.

"Them flyin' chunks raise the dickens sometimes," he observed. "Oh, yes, now an' then a man gets laid out. There's some things you got to take a chance on. Maybe you get cut with an axe, or a limb drops on you, or you get in the way of a breakin' line,—though a man ain't got any business in the bight of a line. A man don't stand much show when the end of a inch 'n' a quarter cable snaps at him like a whiplash. I seen a feller on Howe Sound cut square in two with a cable-end once. A broken block's the worst, though. That generally gets the riggin' slinger, but a piece of it's liable to hit anybody. You see them big iron pulley blocks the haul-back cable works in? Well, sometimes they have to anchor a snatch block to a stump an' run the main line through it at an angle to get a log out the way you want. Suppose the block breaks when I'm givin' it to her? Chunks uh that broken cast iron'll fly like bullets. Yes, sir, broken blocks is bad business. Maybe you noticed the boys used the snatch block two or three times this afternoon? We've been lucky in this camp all spring. Nobody so much as nicked himself with an axe. Breaks in the gear don't come very often, anyway, with an outfit in first-class shape. We got good gear an' a good crew—about as *skookum* a bunch as I ever saw in the woods."

Two hundred yards distant Charlie Benton rose on a stump and semaphored with his arms. The engineer whistled answer and stood to his levers; the main line began to spool slowly in on the drum. Another signal, and he shut off. Another signal, after a brief wait, and the drum rolled faster, the line tautened like a fiddle-string, and the ponderous machine vibrated with the strain of its effort.

Suddenly the line came slack. Stella, watching for the log to appear, saw her brother leap backward off the stump, saw the cable whip sidewise, mowing down a clump of saplings that stood in the bight of the line, before the engineer could cut off the power. In that return of comparative silence there rose above the sibilant hiss of the blow-off valve a sudden commotion of voices.

"Damn!" the donkey engineer peered over the brush. "That don't sound good. I guess somebody got it in the neck."

Almost immediately Sam Davis and two other men came running.

"What's up?" the engineer called as they passed on a dog trot.

"Block broke," Davis answered over his shoulder. "Piece of it near took a leg off Jim Renfrew."

Stella stood a moment, hesitating.

"I may be able to do something. I'll go and see," she said.

"Better not," the engineer warned. "Liable to run into something that'll about turn your stomach. What was I tellin' about a broken block? Them ragged pieces of flyin' iron sure mess a man up. They'll bring a bed spring, an' pack him down to the boat, an' get him to a doctor quick as they can. That's all. You couldn't do nothin'."

Nevertheless she went. Renfrew was the rigging slinger working with Charlie, a big, blond man who blushed like a schoolboy when Benton introduced him to her. Twenty minutes before he had gone trotting after the haul-back, sound and hearty, laughing at some sally of her brother's. It seemed a trifle incredible that he should lie mangled and bleeding among the green forest growth, while his fellows hurried for a stretcher.

Two hundred yards at right angles from where Charlie had stood giving signals she found a little group under a branchy cedar. Renfrew lay on his back, mercifully unconscious. Benton squatted beside him, twisting a silk handkerchief with a stick tightly above the wound. His hands and Renfrew's clothing and the mossy ground was smeared with blood. Stella looked over his shoulder. The overalls were cut away. In the thick of the man's thigh stood a ragged gash she could have laid both hands in. She drew back.

Benton looked up.

"Better keep away," he advised shortly. "We've done all that can be done."

She retreated a little and sat down on a root, half-sickened. The other two men stood up. Benton sat back, his first-aid work done, and rolled a cigarette with fingers that shook a little. Off to one side she saw the fallers climb up on their springboards. Presently arose the ringing whine of the thin steel blade, the chuck of axes where the swampers attacked a fallen tree. No matter, she thought, that injury came to one, that death might hover near, the work went on apace, like action on a battlefield.

A few minutes thereafter the two men who had gone with Sam Davis returned with the spring from Benton's bed and a light mattress. They laid the injured logger on this and covered him with a blanket. Then four of them picked it up. As they started, Stella heard one say to her brother:

"Matt's jagged."

"What?" Benton exploded. "Where'd it come from?"

"One uh them Hungry Bay shingle-bolt cutters's in camp," the logger answered. "Maybe he brought a bottle. I didn't stop to see. But Matt's sure got a tank full."

Benton ripped out an angry oath, passed his men, and strode away down the path. Stella fell in behind him, wakened to a sudden uneasiness at the wrathful set of his features. She barely kept in sight, so rapidly did he move.

Sam Davis had smoke pouring from the *Chickamin's* stack, but the kitchen pipe lifted no blue column, though it was close to five o'clock. Benton made straight for the cookhouse. Stella followed, a trifle uncertainly. A glimpse past Charlie as he came out showed her Matt staggering aimlessly about the kitchen, red-eyed, scowling, muttering to himself. Benton hurried to the bunkhouse door, much as a hound might follow a scent, peered in, and went on to the corner.

On the side facing the lake he found the source of the cook's intoxication. A tall and swarthy lumberjack squatted on his haunches, gabbling in the

Chinook jargon to a *klootchman* and a wizen-featured old Siwash. The Indian woman was drunk beyond any mistaking, affably drunk. She looked up at Benton out of vacuous eyes, grinned, and extended to him a square-faced bottle of Old Tim gin. The logger rose to his feet.

"H'lo, Benton," he greeted thickly. "How's every-thin'?"

Benton's answer was a quick lurch of his body and a smashing jab of his clenched fist. The blow stretched the logger on his back, with blood streaming from both nostrils. But he was a hardy customer, for he bounced up like a rubber ball, only to be floored even more viciously before he was well set on his feet. This time Benton snarled a curse and kicked him as he lay.

"Charlie, Charlie!" Stella screamed.

If he heard her, he gave no heed.

"Hit the trail, you," he shouted at the logger. "Hit it quick before I tramp your damned face into the ground. I told you once not to come around here feeding booze to my cook. I do all the whisky-drinking that's done in this camp, and don't you forget it. Damn your eyes, I've got troubles enough without whisky."

The man gathered himself up, badly shaken, and holding his hand to his bleeding nose, made off to his rowboat at the float.

"G'wan home," Benton curtly ordered the Siwashes. "Get drunk at your own camp, not in mine. *Sabe?* Beat it."

They scuttled off, the wizened little old man steadying his fat *klootch* along her uncertain way. Down on the lake the chastised logger stood out in his boat, resting once on his oars to shake a fist at Benton. Then Charlie faced about on his shocked and outraged sister.

"Good Heavens!" she burst out. "Is it necessary to be so downright brutal in actions as well as speech?"

"I'm running a logging camp, not a kindergarten," he snapped angrily. "I know what I'm doing. If you don't like it, go in the house where your hyper-sensitive tastes won't be offended."

"Thank you," she responded cuttingly and swung about, angry and hurt—only to have a fresh scare from the drunken cook, who came reeling forward.

"I'm gonna quit," he loudly declared. "I ain't goin' to stick 'round here no more. The job's no good. I want m' time. Yuh hear me, Benton. I'm through. Com-pletely, ab-sho-lutely through. You bet I am. Gimme m' time. I'm a gone goose."

"Quit, then, hang you," Benton growled. "You'll get your check in a minute. You're a fine excuse for a cook, all right—get drunk right on the job. You don't need to show up here again, when you've had your jag out."

"'S all right," Matt declared largely. "'S other jobs. You ain't the whole Pacific coast. Oh, way down 'pon the Swa-a-nee ribber—"

He broke into dolorous song and turned back into the cookhouse. Benton's hard-set face relaxed. He laughed shortly.

"Takes all kinds to make a world," he commented. "Don't look so horrified, Sis. This isn't the regular order of events. It's just an accumulation—and it sort of got me going. Here's the boys."

The four stretcher men set down their burden in the shade of the bunkhouse. Renfrew was conscious now.

"Tough luck, Jim," Benton sympathized. "Does it pain much?"

Renfrew shook his head. White and weakened from shock and loss of blood, nevertheless he bravely disclaimed pain.

"We'll get you fixed up at the Springs," Benton went on. "It's a nasty slash in the meat, but I don't think the bone was touched. You'll be on deck before long. I'll see you through, anyway."

They gave him a drink of water and filled his pipe, joking him about easy days in the hospital while they sweated in the woods. The drunken cook came out, carrying his rolled blankets, began maudlin sympathy, and was promptly squelched, whereupon he retreated to the float, emitting conversation to the world at large. Then they carried Renfrew down to the float, and Davis began to haul up the anchor to lay the *Chickamin* alongside.

While the chain was still chattering in the hawse pipe, the squat black hull of Jack Fyfe's tender rounded the nearest point.

"Whistle him up, Sam," Benton ordered. "Jack can beat our time, and this bleeding must be stopped quick."

The tender veered in from her course at the signal. Fyfe himself was at the wheel. Five minutes effected a complete arrangement, and the *Panther* drew off with the drunken cook singing atop of the pilot house, and Renfrew comfortable in her cabin, and Jack Fyfe's promise to see him properly installed and attended in the local hospital at Roaring Springs.

Benton heaved a sigh of relief and turned to his sister.

"Still mad, Stell?" he asked placatingly and put his arm over her shoulders.

"Of course not," she responded instantly to this kindlier phase. "Ugh! Your hands are all bloody, Charlie."

"That's so, but it'll wash off," he replied. "Well, we're shy a good woodsman and a cook, and I'll miss 'em both. But it might be worse. Here's where you go to bat, Stella. Get on your apron and lend me a hand in the kitchen, like a good girl. We have to eat, no matter what happens."

CHAPTER VI
THE DIGNITY (?) OF TOIL

By such imperceptible degrees that she was scarce aware of it, Stella took her place as a cog in her brother's logging machine, a unit in the human mechanism which he operated skilfully and relentlessly at top speed to achieve his desired end—one million feet of timber in boomsticks by September the first.

From the evening that she stepped into the breach created by a drunken cook, the kitchen burden settled steadily upon her shoulders. For a week Benton daily expected and spoke of the arrival of a new cook. Fyfe had wired a Vancouver employment agency to send one, the day he took Jim Renfrew down. But either cooks were scarce, or the order went astray, for no rough and ready kitchen mechanic arrived. Benton in the meantime ceased to look for one. He worked like a horse, unsparing of himself, unsparing of others. He rose at half-past four, lighted the kitchen fire, roused Stella, and helped her prepare breakfast, preliminary to his day in the woods. Later he impressed Katy John into service to wait on the table and wash dishes. He labored patiently to teach Stella certain simple tricks of cooking that she did not know.

Quick of perception, as thorough as her brother in whatsoever she set her hand to do, Stella was soon equal to the job. And as the days passed and no camp cook came to their relief, Benton left the job to her as a matter of course.

"You can handle that kitchen with Katy as well as a man," he said to her at last. "And it will give you something to occupy your time. I'd have to pay a cook seventy dollars a month. Katy draws twenty-five. You can credit yourself with the balance, and I'll pay off when the contract money comes in. We might as well keep the coin in the family. I'll feel easier, because you won't get drunk and jump the job in a pinch. What do you say?"

She said the only possible thing to say under the circumstances. But she did not say it with pleasure, nor with any feeling of gratitude. It was hard work, and she and hard work were utter strangers. Her feet ached from continual standing on them. The heat and the smell of stewing meat and vegetables sickened her. Her hands were growing rough and red from dabbling in water, punching bread dough, handling the varied articles of food that go to make up a meal. Upon hands and forearms there stung continually certain small cuts and burns that lack of experience over a hot range inevitably inflicted upon her. Whereas time had promised to hang heavy on her hands, now an hour of idleness in the day became a precious boon.

Yet in her own way she was as full of determination as her brother. She saw plainly enough that she must leave the drone stage behind. She perceived that to be fed and clothed and housed and to have her wishes readily gratified was not an inherent right—that some one must foot the bill—that now for all she received she must return equitable value. At home she had never thought of it in that light; in fact, she had never thought of it at all. Now that she was beginning to get a glimmering of her true economic relation to the world at large, she had no wish to emulate the clinging vine, even if thereby she could have secured a continuance of that silk-lined existence which had been her fortunate lot. Her pride revolted against parasitism. It was therefore a certain personal satisfaction to have achieved self-support at a stroke, insofar as that in the sweat of her brow,—all too literally,—she earned her bread and a compensation besides. But there were times when that solace seemed scarcely to weigh against her growing detest for the endless routine of her task, the exasperating physical weariness and irritations it brought upon her.

For to prepare three times daily food for a dozen hungry men is no mean undertaking. One cannot have in a logging camp the conveniences of a hotel kitchen. The water must be carried in buckets from the creek near by, and wood brought in armfuls from the pile of sawn blocks outside. The low-roofed kitchen shanty was always like an oven. The flies swarmed in their tens of thousands. As the men sweated with axe and saw in the woods, so she sweated in the kitchen. And her work began two hours before their day's labor, and continued two hours after they were done. She slept, like one exhausted and rose full of sleep-heaviness, full of bodily soreness and spiritual protest when the alarm clock raised its din in the cool morning.

"You don't like thees work, do you, Mees Benton?" Katy John said to her one day, in the soft, slurring accent that colored her English. "You wasn't cut out for a cook."

"This isn't work," Stella retorted irritably. "It's simple drudgery. I don't wonder that men cooks take to drink."

Katy laughed.

"Why don't you be nice to Mr. Abbey," she suggested archly. "He'd like to give you a better job than thees—for life. My, but it must be nice to have lots of money like that man's got, and never have to work."

"You'll get those potatoes peeled sooner if you don't talk quite so much, Katy," Miss Benton made reply.

There was that way out, as the Siwash girl broadly indicated. Paul Abbey had grown into the habit of coming there rather more often than mere neighborliness called for, and it was palpable that he did not come to hold converse with Benton or Benton's gang, although he was "hail fellow" with all woodsmen. At first his coming might have been laid to any whim. Latterly Stella herself was unmistakably the attraction. He brought his sister once, a fair-haired girl about Stella's age. She proved an exceedingly self-contained young person, whose speech during the hour of her stay amounted to a dozen or so drawling sentences. With no hint of condescension or superciliousness, she still managed to arouse in Stella a mild degree of resentment. She wore an impeccable pongee silk, simple and costly, and *her* hands had evidently never known the roughening of work. In one way and another Miss Benton straightway conceived an active dislike for Linda Abbey. As her reception of Paul's sister was not conducive to chumminess, Paul did not bring Linda again.

But he came oftener than Stella desired to be bothered with him. Charlie was beginning to indulge in some rather broad joking, which offended and irritated her. She was not in the least attracted to Paul Abbey. He was a nice enough young man; for all she knew, he might be a concentration of all the manly virtues, but he gave no fillip to either her imagination or her emotions. He was too much like a certain type of young fellow she had known in other embodiments. Her instinct warned her that stripped of his worldly goods he would be wholly commonplace. She could be friends with the Paul Abbey kind of man, but when she tried to consider him as a possible lover, she found herself unresponsive, even amused. She was forced to consider it, because Abbey was fast approaching that stage. It was heralded in the look of dumb appeal that she frequently surprised in his gaze, by various signs and tokens, that Stella Benton was too sophisticated to mistake. One of these days he would lay his heart, and hand at her feet.

Sometimes she considered what her life might be if she should marry him. Abbey was wealthy in his own right and heir to more wealth. But—she could not forbear a wry grimace at the idea. Some fateful hour love would flash across her horizon, a living flame. She could visualize the tragedy if it should be too late, if it found her already bound—sold for a mess of pottage at her ease. She did not mince words to herself when she reflected on this matter. She knew herself as a creature of passionate impulses, consciously resenting all restraint. She knew that men and women did mad things under the spur of emotion. She wanted no shackles, she wanted to be free to face the great adventure when it came.

Yet there were times during the weeks that flitted past when it seemed to her that no bondage could be meaner, more repugnant, than that daily slavery in her brother's kitchen; that transcendent conceptions of love and marriage were vain details by comparison with aching feet and sleep-heavy eyes, with the sting of burns, the smart of sweat on her face, all the never-ending trifles that so irritated her. She had been spoiled in the making for so sordid an existence. Sometimes she would sit amid the array of dishes and pans and cooking food and wonder if she really were the same being whose life had been made up of books and music, of teas and dinners and plays, of light, inconsequential chatter with genial, well-dressed folk. There was no one to talk to here and less time to talk. There was nothing to read except a batch of newspapers filtering into camp once a week or ten days. There was not much in this monster stretch of giant timber but heat and dirt and flies and hungry men who must be fed.

If Paul Abbey had chanced to ask her to marry him during a period of such bodily and spiritual rebellion, she would probably have committed herself to that means of escape in sheer desperation. For she did not harden to the work; it steadily sapped both her strength and patience. But he chose an ill time for his declaration. Stella had overtaken her work and snared a fleeting hour of idleness in mid-afternoon of a hot day in early August. Under a branchy alder at the cook-house-end she piled all the pillows she could commandeer in their quarters and curled herself upon them at grateful ease. Like a tired animal, she gave herself up to the pleasure of physical relaxation, staring at a perfect turquoise sky through the whispering leaves above. She was not even thinking. She was too tired to think, and for the time being too much at peace to permit thought that would, in the very nature of things, be disturbing.

Abbey maintained for his own pleasure a fast motorboat. He slid now into the bay unheard, tied up beside the float, walked to the kitchen, glanced in, then around the corner, and smilingly took a seat on the grass near her.

"It's too perfect a day to loaf in the shade," he observed, after a brief exchange of commonplaces. "Won't you come out for a little spin on the lake? A ride in the *Wolf* will put some color in your cheeks."

"If I had time," she said, "I would. But loggers must eat though the heavens fall. In about twenty minutes I'll have to start supper. I'll have color enough, goodness knows once I get over that stove."

Abbey picked nervously at a blade of grass for a minute.

"This is a regular dog's life for you," he broke out suddenly.

"Oh, hardly that," she protested. "It's a little hard on me because I haven't been used to it, that's all."

"It's Chinaman's work," he said hotly. "Charlie oughtn't to let you stew in that kitchen."

Stella said nothing; she was not moved to the defence of her brother. She was loyal enough to her blood, but not so intensely loyal that she could defend him against criticism that struck a responsive chord in her own mind. She was beginning to see that, being useful, Charlie was making use of her. His horizon had narrowed to logs that might be transmuted into money. Enslaved himself by his engrossing purposes, he thought nothing of enslaving others to serve his end. She had come to a definite conclusion about that, and she meant to collect her wages when he sold his logs, collect also the ninety dollars of her money he had coolly appropriated, and try a different outlet. If one must work, one might at least seek work a little to one's taste. She therefore dismissed Abbey's comment carelessly:

"Some one has to do it."

A faint flush crept slowly up into his round, boyish face. He looked at her with disconcerting steadiness. Perhaps something in his expression gave her the key to his thought, or it may have been that peculiar psychical receptiveness which in a woman we are pleased to call intuition; but at any rate Stella divined what was coming and would have forestalled it by rising. He prevented that move by catching her hands.

"Look here, Stella," he blurted out, "it just grinds me to death to see you slaving away in this camp, feeding a lot of roughnecks. Won't you marry me and cut this sort of thing out? We'd be no end good chums."

She gently disengaged her hands, her chief sensation one of amusement, Abbey was in such an agony of blushing diffidence, all flustered at his own temerity. Also, she thought, a trifle precipitate. That was not the sort of wooing to carry her off her feet. For that matter she was quite sure nothing Paul Abbey could do or say would ever stir her pulses. She had to put an end to the situation, however. She took refuge in a flippant manner.

"Thanks for the compliment, Mr. Abbey," she smiled. "But really I couldn't think of inflicting repentance at leisure on you in that offhand way. You wouldn't want me to marry you just so I could resign the job of chef, would you?"

"Don't you like me?" he asked plaintively.

"Not that way," she answered positively.

"You might try," he suggested hopefully. "Honest, I'm crazy about you. I've liked you ever since I saw you first. I wouldn't want any greater privilege than to marry you and take you away from this sort of thing. You're too good for it. Maybe I'm kind of sudden, but I know my own mind. Can't you take a chance with me?"

"I'm sorry," she said gently, seeing him so sadly in earnest. "It isn't a question of taking a chance. I don't care for you. I haven't got any feeling but the mildest sort of friendliness. If I married you, it would only be for a home, as the saying is. And I'm not made that way. Can't you see how impossible it would be?"

"You'd get to like me," he declared. "I'm just as good as the next man."

His smooth pink-and-white skin reddened again.

"That sounds a lot like tooting my own horn mighty strong," said he. "But I'm in dead earnest. If there isn't anybody else yet, you could like me just as well as the next fellow. I'd be awfully good to you."

"I daresay you would," she said quietly. "But I couldn't be good to you. I don't want to marry you, Mr. Abbey. That's final. All the feeling I have for you isn't enough for any woman to marry on."

"Maybe not," he said dolefully. "I suppose that's the way it goes. Hang it, I guess I was a little too sudden. But I'm a stayer. Maybe you'll change your mind some time."

He was standing very near her, and they were both so intent upon the momentous business that occupied them that neither noticed Charlie Benton until his hail startled them to attention.

"Hello, folks," he greeted and passed on into the cook shanty, bestowing upon Stella, over Abbey's shoulder, a comprehensive grin which nettled her exceedingly. Her peaceful hour had been disturbed to no purpose. She did not want to love or be loved. For the moment she felt old beyond her years, mature beyond the comprehension of any man. If she had voiced her real attitude toward Paul Abbey, she would have counseled him to run and play, "like a good little boy."

Instead she remarked: "I must get to work," and left her downcast suitor without further ceremony.

As she went about her work in the kitchen, she saw Abbey seat himself upon a log in the yard, his countenance wreathed in gloom. He was presently joined by her brother. Glancing out, now and then, she made a guess at the meat of their talk, and her lip curled slightly. She saw them walk down to Abbey's launch, and Charlie delivered an encouraging slap on Paul's shoulder as he embarked. Then the speedy craft tore out of the bay at a headlong gait, her motor roaring in unmuffled exhaust, wide wings of white spray arching off her flaring bows.

"The desperate recklessness of thwarted affection—fiddlesticks!" Miss Benton observed in sardonic mood. Her hands were deep in pie dough. She thumped it viciously. The kitchen and the flies and all the rest of it rasped at her nerves again.

Charlie came into the kitchen, hunted a cookie out of the tin box where such things were kept, and sat swinging one leg over a corner of the table, eying her critically while he munched.

"So you turned Paul down, eh?" he said at last. "You're the prize chump. You've missed the best chance you'll ever have to put yourself on Easy Street."

CHAPTER VII
SOME NEIGHBORLY ASSISTANCE

For a week thereafter Benton developed moods of sourness, periods of scowling thought. He tried to speed up his gang, and having all spring driven them at top speed, the added straw broke the back of their patience, and Stella heard some sharp interchanges of words. He quelled one incipient mutiny through sheer dominance, but it left him more short of temper, more crabbedly moody than ever. Eventually his ill-nature broke out against Stella over some trifle, and she—being herself an aggrieved party to his transactions—surprised her own sense of the fitness of things by retaliating in kind.

"I'm slaving away in your old camp from daylight till dark at work I despise, and you can't even speak decently to me," she flared up. "You act like a perfect brute lately. What's the matter with you?"

Benton gnawed at a finger nail in silence.

"Hang it, I guess you're right," he admitted at last. "But I can't help having a grouch. I'm going to fall behind on this contract, the best I can do."

"Well," she replied tartly. "I'm not to blame for that. I'm not responsible for your failure. Why take it out on me?"

"I don't, particularly," he answered. "Only—can't you *sabe*? A man gets on edge when he works and sweats for months and sees it all about to come to nothing."

"So does a woman," she made pointed retort.

Benton chose to ignore the inference.

"If I fall down on this, it'll just about finish me," he continued glumly. "These people are not going to allow me an inch leeway. I'll have to deliver on that contract to the last stipulated splinter before they'll pay over a dollar. If I don't have a million feet for 'em three weeks from to-day, it's all off, and maybe a suit for breach of contract besides. That's the sort they are. If they can wiggle out of taking my logs, they'll be to the good, because they've made other contracts down the coast at fifty cents a thousand less. And the aggravating thing about it is that if I could get by with this deal, I can close a five-million-foot contract with the Abbey-Monohan outfit, for delivery next spring. I must have the money for this before I can undertake the bigger contract."

"Can't you sell your logs if these other people won't take them?" she asked, somewhat alive now to his position—and, incidentally, her own interest therein.

"In time, yes," he said. "But when you go into the open market with logs, you don't always find a buyer right off the reel. I'd have to hire 'em towed from here to Vancouver, and there's some bad water to get over. Time is money to me right now, Stell. If the thing dragged over two or three months, by the time they were sold and all expenses paid, I might not have anything left. I'm in debt for supplies, behind in wages When it looks like a man's losing, everybody jumps him. That's business. I may have my outfit seized and sold up if I fall down on this delivery and fail to square up accounts right away. Damn it, if you hadn't given Paul Abbey the cold turn-down, I might have got a boost over this hill. You were certainly a chump."

"I'm not a mere pawn in your game yet," she flared hotly. "I suppose you'd trade me for logs enough to complete your contract and consider it a good bargain."

"Oh, piffle," he answered coolly. "What's the use talking like that. It's your game as much as mine. Where do you get off, if I go broke? You might have done a heap worse. Paul's a good head. A girl that hasn't anything but her looks to get through the world on hasn't any business overlooking a bet like that. Nine girls out of ten marry for what there is in it, anyhow."

"Thank you," she replied angrily. "I'm not in the market on that basis."

"All this stuff about ideal love and soul communion and perfect mating is pure bunk, it seems to me," Charlie tacked off on a new course of thought. "A man and a woman somewhere near of an age generally hit it off all right, if they've got common horse sense—and income enough so they don't have to squabble eternally about where the next new hat and suit's coming from. It's the coin that counts most of all. It sure is, Sis. It's me that knows it, right now."

He sat a minute or two longer, again preoccupied with his problems.

"Well," he said at last, "I've got to get action somehow. If I could get about thirty men and another donkey for three weeks, I'd make it."

He went outside. Up in the near woods the whine of the saws and the sounds of chopping kept measured beat. It was late in the forenoon, and Stella was hard about her dinner preparations. Contract or no contract, money or no money, men must eat. That fact loomed biggest on her daily schedule, left her no room to think overlong of other things. Her huff over, she felt rather sorry for Charlie, a feeling accentuated by sight of him humped on a log in the sun, too engrossed in his perplexities to be where he normally was at that hour, in the thick of the logging, working harder than any of his men.

A little later she saw him put off from the float in the *Chickamin's* dinghy. When the crew came to dinner, he had not returned. Nor was he back when they went out again at one.

Near mid-afternoon, however, he strode into the kitchen, wearing the look of a conqueror.

"I've got it fixed," he announced.

Stella looked up from a frothy mass of yellow stuff that she was stirring in a pan.

"Got what fixed?" she asked.

"Why, this log business," he said. "Jack Fyfe is going to put in a crew and a donkey, and we're going to everlastingly rip the innards out of these woods. I'll make delivery after all."

"That's good," she remarked, but noticeably without enthusiasm. The heat of that low-roofed shanty had taken all possible enthusiasm for anything out of her for the time being. Always toward the close of each day she was gripped by that feeling of deadly fatigue, in the face of which nothing much mattered but to get through the last hours somehow and drag herself wearily to bed.

Benton playfully tweaked Katy John's ear and went whistling up the trail. It was plain sailing for him now, and he was correspondingly elated.

He tried to talk to Stella that evening when she was through, all about big things in the future, big contracts he could get, big money he could see his way to make. It fell mostly on unappreciative ears. She was tired, so tired that his egotistical chatter irritated her beyond measure. What she would have welcomed with heartfelt gratitude was not so much a prospect of future affluence in which she might or might not share as a lightening of her present burden. So far as his conversation ran, Benton's sole concern seemed to be more equipment, more men, so that he might get out more logs. In the midst of this optimistic talk, Stella walked abruptly into her room.

Noon of the next day brought the *Panther* coughing into the bay, flanked on the port side by a scow upon which rested a twin to the iron monster that jerked logs into her brother's chute. To starboard was made fast a like scow. That was housed over, a smoking stovepipe stuck through the roof, and a capped and aproned cook rested his arms on the window sill as they floated in. Men to the number of twenty or more clustered about both scows and the *Panther's* deck, busy with pipe and cigarette and rude jest. The clatter of their voices uprose through the noon meal. But when the donkey scow thrust its blunt nose against the beach, the chaff and laughter died into silent, capable action.

"A Seattle yarder properly handled can do anything but climb a tree," Charlie had once boasted to her, in reference to his own machine.

It seemed quite possible to Stella, watching Jack Fyfe's crew at work. Steam was up in the donkey. They carried a line from its drum through a snatch block ashore and jerked half a dozen logs crosswise before the scow in a matter of minutes. Then the same cable was made fast to a sturdy fir, the engineer stood by, and the ponderous machine slid forward on its own skids, like an up-ended barrel on a sled, down off the scow, up the bank, smashing brush, branches, dead roots, all that stood in its path, drawing steadily up to the anchor tree as the cable spooled up on the drum.

A dozen men tailed on to the inch and a quarter cable and bore the loose end away up the path. Presently one stood clear, waving a signal. Again the donkey began to puff and quiver, the line began to roll up on the drum, and the big yarder walked up the slope under its own power, a locomotive unneedful of rails, making its own right of way. Upon the platform built over the skids were piled the tools of the crew, sawed blocks for the fire box, axes, saws, grindstones, all that was necessary in their task. At one o'clock they made their first move. At two the donkey was vanished into that region where the chute-head lay, and the great firs stood waiting the slaughter.

By mid-afternoon Stella noticed an acceleration of numbers in the logs that came hurtling lakeward. Now at shorter intervals arose the grinding sound of their arrival, the ponderous splash as each leaped to the water. It was a good thing, she surmised—for Charlie Benton. She could not see where it made much difference to her whether ten logs a day or a hundred came down to the boomsticks.

Late that afternoon Katy vanished upon one of her periodic visits to the camp of her kindred around the point. Bred out of doors, of a tribe whose immemorial custom it is that the women do all the work, the Siwash girl was strong as an ox, and nearly as bovine in temperament and movements. She could lift with ease a weight that taxed Stella's strength, and Stella Benton was no weakling, either. It was therefore a part of Katy's routine to keep water pails filled from the creek and the wood box supplied, in addition to washing dishes and carrying food to the table. Katy slighted these various tasks occasionally. She needed oversight, continual admonition, to get any job done in time. She was slow to the point of exasperation. Nevertheless, she lightened the day's labor, and Stella put up with her slowness since she needs must or assume the entire burden herself. This time Katy thoughtlessly left with both water pails empty.

Stella was just picking them up off the bench when a shadow darkened the door, and she looked around to see Jack Fyfe.

"How d' do," he greeted.

He had seemed a short man. Now, standing within four feet of her, she perceived that this was an illusion created by the proportion and thickness of his body. He was, in fact, half a head taller than she, and Stella stood five feet five. His gray eyes met hers squarely, with a cool, impersonal quality of gaze. There was neither smirk nor embarrassment in his straightforward glance. He was, in effect, "sizing her up" just as he would have looked casually over a logger asking him for a job. Stella sensed that, and resenting it momentarily, failed to match his manner. She flushed. Fyfe smiled, a broad, friendly grin, in which a wide mouth opened to show strong, even teeth.

"I'm after a drink," he said quite impersonally, and coolly taking the pails out of her hands, walked through the kitchen and down to the creek. He was back in a minute, set the filled buckets in their place, and helped himself with a dipper.

"Say," he asked easily, "how do you like life in a logging camp by this time? This is sure one hot job you've got."

"Literally or slangily?" she asked in a flippant tone. Fyfe's reputation, rather vividly colored, had reached her from various sources. She was not quite sure whether she cared to countenance him or not. There was a disturbing quality in his glance, a subtle suggestion of force about him that she felt without being able to define in understandable terms. In any case she felt more than equal to the task of squelching any effort at familiarity, even if Jack Fyfe were, in a sense, the convenient god in her brother's machine. Fyfe chuckled at her answer.

"Both," he replied shortly and went out.

She saw him a little later out on the bay in the *Panther's* dink, standing up in the little boat, making long, graceful casts with a pliant rod. She perceived that this manner of fishing was highly successful, insomuch as at every fourth or fifth cast a trout struck his fly, breaking water with a vigorous splash. Then the bamboo would arch as the fish struggled, making sundry leaps clear of the water, gleaming like silver each time he broke the surface, but coming at last tamely to Jack Fyfe's landing net. Of outdoor sports she knew most about angling, for her father had been an ardent fly-caster. And she had observed with a true angler's scorn the efforts of her brother's loggers to catch the lake trout with a baited hook, at which they had scant success. Charlie never fished. He had neither time nor inclination for such fooling, as he termed it. Fyfe stopped fishing when the donkeys whistled six. It happened that when he drew in to his cookhouse float, Stella was standing in her kitchen door. Fyfe looked up at her and held aloft a dozen trout strung by the gills on a stick, gleaming in the sun.

"Vanity," she commented inaudibly. "I wonder if he thinks I've been admiring his skill as a fisherman?"

Nevertheless she paid tribute to his skill when ten minutes later he sent a logger with the entire catch to her kitchen. They looked toothsome, those lakers, and they were. She cooked one for her own supper and relished it as a change from the everlasting bacon and ham. In the face of that million feet of timber, Benton hunted no deer. True, the Siwashes had once or twice brought in some venison. That, with a roast or two of beef from town, was all the fresh meat she had tasted in two months. There were enough trout to make a breakfast for the crew. She ate hers and mentally thanked Jack Fyfe.

Lying in her bed that night, in the short interval that came between undressing and wearied sleep, she found herself wondering with a good deal more interest about Jack Fyfe than she had ever bestowed upon—well, Paul Abbey, for instance.

She was quite positive that she was going to dislike Jack Fyfe if he were thrown much in her way. There was something about him that she resented. The difference between him and the rest of the rude crew among which she must perforce live was a question of degree, not of kind. There was certainly some compelling magnetism about the man. But along with it went what she considered an almost brutal directness of speech and action. Part of this conclusion came from hearsay, part from observation, limited though her opportunities had been for the latter. Miss Stella Benton, for all her poise, was not above jumping at conclusions. There was something about Jack Fyfe that she resented. She irritably dismissed it as a foolish impression, but the fact remained that the mere physical nearness of him seemed to put her on the defensive, as if he were in reality a hunter and she the hunted.

Fyfe joined Charlie Benton about the time she finished work. The three of them sat on the grass before Benton's quarters, and every time Jack Fyfe's eyes rested on her she steeled herself to resist—what, she did not know. Something intangible, something that disturbed her. She had never experienced anything like that before; it tantalized her, roused her curiosity. There was nothing occult about the man. He was nowise fascinating, either in face or manner. He made no bid for her attention. Yet during the half hour he sat there, Stella's mind revolved constantly about him. She recalled all that she had heard of him, much of it, from her point of view, highly discreditable. Inevitably she fell to comparing him with other men she knew.

She had, in a way, unconsciously been prepared for just such a measure of concentration upon Jack Fyfe. For he was a power on Roaring Lake, and power,—physical, intellectual or financial,—exacts its own tribute of consideration. He was a fighter, a dominant, hard-bitten woodsman, so the tale ran. He had gathered about him the toughest crew on the Lake, himself, upon occasion, the most turbulent of all. He controlled many square miles of big timber, and he had gotten it all by his own effort in the eight years since he came to Roaring Lake as a hand logger. He was slow of speech, chain-lightning in action, respected generally, feared a lot. All these things her brother and Katy John had sketched for Stella with much verbal embellishment.

There was no ignoring such a man. Brought into close contact with the man himself, Stella felt the radiating force of his personality. There it was, a thing to be reckoned with. She felt that whenever Jack Fyfe's gray eyes rested impersonally on her. His pleasant, freckled face hovered before her until she fell asleep, and in her sleep she dreamed again of him throwing that drunken logger down the Hot Springs slip.

CHAPTER VIII
DURANCE VILE

By September first a growing uneasiness hardened into distasteful certainty upon Stella. It had become her firm resolve to get what money was due her when Charlie marketed his logs and try another field of labor. That camp on Roaring Lake was becoming a nightmare to her. She had no inherent dislike for work. She was too vibrantly alive to be lazy. But she had had an overdose of unaccustomed drudgery, and she was growing desperate. If there had been anything to keep her mind from continual dwelling on the manifold disagreeableness she had to cope with, she might have felt differently, but there was not. She ate, slept, worked, — ate, slept, and worked again, — till every fibre of her being cried out in protest against the deadening round. She was like a flower striving to attain its destiny of bloom in soil overrun with rank weeds. Loneliness and hard, mean work, day after day, in which all that had ever seemed desirable in life had neither place nor consideration, were twin evils of isolation and flesh-wearying labor, from which she felt that she must get away, or go mad.

But she did not go. Benton left to make his delivery to the mill company, the great boom of logs gliding slowly along in the wake of a tug, the *Chickamin* in attendance. Benton's crew accompanied the boom. Fyfe's gang loaded their donkey and gear aboard the scow and went home. The bay lay all deserted, the woods silent. For the first time in three months she had all her hours free, only her own wants to satisfy. Katy John spent most of her time in the smoky camp of her people. Stella loafed. For two days she did nothing, gave herself up to a physical torpor she had never known before. She did not want to read, to walk about, or even lift her eyes to the bold mountains that loomed massive across the lake. It was enough to lie curled among pillows under the alder and stare drowsily at the blue September sky, half aware of the drone of a breeze in the firs, the flutter of birds' wings, and the lap of water on the beach.

Presently, however, the old restless energy revived. The spring came back to her step and she shed that lethargy like a cast-off garment. And in so doing her spirit rose in hot rebellion against being a prisoner to deadening drudgery, against being shut away from all the teeming life that throve and trafficked beyond the solitude in which she sat immured. When Charlie came back, there was going to be a change. She repeated that to herself with determination. Between whiles she rambled about in the littered clearing, prowled along the beaches, and paddled now and then far outside the bay in a flat-bottomed skiff, restless, full of plans. So far as she saw, she would have to face some city alone, but she viewed that prospect with a total absence of the helpless feeling which harassed her so when she first took train for her brother's camp. She had passed through what she termed a culinary inferno. Nothing, she considered, could be beyond her after that unremitting drudgery.

But Benton failed to come back on the appointed day. The four days lengthened to a week. Then the *Panther*, bound up-lake, stopped to leave a brief note from Charlie, telling her business had called him to Vancouver.

Altogether it was ten days before the *Chickamin* whistled up the bay. She slid in beside the float, her decks bristling with men like a passenger craft. Stella, so thoroughly sated with loneliness that she temporarily forgot her grievances, flew to meet her brother. But one fair glimpse of the disembarking crew turned her back. They were all in varying stages of liquor—from two or three who had to be hauled over the float and up to the bunkhouse like sacks of bran, to others who were so happily under the influence of John Barleycorn that every move was some silly antic. She retreated in disgust. When Charlie reached the cabin, he himself proved to be fairly mellow, in the best of spirits—speaking truly in the double sense.

"Hello, lady," he hailed jovially. "How did you fare all by your lonesome this long time? I didn't figure to be gone so long, but there was a lot to attend to. How are you, anyway?"

"All right," she answered coolly. "You evidently celebrated your log delivery in the accepted fashion."

"Don't you believe it," he grinned amiably. "I had a few drinks with the boys on the way up, that's all. No, sir, it was straight business with a capital B all the time I was gone. I've got a good thing in hand, Sis—big money in sight. Tell you about it later. Think you and Katy can rustle grub for this bunch by six?"

"Oh, I suppose so," she said shortly. It was on the tip of her tongue to tell him then and there that she was through,—like Matt, the cook, that memorable afternoon, "completely an' ab-sho-lutely through." She refrained. There was no use in being truculent. But that drunken crowd looked formidable in numbers.

"How many extra?" she asked mechanically.

"Thirty men, all told," Benton returned briskly. "I tell you I'm sure going to rip the heart out of this limit before spring. I've signed up a six-million-foot contract for delivery as soon as the logs'll go over Roaring Rapids in the spring. Remember what I told you when you came? You stick with me, and you'll wear diamonds. I stand to clean up twenty thousand on the winter's work."

"In that case, you should be able to hire a real cook," she suggested, a spice of malice in her tone.

"I sure will, when it begins to come right," he promised largely. "And I'll give you a soft job keeping books then. Well, I'll lend you a hand for to-night. Where's the Siwash maiden?"

"Over at the camp; there she comes now," Stella replied. "Will you start a fire, Charlie, while I change my dress?"

"You look like a peach in that thing." He stood off a pace to admire. "You're some dame, Stell, when you get on your glad rags."

She frowned at her image in the glass behind the closed door of her room as she set about unfastening the linen dress she had worn that afternoon. Deep in her trunk, along with much other unused finery, it had reposed all summer. That ingrained instinct to be admired, to be garbed fittingly and well, came back to her as soon as she was rested. And though there were none but squirrels and bluejays and occasionally Katy John to cast admiring eyes upon her, it had pleased her for a week to wear her best, and wander about the beaches and among the dusky trunks of giant fir, a picture of blooming, well-groomed womanhood. She took off the dress and threw it on the bed with a resentful rush of feeling. The treadmill gaped for her again. But not for long. She was through with that. She was glad that Charlie's prospects pleased him. He could not call on her to help him out of a hole now. She would tell him her decision to-night. And as soon as he could get a cook to fill her place, then good-by to Roaring Lake, good-by to kitchen smells and flies and sixteen hours a day over a hot stove.

She wondered why such a loathing of the work afflicted her; if all who earned their bread in the sweat of their brow were ridden with that feeling,—woodsmen, cooks, chauffeurs, the slaves of personal service and the great industrial mills alike? Her heart went out to them if they were. But she was quite sure that work could be otherwise than repellent, enslaving. She recalled that cooks and maids had worked in her father's house with no sign of the revolt that now assailed her. But it seemed to her that their tasks had been light compared with the job of cooking in Charlie Benton's camp.

Curiously enough, while she changed her clothes, her thoughts a jumble of present things she disliked and the unknown that she would have to face alone in Vancouver, she found her mind turning on Jack Fyfe. During his three weeks' stay, they had progressed less in the direction of acquaintances than she and Paul Abbey had done in two meetings. Fyfe talked to her now and then briefly, but he looked at her more than he talked. Where his searching gaze disturbed, his speech soothed, it was so coolly impersonal. That, she deemed, was merely another of his odd contradictions. He was contradictory. Stella classified Jack Fyfe as a creature of unrestrained passions. She recognized, or thought she recognized, certain dominant, primitive characteristics, and they did not excite her admiration. Men admired him—those who were not afraid of him. If he had been of more polished clay, she could readily have grasped this attitude. But in her eyes he was merely a rude, masterful man, uncommonly gifted with physical strength, dominating other rude, strong men by sheer brute force. And she herself rather despised sheer brute force. The iron hand should fitly be concealed beneath the velvet glove.

Yet in spite of the bold look in his eyes that always confused and irritated her, Fyfe had never singled her out for the slightest attention of the kind any man bestows upon an attractive woman. Stella was no fool. She knew that she was attractive, and she knew why. She had been prepared to repulse, and there had been nothing to repulse. Once during Charlie's absence he had come in a rowboat, hailed her from the beach, and gone away without disembarking when she told him Benton was not back. He was something of an enigma, she confessed to herself, after all. Perhaps that was why he came so frequently into her mind. Or perhaps, she told herself, there was so little on Roaring Lake to think about that one could not escape the personal element. As if any one ever could. As if life were made up of anything but the impinging of one personality upon another. That was something Miss Stella Benton had yet to learn. She was still mired in the rampant egotism of untried youth, as yet the sublime individualist.

That side of her suffered a distinct shock later in the evening. When supper was over, the work done, and the loggers' celebration was slowly subsiding in the bunkhouse, she told Charlie with blunt directness what she wanted to do. With equally blunt directness he declared that he would not permit it. Stella's teeth came together with an angry little click.

"I'm of age, Charlie," she said to him. "It isn't for you to say what you will or will not *permit* me to do. I want that money of mine that you used— and what I've earned. God knows I *have* earned it. I can't stand this work, and I don't intend to. It isn't work; it's slavery."

"But what can you do in town?" he countered. "You haven't the least idea what you'd be going up against, Stell. You've never been away from home, and you've never had the least training at anything useful. You'd be on your uppers in no time at all. You wouldn't have a ghost of a chance."

"I have such a splendid chance here," she retorted ironically. "If I could get in any position where I'd be more likely to die of sheer stagnation, to say nothing of dirty drudgery, than in this forsaken hole, I'd like to know how. I don't think it's possible."

"You could be a whole lot worse off, if you only knew it," Benton returned grumpily. "If you haven't got any sense about things, I have. I know what a rotten hole Vancouver or any other seaport town is for a girl alone. I won't let you make any foolish break like that. That's flat."

From this position she failed to budge him. Once angered, partly by her expressed intention and partly by the outspoken protest against the mountain of work imposed on her, Charlie refused point-blank to give her either the ninety dollars he had taken out of her purse or the three months' wages due. Having made her request, and having met with this—to her—amazing refusal, Stella sat dumb. There was too fine a streak in her to break out in recrimination. She was too proud to cry.

So that she went to bed in a ferment of helpless rage. Virtually she was a prisoner, as much so as if Charlie had kidnaped her and held her so by brute force. The economic restraint was all potent. Without money she could not even leave the camp. And when she contemplated the daily treadmill before her, she shuddered.

At least she could go on strike. Her round cheek flushed with the bitterest anger she had ever known, she sat with eyes burning into the dark of her sordid room, and vowed that the thirty loggers should die of slow starvation if they did not eat until she cooked another meal for them.

CHAPTER IX
JACK FYFE'S CAMP

She was still hot with the spirit of mutiny when morning came, but she cooked breakfast. It was not in her to act like a petulant child. Morning also brought a different aspect to things, for Charlie told her while he helped prepare breakfast that he was going to take his crew and repay in labor the help Jack Fyfe had given him.

"While we're there, Jack's cook will feed all hands," said he. "And by the time we're through there, I'll have things fixed so it won't be such hard going for you here. Do you want to go along to Jack's camp?"

"No," she answered shortly. "I don't. I would much prefer to get away from this lake altogether, as I told you last night."

"You might as well forget that notion," he said stubbornly. "I've got a little pride in the matter. I don't want my sister drudging at the only kind of work she'd be able to earn a living at."

"You're perfectly willing to have me drudge here," she flashed back.

"That's different," he defended. "And it's only temporary. I'll be making real money before long. You'll get your share if you'll have a little patience and put your shoulder to the wheel. Lord, I'm doing the best I can."

"Yes—for yourself," she returned. "You don't seem to consider that I'm entitled to as much fair play as you'd have to accord one of your men. I don't want you to hand me an easy living on a silver salver. All I want of you is what is mine, and the privilege of using my own judgment. I'm quite capable of taking care of myself."

If there had been opportunity to enlarge on that theme, they might have come to another verbal clash. But Benton never lost sight of his primary object. The getting of breakfast and putting his men about their work promptly was of more importance to him than Stella's grievance. So the incipient storm dwindled to a sullen mood on her part. Breakfast over, Benton loaded men and tools aboard a scow hitched beside the boat. He repeated his invitation, and Stella refused, with a sarcastic reflection on the company she would be compelled to keep there.

The *Chickamin* with her tow drew off, and she was alone again.

"Marooned once more," Stella said to herself when the little steamboat slipped behind the first jutting point. "Oh, if I could just be a man for a while."

Marooned seemed to her the appropriate term. There were the two old Siwashes and their dark-skinned brood. But they were little more to Stella than the insentient boulders that strewed the beach. She could not talk to them or they to her. Long since she had been surfeited with Katy John. If there were any primitive virtues in that dusky maiden they were well buried under the white man's schooling. Katy's demand upon life was very simple and in marked contrast to Stella Benton's. Plenty of grub, no work, some cheap finery, and a man white or red, no matter, to make eyes at. Her horizon was bounded by Roaring Lake and the mission at Skookumchuck. She was therefore no mitigation of Stella's loneliness.

Nevertheless Stella resigned herself to make the best of it, and it proved a poor best. She could not detach herself sufficiently from the sordid realities to lose herself in day-dreaming. There was not a book in the camp save some ten-cent sensations she found in the bunkhouse, and these she had exhausted during Charlie's first absence. The uncommon stillness of the camp oppressed her more than ever. Even the bluejays and squirrels seemed to sense its abandonment, seemed to take her as part of the inanimate fixtures, for they frisked and chattered about with uncommon fearlessness. The lake lay dead gray, glassy as some great irregular window in the crust of the earth. Only at rare intervals did sail or smoke dot its surface, and then far offshore. The woods stood breathless in the autumn sun. It was like being entombed. And there would be a long stretch of it, with only a recurrence of that deadly grind of kitchen work when the loggers came home again.

Some time during the next forenoon she went southerly along the lake shore on foot without object or destination, merely to satisfy in some measure the restless craving for action. Colorful turns of life, the more or less engrossing contact of various personalities, some new thing to be done, seen, admired, discussed, had been a part of her existence ever since she could remember. None of this touched her now. A dead weight of monotony rode her hard. There was the furtive wild life of the forest, the light of sun and sky, and the banked green of the forest that masked the steep granite slopes. She appreciated beauty, craved it indeed, but she could not satisfy her being with scenic effects alone. She craved, without being wholly aware of it, or altogether admitting it to herself, some human distraction in all that majestic solitude.

It was forthcoming. When she returned to camp at two o'clock, driven in by hunger, Jack Fyfe sat on the doorstep.

"How-de-do. I've come to bring you over to my place," he announced quite casually.

"Thanks. I've already declined one pressing invitation to that effect," Stella returned drily. His matter-of-fact assurance rather nettled her.

"A woman always has the privilege of changing her mind," Fyfe smiled. "Charlie is going to be at my camp for at least three weeks. It'll rain soon, and the days'll be pretty gray and dreary and lonesome. You might as well pack your war-bag and come along."

She stood uncertainly. Her tongue held ready a blunt refusal, but she did not utter it; and she did not know why. She did have a glimpse of the futility of refusing, only she did not admit that refusal might be of no weight in the matter. With her mind running indignantly against compulsion, nevertheless her muscles involuntarily moved to obey. It irritated her further that she should feel in the least constrained to obey the calmly expressed wish of this quiet-spoken woodsman. Certain possible phases of a lengthy sojourn in Jack Fyfe's camp shot across her mind. He seemed of uncanny perception, for he answered this thought before it was clearly formed.

"Oh, you'll be properly chaperoned, and you won't have to mix with the crew," he drawled. "I've got all kinds of room. My boss logger's wife is up from town for a while. She's a fine, motherly old party, and she keeps us all in order."

"I haven't had any lunch," she temporized. "Have you?"

He shook his head.

"I rowed over here before twelve. Thought I'd get you back to camp in time for dinner. You know," he said with a twinkle in his blue eyes, "a logger never eats anything but a meal. A lunch to us is a snack that you put in your pocket. I guess we lack tone out here. We haven't got past the breakfast-dinner-supper stage yet; too busy making the country fit to live in."

"You have a tremendous job in hand," she observed.

"Oh, maybe," he laughed. "All in the way you look at it. Suits some of us. Well, if we get to my camp before three, the cook might feed us. Come on. You'll get to hating yourself if you stay here alone till Charlie's through."

Why not? Thus she parleyed with herself, one half of her minded to stand upon her dignity, the other part of her urging acquiescence in his wish that was almost a command. She was tempted to refuse just to see what he would do, but she reconsidered that. Without any logical foundation for the feeling, she was shy of pitting her will against Jack Fyfe's. Hitherto quite sure of herself, schooled in self-possession, it was a new and disturbing experience to come in contact with that subtle, analysis-defying quality which carries the possessor thereof straight to his or her goal over all opposition, which indeed many times stifles all opposition. Force of character, overmastering personality, emanation of sheer will, she could not say in what terms it should be described. Whatever it was, Jack Fyfe had it. It existed, a factor to be reckoned with when one dealt with him. For within twenty minutes she had packed a suitcase full of clothes and was embarked in his rowboat.

He sent the lightly built craft easily through the water with regular, effortless strokes. Stella sat in the stern, facing him. Out past the north horn of the bay, she broke the silence that had fallen between them.

"Why did you make a point of coming for me?" she asked bluntly.

Fyfe rested on his oars a moment, looking at her in his direct, unembarrassed way.

"I wintered once on the Stickine," he said. "My partner pulled out before Christmas and never came back. It was the first time I'd ever been alone in my life. I wasn't a much older hand in the country than you are. Four months without hearing the sound of a human voice. Stark alone. I got so I talked to myself out loud before spring. So I thought—well, I thought I'd come and bring you over to see Mrs. Howe."

Stella sat gazing at the slow moving panorama of the lake shore, her chin in her hand.

"Thank you," she said at last, and very gently.

Fyfe looked at her a minute or more, a queer, half-amused expression creeping into his eyes.

"Well," he said finally, "I might as well tell the whole truth. I've been thinking about you quite a lot lately, Miss Stella Benton, or I wouldn't have thought about you getting lonesome."

He smiled ever so faintly, a mere movement of the corners of his mouth, at the pink flush which rose quickly in her cheeks, and then resumed his steady pull at the oars.

Except for a greater number of board shacks and a larger area of stump and top-littered waste immediately behind it, Fyfe's headquarters, outwardly, at least, differed little from her brother's camp. Jack led her to a long, log structure with a shingle roof, which from its more substantial appearance she judged to be his personal domicile. A plump, smiling woman of forty greeted her on the threshold. Once within, Stella perceived that there was in fact considerable difference in Mr. Fyfe's habitation. There was a great stone fireplace, before which big easy-chairs invited restful lounging. The floor was overlaid with thick rugs which deadened her footfalls. With no pretense of ornamental decoration, the room held an air of homely comfort.

"Come in here and lay off your things," Mrs. Howe beamed on her. "If I'd 'a' known you were livin' so close, we'd have been acquainted a week ago; though I ain't got rightly settled here myself. My land, these men are such clams. I never knowed till this mornin' there was any white woman at this end of the lake besides myself."

She showed Stella into a bedroom. It boasted an enamel washstand with taps which yielded hot and cold water, neatly curtained windows, and a deep-seated Morris chair. Certainly Fyfe's household accommodation was far superior to Charlie Benton's. Stella expected the man's home to be rough and ready like himself, and in a measure it was, but a comfortable sort of rough and readiness. She took off her hat and had a critical survey of herself in a mirror, after which she had just time to brush her hair before answering Mrs. Howe's call to a "cup of tea."

The cup of tea resolved itself into a well-cooked and well-served meal, with china and linen and other unexpected table accessories which agreeably surprised, her. Inevitably she made comparisons, somewhat tinctured with natural envy. If Charlie would fix his place with a few such household luxuries, life in their camp would be more nearly bearable, despite the long hours of disagreeable work. As it was—well, the unrelieved discomforts were beginning to warp her out-look on everything.

Fyfe maintained his habitual sparsity of words while they ate the food Mrs. Howe brought on a tray hot from the cook's outlying domain. When they finished, he rose, took up his hat and helped himself to a handful of cigars from a box on the fireplace mantel.

"I guess you'll be able to put in the time, all right," he remarked. "Make yourself at home. If you take a notion to read, there's a lot of books and magazines in my room. Mrs. Howe'll show you."

He walked out. Stella was conscious of a distinct relief when he was gone. She had somehow experienced a recurrence of that peculiar feeling of needing to be on her guard, as if there were some curious, latent antagonism between them. She puzzled over that a little. She had never felt that way about Paul Abbey, for instance, or indeed toward any man she had ever known. Fyfe's more or less ambiguous remark in the boat had helped to arouse it again. His manner of saying that he had "thought a lot about her" conveyed more than the mere words. She could quite conceive of the Jack Fyfe type carrying things with a high hand where a woman was concerned. He had that reputation in all his other dealings. He was aggressive. He could drink any logger in the big firs off his feet. He had an uncanny luck at cards. Somehow or other in every undertaking Jack Fyfe always came out on top, so the tale ran. There must be, she reasoned, a wide streak of the brute in such a man. It was no gratification to her vanity to have him admire her. It did not dawn upon her that so far she had never got over being a little afraid of him, much less to ask herself why she should be afraid of him.

But she did not spend much time puzzling over Jack Fyfe. Once out of her sight she forgot him. It was balm to her lonely soul to have some one of her own sex for company. What Mrs. Howe lacked in the higher culture she made up in homely perception and unassuming kindliness. Her husband was Fyfe's foreman. She herself was not a permanent fixture in the camp. They had a cottage at Roaring Springs, where she spent most of the time, so that their three children could be in school.

"I was up here all through vacation," she told Stella. "But Lefty he got to howlin' about bein' left alone shortly after school started again, so I got my sister to look after the kids for a spell, while I stay. I'll be goin' down about the time Mr. Benton's through here."

Stella eventually went out to take a look around the camp. A hard-beaten path led off toward where rose the distant sounds of logging work, the ponderous crash of trees, and the puff of the donkeys. She followed that a little way and presently came to a knoll some three hundred yards above the beach. There she paused to look and wonder curiously.

For the crest of this little hillock had been cleared and graded level and planted to grass over an area four hundred feet square. It was trimmed like a lawn, and in the center of this vivid green block stood an unfinished house foundation of gray stone. No stick of timber, no board or any material for further building lay in sight. The thing stood as if that were to be all. And it was not a new undertaking temporarily delayed. There was moss creeping over the thick stone wall, she discovered when she walked over it. Whoever had laid that foundation had done it many a moon before. Yet the sward about was kept as if a gardener had it in charge.

A noble stretch of lake and mountain spread out before her gaze. Straight across the lake two deep clefts in the eastern range opened on the water, five miles apart. She could see the white ribbon of foaming cascades in each. Between lifted a great mountain, and on the lakeward slope of this stood a terrible scar of a slide, yellow and brown, rising two thousand feet from the shore. A vaporous wisp of cloud hung along the top of the slide, and above this aërial banner a snow-capped pinnacle thrust itself high into the infinite blue.

"What an outlook," she said, barely conscious that she spoke aloud. "Why do these people build their houses in the bush, when they could live in the open and have something like this to look at. They would, if they had any sense of beauty."

"Sure they haven't? Some of them might have, you know, without being able to gratify it."

She started, to find Jack Fyfe almost at her elbow, the gleam of a quizzical smile lighting his face.

"I daresay that might be true," she admitted.

Fyfe's gaze turned from her to the huge sweep of lake and mountain chain. She saw that he was outfitted for fishing, creel on his shoulder, unjointed rod in one hand. By means of his rubber-soled waders he had come upon her noiselessly.

"It's truer than you think, maybe," he said at length. "You don't want to come along and take a lesson in catching rainbows, I suppose?"

"Not this time, thanks," she shook her head.

"I want to get enough for supper, so I'd better be at it," he remarked. "Sometimes they come pretty slow. If you should want to go up and watch the boys work, that trail will take you there."

He went off across the grassy level and plunged into the deep timber that rose like a wall beyond. Stella looked after.

"It is certainly odd," she reflected with some irritation, "how that man affects me. I don't think a woman could ever be just friends with him. She'd either like him a lot or dislike him intensely. He isn't anything but a logger, and yet he has a presence like one of the lords of creation. Funny."

Then she went back to the house to converse upon domestic matters with Mrs. Howe until the shrilling of the donkey whistle brought forty-odd lumberjacks swinging down the trail.

Behind them a little way came Jack Fyfe with sagging creel. He did not stop to exhibit his catch, but half an hour later they were served hot and crisp at the table in the big living room, where Fyfe, Stella and Charlie Benton, Lefty Howe and his wife, sat down together.

A flunkey from the camp kitchen served the meal and cleared it away. For an hour or two after that the three men sat about in shirt-sleeved ease, puffing at Jack Fyfe's cigars. Then Benton excused himself and went to bed. When Howe and his wife retired, Stella did likewise. The long twilight had dwindled to a misty patch of light sky in the northwest, and she fell asleep more at ease than she had been for weeks. Sitting in Jack Fyfe's living room through that evening she had begun to formulate a philosophy to fit her enforced environment—to live for the day only, and avoid thought of the future until there loomed on the horizon some prospect of a future worth thinking about. The present looked passable enough, she thought, if she kept her mind strictly on it alone.

And with that idea to guide her, she found the days slide by smoothly. She got on famously with Mrs. Howe, finding that woman full of virtues unsuspected in her type. Charlie was in his element. His prospects looked so rosy that they led him into egotistic outlines of what he intended to accomplish. To him the future meant logs in the water, big holdings of timber, a growing bank account. Beyond that,—what all his concentrated effort should lead to save more logs and more timber,—he did not seem to go. Judged by his talk, that was the ultimate, economic power,—money and more money. More and more as Stella listened to him, she became aware that he was following in his father's footsteps; save that he aimed at greater heights and that he worked by different methods, juggling with natural resources where their father had merely juggled with prices and tokens of product, their end was the same—not to create or build up, but to grasp, to acquire. That was the game. To get and to hold for their own use and benefit and to look upon men and things, in so far as they were of use, as pawns in the game.

She wondered sometimes if that were a characteristic of all men, if that were the big motif in the lives of such men as Paul Abbey and Jack Fyfe, for instance; if everything else, save the struggle of getting and keeping money, resolved itself into purely incidental phases of their existence? For herself she considered that wealth, or the getting of wealth, was only a means to an end.

Just what that end might be she found a little vague, rather hard to define in exact terms. It embraced personal leisure and the good things of life as a matter of course, a broader existence, a large-handed generosity toward the less fortunate, an intellectual elevation entirely unrelated to gross material things. Life, she told herself pensively, ought to mean something more than ease and good clothes, but what more she was chary of putting into concrete form. It hadn't meant much more than that for her, so far. She was only beginning to recognize the flinty facts of existence. She saw now that for her there lay open only two paths to food and clothing: one in which, lacking all training, she must earn her bread by daily toil, the other leading to marriage. That, she would have admitted, was a woman's natural destiny, but one didn't pick a husband or lover as one chose a gown or a hat. One went along living, and the thing happened. Chance ruled there, she believed. The morality of her class prevented her from prying into this question of mating with anything like critical consideration. It was only to be thought about sentimentally, and it was easy for her to so think. Within her sound and vigorous body all the heritage of natural human impulses bubbled warmly, but she recognized neither their source nor their ultimate fruits.

Often when Charlie was holding forth in his accustomed vein, she wondered what Jack Fyfe thought about it, what he masked behind his brief sentences or slow smile. Latterly her feeling about him, that involuntary bracing and stiffening of herself against his personality, left her. Fyfe seemed to be more or less self-conscious of her presence as a guest in his house. His manner toward her remained always casual, as if she were a man, and there was no question of sex attraction or masculine reaction to it between them. She liked him better for that; and she did admire his wonderful strength, the tremendous power invested in his magnificent body, just as she would have admired a tiger, without caring to fondle the beast.

Altogether she spent a tolerably pleasant three weeks. Autumn's gorgeous paintbrush laid wonderful coloring upon the maple and alder and birch that lined the lake shore. The fall run of the salmon was on, and every stream was packed with the silver horde, threshing through shoal and rapid to reach the spawning ground before they died. Off every creek mouth and all along the lake the seal followed to prey on the salmon, and sea-trout and lakers alike swarmed to the spawning beds to feed upon the roe. The days shortened. Sometimes a fine rain would drizzle for hours on end, and when it would clear, the saw-toothed ranges flanking the lake would stand out all freshly robed in white,—a mantle that crept lower on the fir-clad slopes after each storm. The winds that whistled off those heights nipped sharply.

Early in October Charlie Benton had squared his neighborly account with Jack Fyfe. With crew and equipment he moved home, to begin work anew on his own limit.

Katy John and her people came back from the salmon fishing. Jim Renfrew, still walking with a pronounced limp, returned from the hospital. Charlie wheedled Stella into taking up the cookhouse burden again. Stella consented; in truth she could do nothing else. Charlie spent a little of his contract profits in piping water to the kitchen, in a few things to brighten up and make more comfortable their own quarters.

"Just as soon as I can put another boom over the rapids, Stell," he promised, "I'll put a cook on the job. I've got to sail a little close for a while. With this crew I ought to put a million feet in the water in six weeks. Then I'll be over the hump, and you can take it easy. But till then—"

"Till then I may as well make myself useful," Stella interrupted caustically.

"Well, why not?" Benton demanded impatiently. "Nobody around here works any harder than I do."

And there the matter rested.

CHAPTER X
ONE WAY OUT

That was a winter of big snow. November opened with rain. Day after day the sun hid his face behind massed, spitting clouds. Morning, noon, and night the eaves of the shacks dripped steadily, the gaunt limbs of the hardwoods were a line of coursing drops, and through all the vast reaches of fir and cedar the patter of rain kept up a dreary monotone. Whenever the mist that blew like rolling smoke along the mountains lifted for a brief hour, there, creeping steadily downward, lay the banked white.

Rain or shine, the work drove on. From the peep of day till dusk shrouded the woods, Benton's donkey puffed and groaned, axes thudded, the thin, twanging whine of the saws rose. Log after log slid down the chute to float behind the boomsticks; and at night the loggers trooped home, soaked to the skin, to hang their steaming mackinaws around the bunkhouse stove. When they gathered in the mess-room they filled it with the odor of sweaty bodies and profane grumbling about the weather.

Early in December Benton sent out a big boom of logs with a hired stern-wheeler that was no more than out of Roaring Lake before the snow came. The sleety blasts of a cold afternoon turned to great, moist flakes by dark, eddying thick out of a windless night. At daybreak it lay a foot deep and snowing hard. Thenceforth there was no surcease. The white, feathery stuff piled up and piled up, hour upon hour and day after day, as if the deluge had come again. It stood at the cabin eaves before the break came, six feet on the level. With the end of the storm came a bright, cold sky and frost,—not the bitter frost of the high latitudes, but a nipping cold that held off the melting rains and laid a thin scum of ice on every patch of still water.

Necessarily, all work ceased. The donkey was a shapeless mound of white, all the lines and gear buried deep. A man could neither walk on that yielding mass nor wallow through it. The logging crew hailed the enforced rest with open relief. Benton grumbled. And then, with the hours hanging heavy on his hands, he began to spend more and more of his time in the bunkhouse with the "boys," particularly in the long evenings.

Stella wondered what pleasure he found in their company, but she never asked him, nor did she devote very much thought to the matter. There was but small cessation in her labors, and that only because six or eight of the men drew their pay and went out. Benton managed to hold the others against the thaw that might open up the woods in twenty-four hours, but the smaller size of the gang only helped a little, and did not assist her mentally at all. All the old resentment against the indignity of her position rose and smoldered. To her the days were full enough of things that she was terribly weary of doing over and over, endlessly. She was always tired. No matter that she did, in a measure, harden to her work, grow callously accustomed to rising early and working late. Always her feet were sore at night, aching intolerably. Hot food, sharp knives, and a glowing stove played havoc with her hands. Always she rose in the morning heavy-eyed and stiff-muscled. Youth and natural vigor alone kept her from breaking down, and to cap the strain of toil, she was soul-sick with the isolation. For she was isolated; there was not a human being in the camp, Katy John included, with whom she exchanged two dozen words a day.

Before the snow put a stop to logging, Jack Fyfe dropped in once a week or so. When work shut down, he came oftener, but he never singled Stella out for any particular attention. Once he surprised her sitting with her elbows on the kitchen table, her face buried in her palms. She looked up at his quiet entrance, and her face must have given him his cue. He leaned a little toward her.

"How long do you think you can stand it?" he asked gently.

"God knows," she answered, surprised into speaking the thought that lay uppermost in her mind, surprised beyond measure that Be should read that thought.

He stood looking down at her for a second or two. His lips parted, but he closed them again over whatever rose to his tongue and passed silently through the dining room and into the bunkhouse, where Benton had preceded him a matter of ten minutes.

It lacked a week of Christmas. That day three of Benton's men had gone in the *Chickamin* to Roaring Springs for supplies. They had returned in mid-afternoon, and Stella guessed by the new note of hilarity in the bunkhouse that part of the supplies had been liquid. This had happened more than once since the big snow closed in. She remembered Charlie's fury at the logger who started Matt the cook on his spree, and she wondered at this relaxation, but it was not in her province, and she made no comment.

Jack Fyfe stayed to supper that evening. Neither he nor Charlie came back to Benton's quarters when the meal was finished. While she stacked up the dishes, Katy John observed:

"Goodness sakes, Miss Benton, them fellers was fresh at supper. They was half-drunk, some of them. I bet they'll be half a dozen fights before mornin'."

Stella passed that over in silence, with a mental turning up of her nose. It was something she could neither defend nor excuse. It was a disgusting state of affairs, but nothing she could change. She kept harking back to it, though, when she was in her own quarters, and Katy John had vanished for the night into her little room off the kitchen. Tired as she was, she remained wakeful, uneasy. Over in the bunkhouse disturbing sounds welled now and then into the cold, still night,—incoherent snatches of song, voices uproariously raised, bursts of laughter. Once, as she looked out the door, thinking she heard footsteps crunching in the snow, some one rapped out a coarse oath that drove her back with burning face.

As the evening wore late, she began to grow uneasily curious to know in what manner Charlie and Jack Fyfe were lending countenance to this minor riot, if they were even participating in it. Eleven o'clock passed, and still there rose in the bunkhouse that unabated hum of voices.

Suddenly there rose a brief clamor. In the dead silence that followed, she heard a thud and the clinking smash of breaking glass, a panted oath, sounds of struggle.

Stella slipped on a pair of her brother's gum boots and an overcoat, and ran out on the path beaten from their cabin to the shore. It led past the bunkhouse, and on that side opened two uncurtained windows, yellow squares that struck gleaming on the snow. The panes of one were broken now, sharp fragments standing like saw teeth in the wooden sash.

She stole warily near and looked in. Two men were being held apart; one by three of his fellows, the other *by* Jack Fyfe alone. Fyfe grinned mildly, talking to the men in a quiet, pacific tone.

"Now you know that was nothing to scrap about," she heard him say, "You're both full of fighting whisky, but a bunkhouse isn't any place to fight. Wait till morning. If you've still got it in your systems, go outside and have it out. But you shouldn't disturb our game and break up the furniture. Be gentlemen, drunk or sober. Better shake hands and call it square."

"Aw, let 'em go to it, if they want to."

Charlie's voice, drink-thickened, harsh, came from a earner of the room into which she could not see until she moved nearer. By the time she picked him out, Fyfe resumed his seat at the table where three others and Benton waited with cards in their hands, red and white chips and money stacked before them.

She knew enough of cards to realize that a stiff poker game was on the board when she had watched one hand dealt and played. It angered her, not from any ethical motive, but because of her brother's part in it. He had no funds to pay a cook's wages, yet he could afford to lose on one hand as much as he credited her with for a month's work. She could slave at the kitchen job day in and day out to save him forty-five dollars a month. He could lose that without the flicker of an eyelash, but he couldn't pay her wages on demand. Also she saw that he had imbibed too freely, if the redness of his face and the glassy fixedness of his eyes could be read aright.

"Pig!" she muttered. "If that's his idea of pleasure. Oh, well, why should I care? I don't, so far as he's concerned, if I could just get away from this beast of a place myself."

Abreast of her a logger came to the broken window with a sack to bar out the frosty air. And Stella, realizing suddenly that she was shivering with the cold, ran back to the cabin and got into her bed.

But she did not sleep, save in uneasy periods of dozing, until midnight was long past. Then Fyfe and her brother came in, and by the sounds she gathered that Fyfe was putting Charlie to bed. She heard his deep, drawly voice urging the unwisdom of sleeping with calked boots on, and Beaton's hiccupy response. The rest of the night she slept fitfully, morbidly imagining terrible things. She was afraid, that was the sum and substance of it. Over in the bunkhouse the carousal was still at its height. She could not rid herself of the sight of those two men struggling to be at each other like wild beasts, the bloody face of the one who had been struck, the coarse animalism of the whole whisky-saturated gang. It repelled and disgusted and frightened her.

The night frosts had crept through the single board walls of Stella's room and made its temperature akin to outdoors when the alarm wakened her at six in the morning. She shivered as she dressed. Katy John was blissfully devoid of any responsibility, for seldom did Katy rise first to light the kitchen fire. Yet Stella resented less each day's bleak beginning than she did the enforced necessity of the situation; the fact that she was enduring these things practically under compulsion was what galled.

A cutting wind struck her icily as she crossed the few steps of open between cabin and kitchen. Above no cloud floated, no harbinger of melting rain. The cold stars twinkled over snow-blurred forest, struck tiny gleams from stumps that were now white-capped pillars. A night swell from the outside waters beat, its melancholy dirge on the frozen beach. And, as she always did at that hushed hour before dawn, she experienced a physical shrinking from those grim solitudes in which there was nothing warm and human and kindly, nothing but vastness of space upon which silence lay like a smothering blanket, in which she, the human atom, was utterly negligible, a protesting mote in the inexorable wilderness. She knew this to be merely a state of mind, but situated as she was, it bore upon her with all the force of reality. She felt like a prisoner who above all things desired some mode of escape.

A light burned in the kitchen. She thanked her stars that this bitter cold morning she would not have to build a fire with freezing fingers while her teeth chattered, and she hurried in to the warmth heralded by a spark-belching stovepipe. But the Siwash girl had not risen to the occasion. Instead, Jack Fyfe sat with his feet on the oven door, a cigar in one corner of his mouth. The kettle steamed. Her porridge pot bubbled ready for the meal.

"Good morning," he greeted. "Mind my preempting your job?"

"Not at all," she answered. "You can have it for keeps if you want."

"No, thanks," he smiled. "I'm sour on my own cooking. Had to eat too much of it in times gone by. I wouldn't be stoking up here either, only I got frozen out. Charlie's spare bed hasn't enough blankets for me these cold nights."

He drew his chair aside to be out of the way as she hurried about her breakfast preparations. All the time she was conscious that his eyes were on her, and also that in them lurked an expression of keen interest. His freckled mask of a face gave no clue to his thoughts; it never did, so far as she had ever observed. Fyfe had a gambler's immobility of countenance. He chucked the butt of his cigar in the stove and sat with hands clasped over one knee for some time after Katy John appeared and began setting the dining room table with a great clatter of dishes.

He arose to his feet then. Stella stood beside the stove, frying bacon. A logger opened the door and walked in. He had been one to fare ill in the night's hilarity, for a discolored patch encircled one eye, and his lips were split and badly swollen. He carried a tin basin.

"Kin I get some hot water?" he asked.

Stella silently indicated the reservoir at one end of the range. The man ladled his basin full. The fumes of whisky, the unpleasant odor of his breath offended her, and she drew back. Fyfe looked at her as the man went out.

"What?" he asked.

She had muttered something, an impatient exclamation of disgust. The man's appearance disagreeably reminded her of the scene she had observed through the bunkhouse window. It stung her to think that her brother was fast putting himself on a par with them—without their valid excuse of type and training.

"Oh, nothing," she said wearily, and turned to the sputtering bacon.

Fyfe put his foot up on the stove front and drummed a tattoo on his mackinaw clad knee.

"Aren't you getting pretty sick of this sort of work, these more or less uncomfortable surroundings, and the sort of people you have to come in contact with?" he asked pointedly.

"I am," she returned as bluntly, "but I think that's rather an impertinent question, Mr. Fyfe."

He passed imperturbably over this reproof, and his glance turned briefly toward the dining room. Katy John was still noisily at work.

"You hate it," he said positively. "I know you do. I've seen your feelings many a time. I don't blame you. It's a rotten business for a girl with your tastes and bringing up. And I'm afraid you'll find it worse, if this snow stays long. I know what a logging camp is when work stops, and whisky creeps in, and the boss lets go his hold for the time being."

"That may be true," she returned gloomily, "but I don't see why you should enumerate these disagreeable things for my benefit."

"I'm going to show you a way out," he said softly. "I've been thinking it over for quite a while. I want you to marry me."

Stella gasped.

"Mr. Fyfe."

"Listen," he said peremptorily, leaning closer to her and lowering his voice. "I have an idea that you're going to say you don't love me. Lord, *I* know that. But you *hate* this. It grates against every inclination of yours like a file on steel. I wouldn't jar on you like that. I wouldn't permit you to live in surroundings that would. That's the material side of it. Nobody can live on day dreams. I like you, Stella Benton, a whole lot more than I'd care to say right out loud. You and I together could make a home we'd be proud of. I want you, and you want to get away from this. It's natural. Marry me and play the game fair, and I don't think you'll be sorry. I'm putting it as baldly as I can. You stand to win everything with nothing to lose—but your domestic chains—" the gleam of a smile lit up his features for a second. "Won't you take a chance?" "No," she declared impulsively. "I won't be a party to any such cold-blooded transaction."

"You don't seem to understand me," he said soberly. "I don't want to hand out any sentiment, but it makes me sore to see you wasting yourself on this sort of thing. If you must do it, why don't you do it for somebody who'll make it worth while? If you'd use the brains God gave you, you know that lots of couples have married on flimsier grounds than we'd have. How can a man and a woman really know anything about each other till they've lived together? Just because we don't marry with our heads in the fog is no reason we shouldn't get on fine. What are you going to do? Stick here at this till you go crazy? You won't get away. You don't realize what a one-idea, determined person this brother of yours is. He has just one object in life, and he'll use everything and everybody in sight to attain that object. He means to succeed and he will. You're purely incidental; but he has that perverted, middle-class family pride that will make him prevent you from getting out and trying your own wings. Nature never intended a woman like you to be a celibate, any more than I was so intended. And sooner or late you'll marry somebody—if only to hop out of the fire into the frying pan."

"I hate you," she flashed passionately, "when you talk like that."

"No, you don't," he returned quietly. "You hate what I say, because it's the truth—and it's humiliating to be helpless. You think I don't *sabe?* But I'm putting a weapon into your hand. Let's put it differently; leave out the sentiment for a minute. We'll say that I want a housekeeper, preferably an ornamental one, because I like beautiful things. You want to get away from this drudgery. That's what it is, simple drudgery. You crave lots of things you can't get by yourself, but that you could help me get for you. There's things lacking in your life, and so is there in mine. Why shouldn't we go partners? You think about it."

"I don't need to," she answered coolly. "It wouldn't work. You don't appear to have any idea what it means for a woman to give herself up body and soul to a man she doesn't care for. For me it would be plain selling myself. I haven't the least affection for you personally. I might even detest you."

"You wouldn't," he said positively.

"What makes you so sure of that?" she demanded.

"It would sound conceited if I told you why," he drawled. "Listen. We're not gods and goddesses, we human beings. We're not, after all, in our real impulses, so much different from the age when a man took his club and went after a female that looked good to him. They mated, and raised their young, and very likely faced on an average fewer problems than arise in modern marriages supposedly ordained in Heaven. You'd have the one big problem solved,—the lack of means to live decently,—which wrecks more homes than anything else, far more than lack of love. Affection doesn't seem to thrive on poverty. What is love?"

His voice took on a challenging note.

Stella shook her head. He puzzled her, wholly serious one minute, a whimsical smile twisting up the corners of his mouth the next. And he surprised her too by his sureness of utterance on subjects she had not supposed would enter such a man's mind.

"I don't know," she answered absently, turning over strips of bacon with the long-handled fork.

"There you are," he said. "I don't know either. We'd start even, then, for the sake of argument. No, I guess we wouldn't either, because you're the only woman I've run across so far with whom I could calmly contemplate spending the rest of my life in close contact. That's a fact. To me it's a highly important fact. You don't happen to have any such feeling about me, eh?"

"No. I hadn't even thought of you in that way," Stella answered truthfully.

"You want to think about me," he said calmly. "You want to think about me from every possible angle, because I'm going to come back and ask you this same question every once in a while, so long as you're in reach and doing this dirty work for a thankless boss. You want to think of me as a possible refuge from a lot of disagreeable things. I'd like to have you to chum with, and I'd like to have some incentive to put a big white bungalow on that old foundation for us two," he smiled. "I'll never do it for myself alone. Go on. Take a gambling chance and marry me, Stella. Say yes, and say it now."

But she shook her head resolutely, and as Katy John came in just then, Fyfe took his foot off the stove and went out of the kitchen. He threw a glance over his shoulder at Stella, a broad smile, as if to say that he harbored no grudge, and nursed no wound in his vanity because she would have none of him.

Katy rang the breakfast gong. Five minutes later the tattoo of knives and forks and spoons told of appetites in process of appeasement. Charlie came into the kitchen in the midst of this, bearing certain unmistakable signs. His eyes were inflamed, his cheeks still bearing the flush of liquor. His demeanor was that of a man suffering an intolerable headache and correspondingly short-tempered. Stella barely spoke to him. It was bad enough for a man to make a beast of himself with whisky, but far worse was his gambling streak. There were so many little ways in which she could have eased things with a few dollars; yet he always grumbled when she spoke of money, always put her off with promises to be redeemed when business got better.

Stella watched him bathe his head copiously in cold water and then seat himself at the long table, trying to force food upon an aggrieved and rebellious stomach. Gradually a flood of recklessness welled up in her breast.

"For two pins I would marry Jack Fyfe," she told herself savagely. "*Anything* would be better than this."

CHAPTER XI
THE PLUNGE

Stella went over that queer debate a good many times in the ten days that followed. It revealed Jack Fyfe to her in a new, inexplicable light, at odd variance with her former conception of the man. She could not have visualized him standing with one foot on the stove front speaking calmly of love and marriage if she had not seen him with her own eyes, heard him with somewhat incredulous ears. She had continued to endow him with the attributes of unrestrained passion, of headlong leaping to the goal of his desires, of brushing aside obstacles and opposition with sheer brute force; and he had shown unreckoned qualities of restraint, of understanding. She was not quite sure if this were guile or sensible consideration. He had put his case logically, persuasively even. She was very sure that if he had adopted emotional methods, she would have been repelled. If he had laid siege to her hand and heart in the orthodox fashion, she would have raised that siege in short order. As it stood, in spite of her words to him, there was in her own mind a lack of finality. As she went about her daily tasks, that prospect of trying a fresh fling at the world as Jack Fyfe's wife tantalized her with certain desirable features.

Was it worth while to play the game as she must play it for some time to come, drudge away at mean, sordid work and amid the dreariest sort of environment? At best, she could only get away from Charlie's camp and begin along new lines that might perhaps be little better, that must inevitably lie among strangers in a strange land. To what end? What did she want of life, anyway? She had to admit that she could not say fully and explicitly what she wanted. When she left out her material wants, there was nothing but a nebulous craving for—what? Love, she assumed. And she could not define love, except as some incomprehensible transport of emotion which irresistibly drew a man and a woman together, a divine fire kindled in two hearts. It was not a thing she could vouch for by personal experience. It might never touch and warm her, that divine fire. Instinct did now and then warn her that some time it would wrap her like a flame. But in the meantime—Life had her in midstream of its remorseless, drab current, sweeping her along. A foothold offered. Half a loaf, a single slice of bread even, is better than none.

Jack Fyfe did not happen in again for nearly two weeks and then only to pay a brief call, but he stole an opportunity, when Katy John was not looking, to whisper in Stella's ear:

"Have you been thinking about that bungalow of ours?"

She shook her head, and he went out quietly, without another word. He neither pleaded nor urged, and perhaps that was wisest, for in spite of herself Stella thought of him continually. He loomed always before her, a persistent, compelling factor.

She knew at last, beyond any gainsaying, that the venture tempted, largely perhaps because it contained so great an element of the unknown. To get away from this soul-dwarfing round meant much. She felt herself reasoning desperately that the frying pan could not be worse than the fire, and held at least the merit of greater dignity and freedom from the twin evils of poverty and thankless domestic slavery.

While she considered this, pro and con, shrinking from such a step one hour, considering it soberly the next, the days dragged past in wearisome sequence. The great depth of snow endured, was added to by spasmodic flurries. The frosts held. The camp seethed with the restlessness of the men. In default of the daily work that consumed their superfluous energy, the loggers argued and fought, drank and gambled, made "rough house" in their sleeping quarters till sometimes Stella's cheeks blanched and she expected murder to be done. Twice the *Chickamin* came back from Roaring Springs with whisky aboard, and a protracted debauch ensued. Once a drunken logger shouldered his way into the kitchen to leer unpleasantly at Stella, and, himself inflamed by liquor and the affront, Charlie Benton beat the man until his face was a mass of bloody bruises. That was only one of a dozen brutal incidents. All the routine discipline of the woods seemed to have slipped out of Benton's hands. When the second whisky consignment struck the camp, Stella stayed in her room, refusing to cook until order reigned again. Benton grumblingly took up the burden himself. With Katy's help and that of sundry loggers, he fed the roistering crew, but for his sister it was a two-day period of protesting disgust.

That mood, like so many of her moods, relapsed into dogged endurance. She took up the work again when Charlie promised that no more whisky should be allowed in the camp.

"Though it's ten to one I won't have a corporal's guard left when I want to start work again," he grumbled. "I'm well within my rights if I put my foot down hard on any jinks when there's work, but I have no license to set myself up as guardian of a logger's morals and pocketbook when I have nothing for him to do. These fellows are paying their board. So long as they don't make themselves obnoxious to you, I don't see that it's our funeral whether they're drunk or sober. They'd tell me so quick enough."

To this pronouncement of expediency Stella made no rejoinder. She no longer expected anything much of Charlie, in the way of consideration. So far as she could see, she, his sister, was little more to him than one of his loggers; a little less important than, say, his donkey engineer. In so far as she conduced to the well-being of the camp and effected a saving to his credit in the matter of preparing food, he valued her and was willing to concede a minor point to satisfy her. Beyond that Stella felt that he did not go. Five years in totally different environments had dug a great gulf between them. He felt an arbitrary sense of duty toward her, she knew, but in its manifestations it never lapped over the bounds of his own immediate self-interest.

And so when she blundered upon knowledge of a state of affairs which must have existed under her very nose for some time, there were few remnants of sisterly affection to bid her seek extenuating circumstances.

Katy John proved the final straw. Just by what means Stella grew to suspect any such moral lapse on Benton's part is wholly irrelevant. Once the unpleasant likelihood came to her notice, she took measures to verify her suspicion, and when convinced she taxed her brother with it, to his utter confusion.

"What kind of a man are you?" she cried at last in shamed anger. "Is there nothing too low for you to dabble in? Haven't you any respect for anything or anybody, yourself included?"

"Oh, don't talk like a damned Puritan," Benton growled, though his tanned face was burning. "This is what comes of having women around the camp. I'll send the girl away."

"You—you beast!" she flared—and ran out of the kitchen to seek refuge in her own room and cry into her pillow some of the dumb protest that surged up within her. For her knowledge of passion and the workings of passion as they bore upon the relations of a man and a woman were at once vague and tinctured with inflexible tenets of morality, the steel-hard conception of virtue which is the bulwark of middle-class theory for its wives and daughters and sisters—with an eye consistently blind to the concealed lapses of its men.

Stella Benton passed that morning through successive stages of shocked amazement, of pity, and disgust. As between her brother and the Siwash girl, she saw little to choose. From her virtuous pinnacle she abhorred both.

If she had to continue intimate living with them, she felt that she would be utterly defiled, degraded to their level. That was her first definite conclusion.

After a time she heard Benton come into their living room and light a fire in the heater. She dried her eyes and went out to face him.

"Charlie," she declared desperately, "I can't stay here any longer. It's simply impossible."

"Don't start that song again. We've had it often enough," he answered stubbornly. "You're not going—not till spring. I'm not going to let you go in the frame of mind you're in right now, anyhow. You'll get over that. Hang it, I'm not the first man whose foot slipped. It isn't your funeral, anyway. Forget it."

The grumbling coarseness of this retort left her speechless. Benton got the fire going and went out. She saw him cross to the kitchen, and later she saw Katy John leave the camp with all her belongings in a bundle over her shoulder, trudging away to the camp of her people around the point.

Kipling's pregnant line shot across her mind:

"For the colonel's lady and Judy O'Grady are sisters under their skins."

"I wonder," she mused. "I wonder if we are? I wonder if that poor, little, brown-skinned fool isn't after all as much a victim as I am. She doesn't know better, maybe; but Charlie does, and he doesn't seem to care. It merely embarrasses him to be found out, that's all. It isn't right. It isn't fair, or decent, or anything. We're just for him to—to use."

She looked out along the shores piled high with broken ice and snow, through a misty air to distant mountains that lifted themselves imperiously aloof, white spires against the sky,—over a forest all draped in winter robes; shore, mountains, and forest alike were chill and hushed and desolate. The lake spread its forty-odd miles in a boomerang curve from Roaring Springs to Fort Douglas, a cold, lifeless gray. She sat a long time looking at that, and a dead weight seemed to settle upon her heart. For the second time that day she broke down. Not the shamed, indignant weeping of an hour earlier, but with the essence of all things forlorn and desolate in her choked sobs.

She did not hear Jack Fyfe come in. She did not dream he was there, until she felt his hand gently on her shoulder and looked up. And so deep was her despondency, so keen the unassuaged craving for some human sympathy, some measure of understanding, that she made no effort to remove his hand. She was in too deep a spiritual quagmire to refuse any sort of aid, too deeply moved to indulge in analytical self-fathoming. She had a dim sense of being oddly comforted by his presence, as if she, afloat on uncharted seas, saw suddenly near at hand a safe anchorage and welcoming hands. Afterward she recalled that. As it was, she looked up at Fyfe and hid her wet face in her hands again. He stood silent a few seconds. When he did speak there was a peculiar hesitation in his voice.

"What is it?" he said softly. "What's the trouble now?"

Briefly she told him, the barriers of her habitual reserve swept aside before the essentially human need to share a burden that has grown too great to bear alone.

"Oh, hell," Fyfe grunted, when she had finished. "This isn't any place for you at all."

He slid his arm across her shoulders and tilted her face with his other hand so that her eyes met his. And she felt no desire to draw away or any of that old instinct to be on her guard against him. For all she knew—indeed, by all she had been told—Jack Fyfe was tarred with the same stick as her brother, but she had no thought of resisting him, no feeling of repulsion.

"Will you marry me, Stella?" he asked evenly. "I can free you from this sort of thing forever."

"How can I?" she returned. "I don't want to marry anybody. I don't love you. I'm not even sure I like you. I'm too miserable to think, even. I'm afraid to take a step like that. I should think you would be too."

He shook his head.

"I've thought a lot about it lately," he said. "It hasn't occurred to me to be afraid of how it may turn out. Why borrow trouble when there's plenty at hand? I don't care whether you love me or not, right now. You couldn't possibly be any worse off as my wife, could you?"

"No," she admitted. "I don't see how I could."

"Take a chance then," he urged. "I'll make a fair bargain with you. I'll make life as pleasant for you as I can. You'll live pretty much as you've been brought up to live, so far as money goes. The rest we'll have to work out for ourselves. I won't ask you to pretend anything you don't feel. You'll play fair, because that's the way you're made,—unless I've sized you up wrong. It'll simply be a case of our adjusting ourselves, just as mating couples have been doing since the year one. You've everything to gain and nothing to lose."

"In some ways," she murmured.

"Every way," he insisted. "You aren't handicapped by caring for any other man."

"How do you know?" she asked.

"Just a hunch," Fyfe smiled. "If you did, he'd have beaten me to the rescue long ago—if he were the sort of man you *could* care for."

"No," she admitted. "There isn't any other man, but there might be. Think how terrible it would be if it happened—afterward."

Fyfe shrugged his shoulders.

"Sufficient unto the day," he said. "There is no string on either of us just now. We start even. That's good enough. Will you?"

"You have me at a disadvantage," she whispered. "You offer me a lot that I want, everything but a feeling I've somehow always believed ought to exist, ought to be mutual. Part of me wants to shut my eyes and jump. Part of me wants to hang back. I can't stand this thing I've got into and see no way of getting out of. Yet I dread starting a new train of wretchedness. I'm afraid—whichever way I turn."

Fyfe considered this a moment.

"Well," he said finally, "that's a rather unfortunate attitude. But I'm going into it with my eyes open. I know what I want. You'll be making a sort of experiment. Still, I advise you to make it. I think you'll be the better for making it. Come on. Say yes."

Stella looked up at him, then out over the banked snow, and all the dreary discomforts, the mean drudgery, the sordid shifts she had been put to for months rose up in disheartening phalanx. For that moment Jack Fyfe loomed like a tower of refuge. She trusted him now. She had a feeling that even if she grew to dislike him, she would still trust him. He would play fair. If he said he would do this or that, she could bank on it absolutely.

She turned and looked at him searchingly a long half-minute, wondering what really lay behind the blue eyes that met her own so steadfastly. He stood waiting patiently, outwardly impassive. But she could feel through the thin stuff of her dress a quiver in the fingers that rested on her shoulder, and that repressed sign of the man's pent-up feeling gave her an odd thrill, moved her strangely, swung the pendulum of her impulse.

"Yes," she said.

Fyfe bent a little lower.

"Listen," he said in characteristically blunt fashion. "You want to get away from here. There is no sense in our fussing or hesitating about what we're going to do, is there?"

"No, I suppose not," she agreed.

"I'll send the *Panther* down to the Springs for Lefty Howe's wife," he outlined his plans unhesitatingly. "She'll get up here this evening. To-morrow we will go down and take the train to Vancouver and be married. You have plenty of good clothes, good enough for Vancouver. I know," — with a whimsical smile, — "because you had no chance to wear them out. Then we'll go somewhere, California, Florida, and come back to Roaring Lake in the spring. You'll have all the bad taste of this out of your mouth by that time."

Stella nodded acquiescence. Better to make the plunge boldly, since she had elected to make it.

"All right. I'm going to tell Benton," Fyfe said. "Good-by till to-morrow."

She stood up. He looked at her a long time earnestly, searchingly, one of her hands imprisoned tight between his two big palms. Then, before she was quite aware of his intention, he kissed her gently on the mouth, and was gone.

This turn of events left Benton dumbfounded, to use a trite but expressive phrase. He came in, apparently to look at Stella in amazed curiosity, for at first he had nothing to say. He sat down beside his makeshift desk and pawed over some papers, running the fingers of one hand through his thick brown hair.

"Well, Sis," he blurted out at last. "I suppose you know what you're doing?"

"I think so," Stella returned composedly.

"But why all this mad haste?" he asked. "If you're going to get married, why didn't you let me know, so I could give you some sort of decent send-off."

"Oh, thanks," she returned dryly. "I don't think that's necessary. Not at this stage of the game, as you occasionally remark."

He ruminated upon this a minute, flushing slightly.

"Well, I wish you luck," he said sincerely enough. "Though I can hardly realize this sudden move. You and Jack Fyfe may get on all right. He's a good sort—in his way."

"His way suits me," she said, spurred to the defensive by what she deemed a note of disparagement in his utterance. "If you have any objections or criticisms, you can save your breath—or address them direct to Mr. Fyfe."

"No, thank you," he grinned. "I don't care to get into any argument with *him*, especially as he's going to be my brother-in-law. Fyfe's all right. I didn't imagine he was the sort of man you'd fancy, that's all."

Stella refrained from any comment on this. She had no intention of admitting to Charlie that marriage with Jack Fyfe commended itself to her chiefly as an avenue of escape from a well-nigh intolerable condition which he himself had inflicted upon her. Her pride rose in arms against any such belittling admission. She admitted it frankly to herself,—and to Fyfe,—because Fyfe understood and was content with that understanding. She desired to forget that phase of the transaction. She told herself that she meant honestly to make the best of it.

Benton turned again to his papers. He did not broach the subject again until in the distance the squat hull of the *Panther* began to show on her return from the Springs. Then he came to where Stella was putting the last of her things into her trunk. He had some banknotes in one hand, and a check.

"Here's that ninety I borrowed, Stell," he said. "And a check for your back pay. Things have been sort of lean around here, maybe, but I still think it's a pity you couldn't have stuck it out till it came smoother. I hate to see you going away with a chronic grouch against me. I suppose I wouldn't even be a welcome guest at the wedding?"

"No," she said unforgivingly. "Some things are a little too—too recent."

"Oh," he replied casually enough, pausing in the doorway a second on his way out, "you'll get over that. You'll find that ordinary, everyday living isn't any kid-glove affair."

She sat on the closed lid of her trunk, looking at the check and money. Three hundred and sixty dollars, all told. A month ago that would have spelled freedom, a chance to try her luck in less desolate fields. Well, she tried to consider the thing philosophically; it was no use to bewail what might have been. In her hands now lay the sinews of a war she had forgone all need of waging. It did not occur to her to repudiate her bargain with Jack Fyfe. She had given her promise, and she considered she was bound, irrevocably. Indeed, for the moment, she was glad of that. She was worn out, all weary with unaccustomed stress of body and mind. To her, just then, rest seemed the sweetest boon in the world. Any port in a storm, expressed her mood. What came after was to be met as it came. She was too tired to anticipate.

It was a pale, weary-eyed young woman, dressed in the same plain tailored suit she had worn into the country, who was cuddled to Mrs. Howe's plump bosom when she went aboard the *Panther* for the first stage of her journey.

A slaty bank of cloud spread a somber film across the sky. When the *Panther* laid her ice-sheathed guard-rail against the Hot Springs wharf the sun was down. The lake spread gray and lifeless under a gray sky, and Stella Benton's spirits were steeped in that same dour color.

CHAPTER XII
AND SO THEY WERE MARRIED

Spring had waved her transforming wand over the lake region before the Fyfes came home again. All the low ground, the creeks and hollows and banks, were bright green with new-leaved birch and alder and maple. The air was full of those aromatic exudations the forest throws off when it is in the full tide of the growing time. Shores that Stella had last seen dismal and forlorn in the frost-fog, sheathed in ice, banked with deep snow, lay sparkling now in warm sunshine, under an unflecked arch of blue. All that was left of winter was the white cap on Mount Douglas, snow-filled chasms on distant, rocky peaks. Stella stood on the Hot Springs wharf looking out across the emerald deep of the lake, thinking soberly of the contrast.

Something, she reflected, some part of that desolate winter, must have seeped to the very roots of her being to produce the state of mind in which she embarked upon that matrimonial voyage. A little of it clung to her still. She could look back at those months of loneliness, of immeasurable toil and numberless indignities, without any qualms. There would be no repetition of that. The world at large would say she had done well. She herself in her most cynical moments could not deny that she had done well. Materially, life promised to be generous. She was married to a man who quietly but inexorably got what he wanted, and it was her good fortune that he wanted her to have the best of everything.

She saw him now coming from the hotel, and she regarded him thoughtfully, a powerful figure swinging along with light, effortless steps. He was back on his own ground, openly glad to be back. Yet she could not recall that he had ever shown himself at a disadvantage anywhere they had been together. He wore evening clothes when occasion required as unconcernedly as he wore mackinaws and calked boots among his loggers. She had not yet determined whether his equable poise arose from an unequivocal democracy of spirit, or from sheer egotism. At any rate, where she had set out with subtle misgivings, she had to admit that socially, at least, Jack Fyfe could play his hand at any turn of the game. Where or how he came by this faculty, she did not know. In fact, so far as Jack Fyfe's breeding and antecedents were concerned, she knew little more than before their marriage. He was not given to reminiscence. His people—distant relatives—lived in her own native state of Pennsylvania. He had an only sister who was now in South America with her husband, a civil engineer. Beyond that Fyfe did not go, and Stella made no attempt to pry up the lid of his past. She was not particularly curious.

Her clearest judgment of him was at first hand. He was a big, virile type of man, generous, considerate, so sure of himself that he could be tolerant of others. She could easily understand why Roaring Lake considered Jack Fyfe "square." The other tales of him that circulated there she doubted now. The fighting type he certainly was, aggressive in a clash, but if there were any downright coarseness in him, it had never manifested itself to her. She was not sorry she had married him. If they had not set out blind in a fog of sentiment, as he had once put it, nevertheless they got on. She did not love him,—not as she defined that magic word,—but she liked him, was mildly proud of him. When he kissed her, if there were no mad thrill in it, there was at least a passive contentment in having inspired that affection. For he left her in no doubt as to where he stood, not by what he said, but wholly by his actions.

He joined her now. The *Panther*, glossy black as a crow's wing with fresh paint, lay at the pier-end with their trunks aboard. Stella surveyed those marked with her initials, looking them over with a critical eye, when they reached the deck.

"How in the world did I ever manage to accumulate so much stuff, Jack?" she asked quizzically. "I didn't realize it. We might have been doing Europe with souvenir collecting our principal aim, by the amount of our baggage."

Fyfe smiled, without commenting. They sat on a trunk and watched Roaring Springs fall astern, dwindle to a line of white dots against the great green base of the mountain that rose behind it.

"It's good to get back here," he said at last. "To me, anyway. How about it, Stella? You haven't got so much of a grievance with the world in general as you had when we left, eh?"

"No, thank goodness," she responded fervently.

"You don't look as if you had," he observed, his eyes admiringly upon her.

Nor had she. There was a bloom on the soft contour of her cheek, a luminous gleam in her wide, gray eyes. All the ill wrought by months of drudging work and mental revolt had vanished. She was undeniably good to look at, a woman in full flower, round-bodied, deep-breasted, aglow with the unquenched fires of youth. She was aware that Jack Fyfe found her so and tolerably glad that he did so find her. She had revised a good many of her first groping estimates of him that winter. And when she looked over the port bow and saw in behind Halfway Point the huddled shacks of her brother's camp where so much had overtaken her, she experienced a swift rush of thankfulness that she was—as she was. She slid her gloved hand impulsively into Jack Fyfe's, and his strong fingers shut down on hers closely.

They sat silent until the camp lay abeam. About it there was every sign of activity. A chunky stern-wheeler, with blow-off valve hissing, stood by a boom of logs in the bay, and men were moving back and forth across the swifters, making all ready for a tow. Stella marked a new bunkhouse. Away back on the logging ground in a greater clearing she saw the separate smoke of two donkey engines. Another, a big roader, Fyfe explained, puffed at the water's edge. She could see a string of logs tearing down the skid-road.

"He's going pretty strong, that brother of yours," Fyfe remarked. "If he holds his gait, he'll be a big timberman before you know it."

"He'll make money, I imagine," Stella admitted, "but I don't know what good that will do him. He'll only want more. What is there about money-making that warps some men so, makes them so grossly self-centered? I'd pity any girl who married Charlie. He used to be rather wild at home, but I never dreamed any man could change so."

"You use the conventional measuring-stick on him," her husband answered, with that tolerance which so often surprised her. "Maybe his ways are pretty crude. But he's feverishly hewing a competence—which is what we're all after—out of pretty crude material. And he's just a kid, after all, with a kid's tendency to go to extremes now and then. I kinda like the beggar's ambition and energy."

"But he hasn't the least consideration for anybody or anything," Stella protested. "He rides rough-shod over every one. That isn't either right or decent."

"It's the only way some men can get to the top," Fyfe answered quietly. "They concentrate on the object to be attained. That's all that counts until they're in a secure position. Then, when they stop to draw their breath, sometimes they find they've done lots of things they wouldn't do again. You watch. By and by Charlie Benton will cease to have those violent reactions that offend you so. As it is—he's a youngster, bucking a big game. Life, when you have your own way to hew through it, with little besides your hands and brain for capital, is no silk-lined affair."

She fell into thought over this reply. Fyfe had echoed almost her brother's last words to her. And she wondered if Jack Fyfe had attained that degree of economic power which enabled him to spend several thousand dollars on a winter's pleasuring with her by the exercise of a strong man's prerogative of overriding the weak, bending them to his own inflexible purposes, ruthlessly turning everything to his own advantage? If women came under the same head! She recalled Katy John, and her face burned. Perhaps. But she could not put Jack Fyfe in her brother's category. He didn't fit. Deep in her heart there still lurked an abiding resentment against Charlie Benton for the restraint he had put upon her and the license he had arrogated to himself. She could not convince herself that the lapses of that winter were not part and parcel of her brother's philosophy of life, a coarse and material philosophy.

Presently they were drawing in to Cougar Point, with the weather-bleached buildings of Fyfe's camp showing now among the upspringing second-growth scrub. Fyfe went forward and spoke to the man at the wheel. The *Panther* swung offshore.

"Why are we going out again?" Stella asked.

"Oh, just for fun," Fyfe smiled.

He sat down beside her and slipped one arm around her waist. In a few minutes they cleared the point. Stella was looking away across the lake, at the deep cleft where Silver Creek split a mountain range in twain.

"Look around," said he, "and tell me what you think of the House of Fyfe."

There it stood, snow-white, broad-porched, a new house reared upon the old stone foundation she remembered. The noon sun struck flashing on the windows. About it spread the living green of the grassy square, behind that towered the massive, darker-hued background of the forest.

"Oh," she exclaimed. "What wizard of construction did the work. *That* was why you fussed so long over those plans in Los Angeles. I thought it was to be this summer or maybe next winter. I never dreamed you were having it built right away."

"Well, isn't it rather nice to come home to?" he observed.

"It's dear. A homey looking place," she answered. "A beautiful site, and the house fits, — that white and the red tiles. Is the big stone fireplace in the living room, Jack?"

"Yes, and one in pretty nearly every other room besides," he nodded. "Wood fires are cheerful."

The *Panther* turned her nose shoreward at Fyfe's word.

"I wondered about that foundation the first time I saw it," Stella confessed, "whether you built it, and why it was never finished. There was moss over the stones in places. And that lawn wasn't made in a single season. I know, because dad had a country place once, and he was raging around two or three summers because the land was so hard to get well-grassed."

"No, I didn't build the foundation or make the lawn," Fyfe told her. "I merely kept it in shape. A man named Hale owned the land that takes in the bay and the point when I first came to the lake. He was going to be married. I knew him pretty well. But it was tough going those days. He was in the hole on some of his timber, and he and his girl kept waiting. Meantime he cleared and graded that little hill, sowed it to grass, and laid the foundation. He was about to start building when he was killed. A falling tree caught him. I bought in his land and the timber limits that lie back of it. That's how the foundation came there."

"It's a wonder it didn't grow up wild," Stella mused. "How long ago was that?"

"About five years," Fyfe said. "I kept the grass trimmed. It didn't seem right to let the brush overrun it after the poor devil put that labor of love on it. It always seemed to me that it should be kept smooth and green, and that there should be a big, roomy bungalow there. You see my hunch was correct, too."

She looked up at him in some wonder. She hadn't accustomed herself to associating Jack Fyfe with actions based on pure sentiment. He was too intensely masculine, solid, practical, impassive. He did not seem to realize even that sentiment had influenced him in this. He discussed it too matter-of-factly for that. She wondered what became of the bride-to-be. But that Fyfe could not tell her.

"Hale showed me her picture once," he said, "but I never saw her. Oh, I suppose she's married some other fellow long ago. Hale was a good sort. He was out-lucked, that's all."

The *Panther* slid in to the float. Jack and Stella went ashore. Lefty Howe came down to meet them. Thirty-five or forty men were stringing away from the camp, back to their work in the woods. Some waved greeting to Jack Fyfe, and he waved back in the hail-fellow fashion of the camps.

"How's the frau, Lefty?" he inquired, after they had shaken hands.

"Fine. Down to Vancouver. Sister's sick," Howe answered laconically. "House's all shipshape. Wanta eat here, or up there?"

"Here at the camp, until we get straightened around," Fyfe responded. "Tell Pollock to have something for us in about half an hour. We'll go up and take a look."

Howe went in to convey this message, and the two set off up the path. A sudden spirit of impishness made Jack Fyfe sprint. Stella gathered up her skirt and raced after him, but a sudden shortness of breath overtook her, and she came panting to where Fyfe had stopped to wait.

"You'll have to climb hills and row and swim so you'll get some wind," Fyfe chuckled. "Too much easy living, lady."

She smiled without making any reply to this sally, and they entered the house—the House of Fyfe, that was to be her home.

If the exterior had pleased her, she went from room to room inside with growing amazement. Fyfe had finished it from basement to attic without a word to her that he had any such undertaking in hand. Yet there was scarcely a room in which she could not find the visible result of some expressed wish or desire. Often during the winter they had talked over the matter of furnishings, and she recalled how unconsciously she had been led to make suggestions which he had stored up and acted upon. For the rest she found her husband's taste beyond criticism. There were drapes and rugs and prints and odds and ends that any woman might be proud to have in her home.

"You're an amazing sort of a man, Jack," she said thoughtfully. "Is there anything you're not up to? Even a Chinese servant in the kitchen. It's perfect."

"I'm glad you like it," he said. "I hoped you would."

"Who wouldn't?" she cried impulsively. "I love pretty things. Wait till I get done rearranging."

They introduced themselves to the immobile-featured Celestial when they had jointly and severally inspected the house from top to bottom. Sam Foo gazed at them, listened to their account of themselves, and disappeared. He re-entered the room presently, bearing a package.

"Mist' Chol' Bentlee him leave foh yo'."

Stella looked at it. On the outer wrapping was written:

From C.A. Benton to Mrs. John Henderson Fyfe
A Belated Wedding Gift

She cut the string, and delved into the cardboard box, and gasped. Out of a swathing of tissue paper her hands bared sundry small articles. A little cap and jacket of knitted silk—its double in fine, fleecy yarn—a long silk coat—a bonnet to match,—both daintily embroidered. Other things—a shoal of them—baby things. A grin struggled for lodgment on Fyfe's freckled countenance. His blue eyes twinkled.

"I suppose," he growled, "that's Charlie's idea of a joke, huh?"

Stella turned away from the tiny garments, one little, hood crumpled tight in her hand. She laid her hot face against his breast and her shoulders quivered. She was crying.

"Stella, Stella, what's the matter?" he whispered.

"It's no joke," she sobbed. "It's a—it's a reality."

CHAPTER XIII
IN WHICH EVENTS MARK TIME

From that day on Stella found in her hands the reins over a smooth, frictionless, well-ordered existence. Sam Foo proved himself such a domestic treasure as only the trained Oriental can be. When the labor of an eight room dwelling proved a little too much for him, he urbanely said so. Thereupon, at Fyfe's suggestion, he imported a fellow countryman, another bland, silent-footed model of efficiency in personal service. Thereafter Stella's task of supervision proved a sinecure.

A week or so after their return, in sorting over some of her belongings, she came across the check Charlie had given her: that two hundred and seventy dollars which represented the only money she had ever earned in her life. She studied it a minute, then went out to where her husband sat perched on the verandah rail.

"You might cash this, Jack," she suggested.

He glanced at the slip.

"Better have it framed as a memento," he said, smiling. "You'll never earn two hundred odd dollars so hard again, I hope. No, I'd keep it, if I were you. If ever you should need it, it'll always be good—unless Charlie goes broke."

There never had been any question of money between them. From the day of their marriage Fyfe had made her a definite monthly allowance, a greater sum than she needed or spent.

"As a matter of fact," he went on, "I'm going to open an account in your name at the Royal Bank, so you can negotiate your own paper and pay your own bills by check."

She went in and put away the check. It was hers, earned, all too literally, in the sweat of her brow. For all that it represented she had given service threefold. If ever there came a time when that hunger for independence which had been fanned to a flame in her brother's kitchen should demand appeasement—she pulled herself up short when she found her mind running upon such an eventuality. Her future was ordered. She was married— to be a mother. Here lay her home. All about her ties were in process of formation, ties that with time would grow stronger than any shackles of steel, constraining her to walk in certain ways,—ways that were pleasant enough, certain of ease if not of definite purpose.

Yet now and then she found herself falling into fits of abstraction in which Roaring Lake and Jack Fyfe, all that meant anything to her now, faded into the background, and she saw herself playing a lone hand against the world, making her individual struggle to be something more than the petted companion of a dominant male and the mother of his children. She never quite lost sight of the fact that marriage had been the last resort, that in effect she had taken the avenue her personal charm afforded to escape drudgery and isolation. There was still deep-rooted in her a craving for something bigger than mere ease of living. She knew as well as she knew anything that in the natural evolution of things marriage and motherhood should have been the big thing in her life. And it was not. It was too incidental, too incomplete, too much like a mere breathing-place on life's highway. Sometimes she reasoned with herself bluntly, instead of dreaming, was driven to look facts in the eye because she did dream. Always she encountered the same obstacle, a feeling that she had been defrauded, robbed of something vital; she had forgone that wonderful, passionate drawing together which makes the separate lives of the man and woman who experiences it so fuse that in the truest sense of the word they become one.

Mostly she kept her mind from that disturbing introspection, because invariably it led her to vague dreaming of a future which she told herself—sometimes wistfully—could never be realized. She had shut the door on many things, it seemed to her now. But she had the sense to know that dwelling on what might have been only served to make her morbid, and did not in the least serve to alter the unalterable. She had chosen what seemed to her at the time the least of two evils, and she meant to abide steadfast by her choice.

Charlie Benton came to visit them. Strangely enough to Stella, who had never seen him on Roaring Lake, at least, dressed otherwise than as his loggers, he was sporting a natty gray suit, he was clean shaven, Oxford ties on his feet, a gentleman of leisure in his garb. If he had started on the down grade the previous winter, he bore no signs of it now, for he was the picture of ruddy vigor, clear-eyed, brown-skinned, alert, bubbling over with good spirits.

"Why, say, you look like a tourist," Fyfe remarked after an appraising glance.

"I'm making money, pulling ahead of the game, that's all," Benton retorted cheerfully. "I can afford to take a holiday now and then. I'm putting a million feet a month in the water. That's going some for small fry like me. Say, this house of yours is all to the good, Jack. It's got class, outside and in. Makes a man feel as if he had to live up to it, eh? Mackinaws and calked boots don't go with oriental rugs and oak floors."

"You should get a place like this as soon as possible then," Stella put in drily, "to keep you up to the mark, on edge aesthetically, one might put it."

"Not to say morally," Benton laughed. "Oh, maybe I'll get to it by and by, if the timber business holds up."

Later, when he and Stella were alone together, he said to her:

"You're lucky. You've got everything, and it comes without an effort. You sure showed good judgment when you picked Jack Fyfe. He's a thoroughbred."

"Oh, thank you," she returned, a touch of irony in her voice, a subtlety of inflection that went clean over Charlie's head.

He was full of inquiries about where they had been that winter, what they had done and seen. Also he brimmed over with his own affairs. He stayed overnight and went his way with a brotherly threat of making the Fyfe bungalow his headquarters whenever he felt like it.

"It's a touch of civilization that looks good to me," he declared. "You can put my private mark on one of those big leather chairs, Jack. I'm going to use it often. All you need to make this a social center is a good-looking girl or two—unmarried ones. You watch. When the summer flock comes to the lake, your place is going to be popular."

That observation verified Benton's shrewdness. The Fyfe bungalow did become popular. Two weeks after Charlie's visit, a lean, white cruiser, all brass and mahogany above her topsides, slid up to the float, and two women came at a dignified pace along the path to the house. Stella had met Linda Abbey once, reluctantly, under the circumstances, but it was different now—with the difference that money makes. She could play hostess against an effective background, and she did so graciously. Nor was her graciousness wholly assumed. After all, they were her kind of people: Linda, fair-haired, perfectly gowned, perfectly mannered, sweetly pretty; Mrs. Abbey, forty-odd and looking thirty-five, with that calm self-assurance which wealth and position confer upon those who hold it securely. Stella found them altogether to her liking. It pleased her, too, that Jack happened in to meet them. He was not a scintillating talker, yet she had noticed that when he had anything to say, he never failed to attract and hold attention. His quiet, impersonal manner never suggested stolidness. And she was too keen an observer to overlook the fact that from a purely physical standpoint

Jack Fyfe made an impression always, particularly on women. Throughout that winter it had not disturbed her. It did not disturb her now, when she noticed Linda Abbey's gaze coming back to him with a veiled appraisal in her blue eyes that were so like Fyfe's own in their tendency to twinkle and gleam with no corresponding play of features.

"We'll expect to see a good deal of you this summer," Mrs. Abbey said cordially at leave-taking. "We have a few people up from town now and then to vary the monotony of feasting our souls on scenery. Sometimes we are quite a jolly crowd. Don't be formal. Drop in when you feel the inclination."

When Stella reminded Jack of this some time later, in a moment of boredom, he put the *Panther* at her disposal for the afternoon. But he would not go himself. He had opened up a new outlying camp, and he had directions to issue, work to lay out.

"You hold up the social end of the game," he laughed. "I'll hustle logs."

So Stella invaded the Abbey-Monohan precincts by herself and enjoyed it—for she met a houseful of young people from the coast, and in that light-hearted company she forgot for the time being that she was married and the responsible mistress of a house. Paul Abbey was there, but he had apparently forgotten or forgiven the blow she had once dealt his vanity. Paul, she reflected, was not the sort to mourn a lost love long.

She had the amused experience too of beholding Charlie Benton appear an hour or so before she departed and straightway monopolize Linda Abbey in his characteristically impetuous fashion. Charlie was no diplomat. He believed in driving straight to any goal he selected.

"So *that's* the reason for the outward metamorphosis," Stella reflected. "Well?"

Altogether she enjoyed the afternoon hugely. The only fly in her ointment was a greasy smudge bestowed upon her dress—a garment she prized highly—by some cordage coiled on the *Panther's* deck. The black tender had carried too many cargoes of loggers and logging supplies to be a fit conveyance for persons in party attire. She exhibited the soiled gown to Fyfe with due vexation.

"I hope you'll have somebody scrub down the *Panther* the next time I want to go anywhere in a decent dress," she said ruefully. "That'll never come out. And it's the prettiest thing I've got too."

"Ah, what's the odds?" Fyfe slipped one arm around her waist. "You can buy more dresses. Did you have a good time? That's the thing!"

That ruined gown, however, subsequently produced an able, forty-foot, cruising launch, powerfully engined, easy in a sea, and comfortably, even luxuriously fitted as to cabin. With that for their private use, the *Panther* was left to her appointed service, and in the new boat Fyfe and Stella spent many a day abroad on Roaring Lake. They fished together, explored nooks and bays up and down its forty miles of length, climbed hills together like the bear of the ancient rhyme, to see what they could see. And the *Waterbug* served to put them on intimate terms with their neighbors, particularly the Abbey crowd. The Abbeys took to them wholeheartedly. Fyfe himself was highly esteemed by the elder Abbey, largely, Stella suspected, for his power on Roaring Lake. Abbey *père* had built up a big fortune out of timber. He respected any man who could follow the same path to success. Therefore he gave Fyfe double credit,—for making good, and for a personality that could not be overlooked. He told Stella that once; that is to say, he told her confidentially that her husband was a very "able" young man. Abbey senior was short and double-chinned and inclined to profuse perspiration if he moved in haste over any extended time. Paul promised to be like him, in that respect.

Summer slipped by. There were dances, informal little hops at the Abbey domicile, return engagements at the Fyfe bungalow, laughter and music and Japanese lanterns strung across the lawn. There was tea and tennis and murmuring rivers of small talk. And amid this Stella Fyfe flitted graciously, esteeming it her world, a fair measure of what the future might be. Viewed in that light, it seemed passable enough.

Later, when summer was on the wane, she withdrew from much of this activity, spending those days when she did not sit buried in a book out on the water with her husband. When October ushered in the first of the fall rains, they went to Vancouver and took apartments. In December her son was born.

CHAPTER XIV
A CLOSE CALL AND A NEW ACQUAINTANCE

With the recurrence of spring, Fyfe's household transferred itself to the Roaring Lake bungalow again. Stella found the change welcome, for Vancouver wearied her. It was a little too crude, too much as yet in the transitory stage, in that civic hobbledehoy period which overtakes every village that shoots up over-swiftly to a city's dimensions. They knew people, to be sure, for the Abbey influence would have opened the way for them into any circle. Stella had made many friends and pleasant acquaintances that summer on the lake, but part of that butterfly clique sought pleasanter winter grounds before she was fit for social activity. Apart from a few more or less formal receptions and an occasional auction party, she found it pleasanter to stay at home. Fyfe himself had spent only part of his time in town after their boy was born. He was extending his timber operations. What he did not put into words, but what Stella sensed because she experienced the same thing herself, was that town bored him to death,—such town existence as Vancouver afforded. Their first winter had been different, because they had sought places where there was manifold variety of life, color, amusement. She was longing for the wide reach of Roaring Lake, the immense amphitheater of the surrounding mountains, long before spring.

So she was quite as well pleased when a mild April saw them domiciled at home again. In addition to Sam Foo and Feng Shu, there was a nurse for Jack Junior. Stella did not suggest that; Fyfe insisted on it. He was quite proud of his boy, but he did not want her chained to her baby.

"If the added expense doesn't count, of course a nurse will mean a lot more personal freedom," Stella admitted. "You see, I haven't the least idea of your resources, Jack. All I know about it is that you allow me plenty of money for my individual expenses. And I notice we're acquiring a more expensive mode of living all the time."

"That's so," Fyfe responded. "I never have gone into any details of my business with you. No reason why you shouldn't know what limits there are to our income. You never happened to express any curiosity before. Operating as I did up till lately, the business netted anywhere from twelve to fifteen thousand a year. I'll double that this season. In fact, with the amount of standing timber I control, I could make it fifty thousand a year by expanding and speeding things up. I guess you needn't worry about an extra servant or two."

So, apart from voluntary service on behalf of Jack Junior, she was free as of old to order her days as she pleased. Yet that small morsel of humanity demanded much of her time, because she released through the maternal floodgates a part of that passionate longing to bestow love where her heart willed. Sometimes she took issue with herself over that wayward tendency. By all the rules of the game, she should have loved her husband. He was like a rock, solid, enduring, patient, kind, and generous. He stood to her in the most intimate relation that can exist between a man and a woman. But she never fooled herself; she never had so far as Jack Fyfe was concerned. She liked him, but that was all. He was good to her, and she was grateful.

Sometimes she had a dim sense that under his easy-going exterior lurked a capacity for tremendously passionate outbreak. If she had been compelled to modify her first impression of him as an arrogant, dominant sort of character, scarcely less rough than the brown firs out of which he was hewing a fortune, she knew likewise that she had never seen anything but the sunny side of him. He still puzzled her a little at times; there were odd flashes of depths she could not see into, a quality of unexpectedness in things he would do and say. Even so, granting that in him was embodied so much that other men she knew lacked, she did not love him; there were indeed times when she almost resented him.

Why, she could not perhaps have put into words. It seemed too fantastic for sober summing-up, when she tried. But lurking always in the background of her thoughts was the ghost of an unrealized dream, a nebulous vision which once served to thrill her in secret. It could never be anything but a vision, she believed now, and believing, regretted. The cold facts of her existence couldn't be daydreamed away. She was married, and marriage put a full stop to the potential adventuring of youth. Twenty and maidenhood lies at the opposite pole from twenty-four and matrimony. Stella subscribed to that. She took for her guiding-star—theoretically—the twin concepts of morality and duty as she had been taught to construe them. So she saw no loophole, and seeing none, felt cheated of something infinitely precious. Marriage and motherhood had not come to her as the fruits of love, as the passionately eager fulfilling of her destiny. It had been thrust upon her. She had accepted it as a last resort at a time when her powers of resistance to misfortune were at the ebb.

She knew that this sort of self-communing was a bad thing, that it was bound to sour the whole taste of life in her mouth. As much as possible she thrust aside those vague, repressed longings. Materially she had everything. If she had foregone that bargain with Jack Fyfe, God only knew what long-drawn agony of mind and body circumstances and Charlie Benton's subordination of her to his own ends might have inflicted upon her. That was the reverse of her shield, but one that grew dimmer as time passed. Mostly, she took life as she found it, concentrating upon Jack Junior, a sturdy boy with blue eyes like his father, and who grew steadily more adorable.

Nevertheless she had recurring periods when moodiness and ill-stifled discontent got hold of her. Sometimes she stole out along the cliffs to sit on a mossy boulder, staring with absent eyes at the distant hills. And sometimes she would slip out in a canoe, to lie rocking in the lake swell,—just dreaming, filled with a passive sort of regret. She could not change things now, but she could not help wishing she could.

Fyfe warned her once about getting offshore in the canoe. Roaring Lake, pent in the shape of a boomerang between two mountain ranges, was subject to squalls. Sudden bursts of wind would shoot down its length like blasts from some monster funnel. Stella knew that; she had seen the glassy surface torn into whitecaps in ten minutes, but she was not afraid of the lake nor the lake winds. She was hard and strong. The open, the clean mountain air, and a measure of activity, had built her up physically. She swam like a seal. Out in that sixteen-foot Peterboro she could detach herself from her world of reality, lie back on a cushion, and lose herself staring at the sky. She paid little heed to Fyfe's warning beyond a smiling assurance that she had no intention of courting a watery end.

So one day in mid-July she waved a farewell to Jack Junior, crowing in his nurse's lap on the bank, paddled out past the first point to the north, and pillowing her head on a cushioned thwart, gave herself up to dreamy contemplation on the sky. There was scarce a ripple on the lake. A faint breath of an offshore breeze fanned her, drifting the canoe at a snail's pace out from land. Stella luxuriated in the quiet afternoon. A party of campers cruising the lake had tarried at the bungalow till after midnight. Jack Fyfe had risen at dawn to depart for some distant logging point. Stella, once wakened, had risen and breakfasted with him. She was tired, drowsy, content to lie there in pure physical relaxation. Lying so, before she was aware of it, her eyes closed.

She wakened with a start at a cold touch of moisture on her face,—rain, great pattering drops. Overhead an ominously black cloud hid the face of the sun. The shore, when she looked, lay a mile and a half abeam. To the north and between her and the land's rocky line was a darkening of the lake's surface. Stella reached for her paddle. The black cloud let fall long, gray streamers of rain. There was scarcely a stirring of the air, but that did not deceive her. There was a growing chill, and there was that broken line sweeping down the lake. Behind that was wind, a summer gale, the black squall dreaded by the Siwashes.

She had to buck her way to shore through that. She drove hard on the paddle. She was not afraid, but there rose in her a peculiar tensed-up feeling. Ahead lay a ticklish bit of business. The sixteen-foot canoe dwarfed to pitiful dimensions in the face of that snarling line of wind harried water. She could hear the distant murmur of it presently, and gusty puffs of wind began to strike her.

Then it swept up to her, a ripple, a chop, and very close behind that the short, steep, lake combers with a wind that blew off the tops as each wave-head broke in white, bubbling froth. Immediately she began to lose ground. She had expected that, and it did not alarm her. If she could keep the canoe bow on, there was an even chance that the squall would blow itself out in half an hour. But keeping the canoe bow on proved a task for stout arms. The wind would catch all that forward part which thrust clear as she topped a sea and twist it aside, tending always to throw her broadside into the trough. Spray began to splash aboard. The seas were so short and steep that the Peterboro would rise over the crest of a tall one and dip its bow deep in the next, or leap clear to strike with a slap that made Stella's heart jump. She had never undergone quite that rough and tumble experience in a small craft. She was being beaten farther out and down the lake, and her arms were growing tired. Nor was there any slackening of the wind.

The combined rain and slaps of spray soaked her thoroughly. A puddle gathered about her knees in the bilge, sloshing fore and aft as the craft pitched, killing the natural buoyancy of the canoe so that she dove harder. Stella took a chance, ceased paddling, and bailed with a small can. She got a tossing that made her head swim while she lay in the trough. And when she tried to head up into it again, one comber bigger than its fellows reared up and slapped a barrel of water inboard. The next wave swamped her.

Sunk to the clamps, Stella held fast to the topsides, crouching on her knees, immersed to the hips in water that struck a chill through her flesh. She had the wit to remember and act upon Jack Fyfe's coaching, namely, to sit tight and hang on. No sea that ever ran can sink a canoe. Wood is buoyant. So long as she could hold on, the submerged craft would keep her head and shoulders above water. But it was numbing cold. Fed by glacial streams, Roaring Lake is icy in hottest midsummer.

What with paddling and bailing and the excitement of the struggle, Stella had wasted no time gazing about for other boats. She knew that if any one at the camp saw her, rescue would be speedily effected. Now, holding fast and sitting quiet, she looked eagerly about as the swamped canoe rose loggily on each wave. Almost immediately she was heartened by seeing distinctly some sort of craft plunging through the blow. She had not long to wait after that, for the approaching launch was a lean-lined speeder, powerfully engined, and she was being forced. Stella supposed it was one of the Abbey runabouts. Even with her teeth chattering and numbness fastening itself upon her, she shivered at the chances the man was taking. It was no sea for a speed boat to smash into at thirty miles an hour. She saw it shoot off the top of one wave and disappear in a white burst of spray, slash through the next and bury itself deep again, flinging a foamy cloud far to port and starboard. Stella cried futilely to the man to slow down. She could hang on a long time yet, but her voice carried no distance.

After that she had not long to wait. In four minutes the runabout was within a hundred yards, open exhausts cracking like a machine gun. And then the very thing she expected and dreaded came about. Every moment she expected to see him drive bows under and go down. Here and there at intervals uplifted a comber taller than its fellows, standing, just as it broke, like a green wall. Into one such hoary-headed sea the white boat now drove like a lance. Stella saw the spray leap like a cascade, saw the solid green curl deep over the forward deck and engine hatch and smash the low windshield. She heard the glass crack. Immediately the roaring exhausts died. Amid the whistle of the wind and the murmur of broken water, the launch staggered like a drunken man, lurched off into the trough, deep down by the head with the weight of water she had taken.

The man in her stood up with hands cupped over his mouth.

"Can you hang on a while longer?" he shouted. "Till I can get my boat bailed?"

"I'm all right," she called back.

She saw him heave up the engine hatch. For a minute or two he bailed rapidly. Then he spun the engine, without result. He straightened up at last, stood irresolute a second, peeled off his coat.

The launch lay heavily in the trough. The canoe, rising and clinging on the crest of each wave, was carried forward a few feet at a time, taking the run of the sea faster than the disabled motorboat. So now only a hundred-odd feet separated them, but they could come no nearer, for the canoe was abeam and slowly drifting past.

Stella saw the man stoop and stand up with a coil of line in his hand. Then she gasped, for he stepped on the coaming and plunged overboard in a beautiful, arching dive. A second later his head showed glistening above the gray water, and he swam toward her with a slow, overhand stroke. It seemed an age—although the actual time was brief enough—before he reached her. She saw then that there was method in his madness, for the line strung out behind him, fast to a cleat on the launch. He laid hold of the canoe and rested a few seconds, panting, smiling broadly at her.

"Sorry that whopping wave put me out of commission," he said at last. "I'd have had you ashore by now. Hang on for a minute."

He made the line fast to a thwart near the bow. Holding fast with one hand, he drew the swamped canoe up to the launch. In that continuous roll it was no easy task to get Stella aboard, but they managed it, and presently she sat shivering in the cockpit, watching the man spill the water out of the Peterboro till it rode buoyantly again. Then he went to work at his engine methodically, wiping dry the ignition terminals, all the various connections where moisture could effect a short circuit. At the end of a few minutes, he turned the starting crank. The multiple cylinders fired with a roar.

He moved back behind the wrecked windshield where the steering gear stood.

"Well, Miss Ship-wrecked Mariner," said he lightly, "where do you wish to be landed?"

"Over there, if you please." Stella pointed to where the red roof of the bungalow stood out against the green. "I'm Mrs. Fyfe."

"Ah!" said he. An expression of veiled surprise flashed across his face. "Another potential romance strangled at birth. You know, I hoped you were some local maiden before whom I could pose as a heroic rescuer. Such is life. Odd, too. Linda Abbey—I'm the Monohan tail to the Abbey business kite, you see—impressed me as pilot for a spin this afternoon and backed out at the last moment. I think she smelled this blow. So I went out for a ride by myself. I was glowering at that new house through a glass when I spied you out in the thick of it."

He had the clutch in now, and the launch was cleaving the seas, even at half speed throwing out wide wings of spray. Some of this the wind brought across the cockpit. "Come up into this seat," Monohan commanded. "I don't suppose you can get any wetter, but if you put your feet through this bulkhead door, the heat from the engine will warm you. By Jove, you're fairly shivering."

"It's lucky for me you happened along," Stella remarked, when she was ensconced behind the bulkhead. "I was getting so cold. I don't know how much longer I could have stood it."

"Thank the good glasses that picked you out. You were only a speck on the water, you know, when I sighted you first."

He kept silent after that. All his faculties were centered on the seas ahead which rolled up before the sharp cutwater of the launch. He was making time and still trying to avoid boarding seas. When a big one lifted ahead, he slowed down. He kept one hand on the throttle control, whistling under his breath disconnected snatches of song. Stella studied his profile, clean-cut as a cameo and wholly pleasing. He was almost as big-bodied as Jack Fyfe, and full four inches taller. The wet shirt clinging close to his body outlined well-knit shoulders, ropy-muscled arms. He could easily have posed for a Viking, so strikingly blond was he, with fair, curly hair. She judged that he might be around thirty, yet his face was altogether boyish.

Sitting there beside him, shivering in her wet clothes, she found herself wondering what magnetic quality there could be about a man that focussed a woman's attention upon him whether she willed it or no. Why should she feel an oddly-disturbing thrill at the mere physical nearness of this fair-haired stranger? She did. There was no debating that. And she wondered—wondered if a bolt of that lightning she had dreaded ever since her marriage was about to strike her now. She hoped not. All her emotions had lain fallow. If Jack Fyfe had no power to stir her,—and she told herself Jack had so failed, without asking herself why,—then some other man might easily accomplish that, to her unutterable grief. She had told herself many a time that no more terrible plight could overtake her than to love and be loved and sit with hands folded, foregoing it all. She shrank from so tragic an evolution. It meant only pain, the ache of unfulfilled, unattainable desires. If, she reflected cynically, this man beside her stood for such a motif in her life, he might better have left her out in the swamped canoe.

While she sat there, drawn-faced with the cold, thinking rather amazedly these things which she told herself she had no right to think, the launch slipped into the quiet nook of Cougar Bay and slowed down to the float.

Monohan helped her out, threw off the canoe's painter, and climbed back into the launch.

"You're as wet as I am," Stella said. "Won't you come up to the house and get a change of clothes? I haven't even thanked you."

"Nothing to be thanked for," he smiled up at her. "Only please remember not to get offshore in a canoe again. I mightn't be handy the next time—and Roaring Lake's as fickle as your charming sex. All smiles one minute, storming the next. No, I won't stay this time, thanks. A little wet won't hurt me. I wasn't in the water long enough to get chilled, you know. I'll be home in half an hour. Run along and get dressed, Mrs. Fyfe, and drink something hot to drive that chill away. Good-by."

Stella went up to the house, her hand tingling with his parting grip. Over and above the peril she had escaped rose an uneasy vision of a greater peril to her peace of mind. The platitudes of soul-affinity, of irresistible magnetic attraction, of love that leaped full-blown into reality at the touch of a hand or the glance of an eye, she had always viewed with distrust, holding them the weaknesses of weak, volatile natures. But there was something about this man which had stirred her, nothing that he said or did, merely some elusive, personal attribute. She had never undergone any such experience, and she puzzled over it now. A chance stranger, and his touch could make her pulse leap. It filled her with astonished dismay.

Afterward, dry-clad and warm, sitting in her pet chair, Jack Junior cooing at her from a nest among cushions on the floor, the natural reaction set in, and she laughed at herself. When Fyfe came home, she told him lightly of her rescue.

He said nothing at first, only sat drumming on his chair-arm, his eyes steady on her.

"That might have cost you your life," he said at last. "Will you remember not to drift offshore again?"

"I rather think I shall," she responded. "It wasn't a pleasant experience."

"Monohan, eh?" he remarked after another interval. "So he's on Roaring Lake again."

"Do you know him?" she asked.

"Yes," he replied briefly.

For a minute or so longer he sat there, his face wearing its habitual impassiveness. Then he got up, kissed her with a queer sort of intensity, and went put. Stella gazed after him, mildly surprised. It wasn't quite in his usual manner.

CHAPTER XV
A RESURRECTION

It might have been a week or so later that Stella made a discovery which profoundly affected the whole current of her thought. The long twilight was just beginning. She was curled on the living-room floor, playing with the baby. Fyfe and Charlie Benton sat by a window, smoking, conversing, as they frequently did, upon certain phases of the timber industry. A draft from an open window fluttered some sheet music down off the piano rack, and Stella rescued it from Jack Junior's tiny, clawing hands. Some of the Abbeys had been there the evening before. One bit of music was a song Linda had tried to sing and given up because it soared above her vocal range. Stella rose to put up the music. Without any premeditated idea of playing, she sat down at the piano and began to run over the accompaniment. She could play passably.

"That doesn't seem so very hard," she thought aloud. Benton turned at sound of her words.

"Say, did you never get any part of your voice back, Stell?" he asked. "I never hear you try to sing."

"No," she answered. "I tried and tried long after you left home, but it was always the same old story. I haven't sung a note in five years."

"Linda fell down hard on that song last night," he went on. "There was a time when that wouldn't have been a starter for you, eh? Did you know Stella used to warble like a prima donna, Jack?"

Fyfe shook his head.

"Fact. The governor spent a pot of money cultivating her voice. It was some voice, too. She—"

He broke off to listen. Stella was humming the words of the song, her fingers picking at the melody instead of the accompaniment.

"Why, you can," Benton cried.

"Can what?" She turned on the stool.

"Sing, of course. You got that high trill that Linda had to screech through. You got it perfectly, without effort."

"I didn't," she returned. "Why, I wasn't singing, just humming it over."

"You let out a link or two on those high notes just the same, whether you knew you were doing it or not," her brother returned impatiently. "Go on. Turn yourself loose. Sing that song."

"Oh, I couldn't," Stella said ruefully. "I haven't tried for so long. It's no use. My voice always cracks, and I want to cry."

"Crack fiddlesticks!" Benton retorted. "I know what it used to be. Believe me, it sounded natural, even if you were just lilting. Here."

He came over to the piano and playfully edged her off the stool.

"I'm pretty rusty," he said. "But I can fake what I can't play of this. It's simple enough. You stand up there and sing."

She only stood looking at him.

"Go on," he commanded. "I believe you can sing anything. You have to show me, if you can't."

Stella fingered the sheets reluctantly. Then she drew a deep breath and began.

It was not a difficult selection, merely a bit from a current light opera, with a closing passage that ranged a trifle too high for the ordinary untrained voice to take with ease. Stella sang it effortlessly, the last high, trilling notes pouring out as sweet and clear as the carol of a lark. Benton struck the closing chord and looked up at her. Fyfe leaned forward in his chair. Jack Junior, among his pillows on the floor, waved his arms, kicking and gurgling.

"You did pretty well on that," Charlie remarked complacently. "Now *sing* something. Got any of your old pieces?"

"I wonder if I could?" Stella murmured. "I'm almost afraid to try."

She hurried away to some outlying part of the house, reappearing in a few minutes with a dog-eared bundle of sheets in her hand. From among these she selected three and set them on the rack.

Benton whistled when he glanced over the music.

"The Siren Song," he grunted. "What is it? something new? Lord, look at the scale. Looks like one of those screaming arias from the 'Flying Dutchman.' Some stunt."

"Marchand composed it for the express purpose of trying out voices," Stella said. "It *is* a stunt."

"You'll have to play your own accompaniment," Charlie grinned. "That's too much for me."

"Oh, just so you give me a little support here and there," Stella told him. "I can't sing sitting on a piano stool."

Benton made a face at the music and struck the keys.

It seemed to Stella nothing short of a miracle. She had been mute so long. She had almost forgotten what a tragedy losing her voice had been. And to find it again, to hear it ring like a trumpet. It did! It was too big for the room. She felt herself caught up in a triumphant ecstasy as she sang. She found herself blinking as the last note died away. Her brother twisted about on the piano stool, fumbling for a cigarette.

"And still they say they can't come back," he remarked at last. "Why, you're better than you ever were, Stella. You've got the old sweetness and flexibility that dad used to rave about. But your voice is bigger, somehow different. It gets under a man's skin."

She picked up the baby from the floor, began to play with him. She didn't want to talk. She wanted to think, to gloat over and hug to herself this miracle of her restored voice. She was very quiet, very much absorbed in her own reflections until it was time—very shortly—to put Jack Junior in his bed. That was a function she made wholly her own. The nurse might greet his waking whimper in the morning and minister to his wants throughout the day, but Stella "tucked him in" his crib every night. And after the blue eyes were closed, she sat there, very still, thinking. In a detached way she was conscious of hearing Charlie leave.

Later, when she was sitting beside her dressing table brushing her hair, Fyfe came in. He perched himself on the foot rail of the bed, looking silently at her. She had long grown used to that. It was a familiar trick of his.

"How did it happen that you've never tried your voice lately?" he asked after a time.

"I gave it up long ago," she said. "Didn't I ever tell you that I used to sing and lost my voice?"

"No," he answered. "Charlie did just now. You rather took my breath away. It's wonderful. You'd be a sensation in opera."

"I might have been," she corrected. "That was one of my little dreams. You don't know what a grief it was to me when I got over that throat trouble and found I couldn't sing. I used to try and try—and my voice would break every time. I lost all heart to try after a while. That was when I wanted to take up nursing, and they wouldn't let me. I haven't thought about singing for an age. I've crooned lullabies to Jacky without remembering that I once had volume enough to drown out an accompanist. Dad was awfully proud of my voice."

"You've reason to be proud of it now," Fyfe said slowly. "It's a voice in ten thousand. What are going to do with it?"

Stella drew the brush mechanically through her heavy hair. She had been asking herself that. What could she do? A long road and a hard one lay ahead of her or any other woman who essayed to make her voice the basis of a career. Over and above that she was not free to seek such a career. Fyfe himself knew that, and it irritated her that he should ask such a question. She swung about on him.

"Nothing," she said a trifle tartly. "How can I? Granting that my voice is worth the trouble, would you like me to go and study in the East or abroad? Would you be willing to bear the expense of such an undertaking? To have me leave Jack to nursemaids and you to your logs?"

"So that in the fullness of time I might secure a little reflected glory as the husband of Madame Fyfe, the famous soprano," he replied slowly. "Well, I can't say that's a particularly pleasing prospect."

"Then why ask me what I'm going to do with it?" she flung back impatiently. "It'll be an asset—like my looks—and—and—"

She dropped her face in her hands, choking back an involuntary sob. Fyfe crossed the room at a bound, put his arms around her.

"Stella, Stella!" he cried sharply. "Don't be a fool."

"D—don't be cross, Jack," she whispered. "Please. I'm sorry. I simply can't help it. You don't understand."

"Oh, don't I?" he said savagely. "I understand too well; that's the devil of it. But I suppose that's a woman's way,—to feed her soul with illusions, and let the realities go hang. Look here."

He caught her by the shoulders and pulled her to her feet, facing him. There was a fire in his eye, a hard shutting together of his lips that frightened her a little.

"Look here," he said roughly. "Take a brace, Stella. Do you realize what sort of a state of mind you're drifting into? You married me under more or less compulsion,—compulsion of circumstances,—and gradually you're beginning to get dissatisfied, to pity yourself. You'll precipitate things you maybe don't dream of now, if you keep on. Damn it, I didn't create the circumstances. I only showed you a way out. You took it. It satisfied you for a while; you can't deny it did. But it doesn't any more. You're nursing a lot of illusions, Stella, that are going to make your life full of misery."

"I'm not," she sobbed. "It's because I haven't any illusions that—that—Oh, what's the use of talking, Jack? I'm not complaining. I don't even know what gave me this black mood, just now. I suppose that queer miracle of my voice coming back upset me. I feel—well, as if I were a different person, somehow; as if I had forfeited any right to have it. Oh, it's silly, you'll say. But it's there. I can't help my feeling—or my lack of it."

Fyfe's face whitened a little. His hands dropped from her shoulders.

"Now you're talking to the point," he said quietly. "Especially that last. We've been married some little time now, and if anything, we're farther apart in the essentials of mating than we were at the beginning. You've committed yourself to an undertaking, yet more and more you encourage yourself to wish for the moon. If you don't stop dreaming and try real living, don't you see a lot of trouble ahead for yourself? It's simple. You're slowly hardening yourself against me, beginning to resent my being a factor in your life. It's only a matter of time, if you keep on, until your emotions center about some other man."

"Why do you talk like that?" she said bitterly. "Do you think I've got neither pride nor self-respect?"

"Yes. Both a-plenty," he answered. "But you're a woman, with a rather complex nature even for your sex. If your heart and your head ever clash over anything like that, you'll be in perfect hell until one or the other gets the upper hand. You're a thoroughbred, and high-strung as thoroughbreds are. It takes something besides three meals a day and plenty of good clothes to complete your existence. If I can't make it complete, some other man will make you think he can. Why don't you try? Haven't I got any possibilities as a lover? Can't you throw a little halo of romance about me, for your own sake—if not for mine?"

He drew her up close to him, stroking tenderly the glossy brown hair that flowed about her shoulders.

"Try it, Stella," he whispered passionately. "Try wanting to like me, for a change. I can't make love by myself. Shake off that infernal apathy that's taking possession of you where I'm concerned. If you can't love me, for God's sake fight with me. Do *something!*"

CHAPTER XVI
THE CRISIS

Looking back at that evening as the summer wore on, Stella perceived that it was the starting point of many things, no one of them definitely outstanding by itself but bulking large as a whole. Fyfe made his appeal, and it left her unmoved save in certain superficial aspects. She was sorry, but she was mostly sorry for herself. And she denied his premonition of disaster. If, she said to herself, they got no raptures out of life, at least they got along without friction. In her mind their marriage, no matter that it lacked what she no less than Fyfe deemed an essential to happiness, was a fixed state, final, irrevocable, not to be altered by any emotional vagaries.

No man, she told herself, could make her forget her duty. If it should befall that her heart, lacking safe anchorage, went astray, that would be her personal cross—not Jack Fyfe's. *He* should never know. One might feel deeply without being moved to act upon one's feelings. So she assured herself.

She never dreamed that Jack Fyfe could possibly have foreseen in Walter Monohan a dangerous factor in their lives. A man is not supposed to have uncanny intuitions, even when his wife is a wonderfully attractive woman who does not care for him except in a friendly sort of way. Stella herself had ample warning. From the first time of meeting, the man's presence affected her strangely, made an appeal to her that no man had ever made. She felt it sitting beside him in the plunging launch that day when Roaring Lake reached its watery arms for her. There was seldom a time when they were together that she did not feel it. And she pitted her will against it, as something to be conquered and crushed.

There was no denying the man's personal charm in the ordinary sense of the word. He was virile, handsome, cultured, just such a man as she could easily have centered her heart upon in times past,—just such a man as can set a woman's heart thrilling when he lays siege to her. If he had made an open bid for Stella's affection, she, entrenched behind all the accepted canons of her upbringing, would have recoiled from him, viewed him with wholly distrustful eyes.

But he did nothing of the sort. He was a friend, or at least he became so. Inevitably they were thrown much together. There was a continual informal running back and forth between Fyfe's place and Abbey's. Monohan was a lily of the field, although it was common knowledge on Roaring Lake that he was a heavy stock-holder in the Abbey-Monohan combination. At any rate, he was holidaying on the lake that summer. There had grown up a genuine intimacy between Linda and Stella. There were always people at the Abbeys'; sometimes a few guests at the Fyfe bungalow. Stella's marvellous voice served to heighten her popularity. The net result of it all was that in the following three months source three days went by that she did not converse with Monohan.

She could not help making comparisons between the two men. They stood out in marked contrast, in manner, physique, in everything. Where Fyfe was reserved almost to taciturnity, impassive-featured, save for that whimsical gleam that was never wholly absent from his keen blue eyes, Monohan talked with facile ease, with wonderful expressiveness of face. He was a finished product of courteous generations. Moreover, he had been everywhere, done a little of everything, acquired in his manner something of the versatility of his experience. Physically he was fit as any logger in the camps, a big, active-bodied, clear-eyed, ruddy man.

What it was about him that stirred her so, Stella could never determine. She knew beyond peradventure that he had that power. He had the gift of quick, sympathetic perception,—but so too had Jack Fyfe, she reminded herself. Yet no tone of Jack Fyfe's voice could raise a flutter in her breast, make a faint flush glow in her cheeks, while Monohan could do that. He did not need to be actively attentive. It was only necessary for him to be near.

It dawned upon Stella Fyfe in the fullness of the season, when the first cool October days were upon them, and the lake shores flamed again with the red and yellow and umber of autumn, that she had been playing with fire—and that fire burns.

This did not filter into her consciousness by degrees. She had steeled herself to seeing him pass away with the rest of the summer folk, to take himself out of her life. She admitted that there would be a gap. But that had to be. No word other than friendly ones would ever pass between them. He would go away, and she would go on as before. That was all. She was scarcely aware how far they had traveled along that road whereon travelers converse by glance of eye, by subtle intuitions, eloquent silences. Monohan himself delivered the shock that awakened her to despairing clearness of vision.

He had come to bring her a book, he and Linda Abbey and Charlie together,—a commonplace enough little courtesy. And it happened that this day Fyfe had taken his rifle and vanished into the woods immediately after luncheon. Between Linda Abbey and Charlie Benton matters had so far progressed that it was now the most natural thing for them to seek a corner or poke along the beach together, oblivious to all but themselves. This afternoon they chatted a while with Stella and then gradually detached themselves until Monohan, glancing through the window, pointed them out to his hostess. They were seated on a log at the edge of the lawn, a stone's throw from the house.

"They're getting on," he said. "Lucky beggars. It's all plain sailing for them."

There was a note of infinite regret in his voice, a sadness that stabbed Stella Fyfe like a lance. She did not dare look at him. Something rose chokingly in her throat. She felt and fought against a slow welling of tears to her eyes. Before she sensed that she was betraying herself, Monohan was holding both her hands fast between his own, gripping them with a fierce, insistent pressure, speaking in a passionate undertone.

"Why should we have to beat our heads against a stone wall like this?" he was saying wildly. "Why couldn't we have met and loved and been happy, as we could have been? It was fated to happen. I felt it that day I dragged you out of the lake. It's been growing on me ever since. I've struggled against it, and it's no use. It's something stronger than I am. I love you, Stella, and it maddens me to see you chafing in your chains. Oh, my dear, why couldn't it have been different?"

"You mustn't talk like that," she protested weakly. "You mustn't. It isn't right."

"I suppose it's right for you to live with a man you don't love, when your heart's crying out against it?" he broke out. "My God, do you think I can't see? I don't have to see things; I can feel them. I know you're the kind of woman who goes through hell for her conceptions of right and wrong. I honor you for that, dear. But, oh, the pity of it. Why should it have to be? Life could have held so much that is fine and true for you and me together. For you do care, don't you?"

"What difference does that make?" she whispered. "What difference can it make? Oh, you mustn't tell me these things, I mustn't listen. I mustn't."

"But they're terribly, tragically true," Monohan returned. "Look at me, Stella. Don't turn your face away, dear. I wouldn't do anything that might bring the least shadow on you. I know the pitiful hopelessness of it.

You're fettered, and there's no apparent loophole to freedom. I know it's best for me to keep this locked tight in my heart, as something precious and sorrowful. I never meant to tell you. But the flesh isn't always equal to the task the spirit imposes."

She did not answer him immediately, for she was struggling for a grip on herself, fighting back an impulse to lay her head against him and cry her agony out on his breast. All the resources of will that she possessed she called upon now to still that tumult of emotion that racked her. When she did speak, it was in a hard, strained tone. But she faced the issue squarely, knowing beyond all doubt what she had to face.

"Whether I care or not isn't the question," she said. "I'm neither little enough nor prudish enough to deny a feeling that's big and clean. I see no shame in that. I'm afraid of it—if you can understand that. But that's neither here nor there. I know what I have to do. I married without love, with my eyes wide open, and I have to pay the price. So you must never talk to me of love. You mustn't even see me, if it can be avoided. It's better that way. We can't make over our lives to suit ourselves—at least I can't. I must play the game according to the only rules I know. We daren't—we mustn't trifle with this sort of a feeling. With you—footloose, and all the world before you—it'll die out presently."

"No," he flared. "I deny that. I'm not an impressionable boy. I know myself."

He paused, and the grip of his hands on hers tightened till the pain of it ran to her elbows. Then his fingers relaxed a little.

"Oh, I know," he said haltingly. "I know it's got to be that way. I have to go my road and leave you to yours. Oh, the blank hopelessness of it, the useless misery of it. We're made for each other, and we have to grin and say good-by, go along our separate ways, trying to smile. What a devilish state of affairs! But I love you, dear, and no matter—I—ah—"

His voice flattened out. His hands released hers, he straightened quickly. Stella turned her head. Jack Fyfe stood in the doorway. His face was fixed in its habitual mask. He was biting the end off a cigar. He struck a match and put it to the cigar end with steady fingers as he walked slowly across the big room.

"I hear the kid peeping," he said to Stella quite casually, "and I noticed Martha outside as I came in. Better go see what's up with him."

Trained to repression, schooled in self-control, Stella rose to obey, for under the smoothness of his tone there was the iron edge of command. Her heart apparently ceased to beat. She tried to smile, but she knew that her face was tear-wet. She knew that Jack Fyfe had seen and understood. She had done no wrong, but a terrible apprehension of consequences seized her, a fear that tragedy of her own making might stalk grimly in that room.

In this extremity she banked with implicit faith on the man she had married rather than the man she loved. For the moment she felt overwhelmingly glad that Jack Fyfe was iron—cool, unshakable. He would never give an inch, but he would never descend to any sordid scene. She could not visualize him the jealous, outraged husband, breathing the conventional anathema, but there were elements unreckonable in that room. She knew instinctively that Fyfe once aroused would be deadly in anger and she could not vouch for Monohan's temper under the strain of feeling. That was why she feared.

So she lingered a second or two outside the door, quaking, but there arose only the sound of Fyfe's heavy body settling into a leather chair, and following that the low, even rumble of his voice. She could not distinguish words. The tone sounded ordinary, conversational. She prayed that his intent was to ignore the situation, that Monohan would meet him halfway in that effort. Afterward there would be a reckoning. But for herself she neither thought nor feared. It was a problem to be faced, that was all. And so, the breath of her coming in short, quick respirations, she went to her room. There was no wailing from the nursery. She had known that.

Sitting beside a window, chin in hand, her lower lip compressed between her teeth, she saw Fyfe, after the lapse of ten minutes, leave by the front entrance, stopping to chat a minute with Linda and Charlie Benton, who were moving slowly toward the house. Stella rose to her feet and dabbed at her face with a powdered chamois. She couldn't let Monohan go like that; her heart cried out against it. Very likely they would never meet again.

She flew down the hall to the living room. Monohan stood just within the front door, gazing irresolutely over his shoulder. He took a step or two to meet her. His clean-cut face was drawn into sullen lines, a deep flush mantled his cheek.

"Listen," he said tensely. "I've been made to feel like—like—Well, I controlled myself. I knew it had to be that way. It was unfortunate. I think we could have been trusted to do the decent thing. You and I were bred to do that. I've got a little pride. I can't come here again. And I want to see you once more before I leave here for good. I'll be going away next week. That'll be the end of it—the bitter finish. Will you slip down to the first point south of Cougar Bay about three in the afternoon to-morrow? It'll be the last and only time. He'll have you for life; can't I talk to you for twenty minutes?"

"No," she whispered forlornly. "I can't do that. I—oh, good-by—good-by."

"Stella, Stella," she heard his vibrant whisper follow after. But she ran away through dining room and hall to the bedroom, there to fling herself face down, choking back the passionate protest that welled up within her. She lay there, her face buried in the pillow, until the sputtering exhaust of the Abbey cruiser growing fainter and more faint told her they were gone.

She heard her husband walk through the house once after that. When dinner was served, he was not there. It was eleven o'clock by the time-piece on her mantel when she heard him come in, but he did not come to their room. He went quietly into the guest chamber across the hall.

She waited through a leaden period. Then, moved by an impulse she did not attempt to define, a mixture of motives, pity for him, a craving for the outlet of words, a desire to set herself right before him, she slipped on a dressing robe and crossed the hall. The door swung open noiselessly. Fyfe sat slumped in a chair, hat pulled low on his forehead, hands thrust deep in his pockets. He did not even look up. His eyes stared straight ahead, absent, unseeingly fixed on nothing. He seemed to be unconscious of her presence or to ignore it,—she could not tell which.

"Jack," she said. And when he made no response she said again, tremulously, that unyielding silence chilling her, "Jack."

He stirred a little, but only to take off his hat and lay it on a table beside him. With one hand pushing back mechanically the straight, reddish-tinged hair from his brow, he looked up at her and said briefly, in a tone barren of all emotion:

"Well?"

She was suddenly dumb. Words failed her utterly. Yet there was much to be said, much that was needful to say. They could not go on with a cloud like that over them, a cloud that had to be dissipated in the crucible of words. Yet she could not begin. Fyfe, after a prolonged silence, seemed to grasp her difficulty. Abruptly he began to speak, cutting straight to the heart of his subject, after his fashion.

"It's a pity things had to take his particular turn," said he. "But now that you're face to face with something definite, what do you propose to do about it?"

"Nothing," she answered slowly. "I can't help the feeling. It's there. But I can thrust it into the background, go on as if it didn't exist. There's nothing else for me to do, that I can see. I'm sorry, Jack."

"So am I," he said grimly. "Still, it was a chance we took,—or I took, rather. I seem to have made a mistake or two, in my estimate of both you and myself. That is human enough, I suppose. You're making a bigger mistake than I did though, to let Monohan sweep you off your feet."

There was something that she read for contempt in his tone. It stung her.

"He hasn't swept me off my feet, as you put it," she cried. "Good Heavens, do you think I'm that spineless sort of creature? I've never forgotten I'm your wife. I've got a little self-respect left yet, if I was weak enough to grasp at the straw you threw me in the beginning. I was honest with you then, I'm trying to be honest with you now."

"I know, Stella," he said gently. "I'm not throwing mud. It's a damnably unfortunate state of affairs, that's all. I foresaw something of the sort when we were married. You were candid enough about your attitude. But I told myself like a conceited fool that I could make your life so full that in a little while I'd be the only possible figure on your horizon. I've failed. I've known for some time that I was going to fail. You're not the thin-blooded type of woman that is satisfied with pleasant surroundings and any sort of man. You're bound to run the gamut of all the emotions, sometime and somewhere. I loved you, and I thought in my conceit I could make myself the man, the one man who would mean everything to you."

"Just the same," he continued, "you've been a fool, and I don't see how you can avoid paying the penalty for folly."

"What do you mean?" she asked.

"You haven't tried to play the game," he answered tensely. "For months you've been withdrawing into your shell. You've been clanking your chains and half-heartedly wishing for some mysterious power to strike them off. It wasn't a thing you undertook lightly. It isn't a thing—marriage, I mean— that you hold lightly. That being the case, you would have been wise to try making the best of it, instead of making the worst of it. But you let yourself drift into a state of mind where you—well, you see the result. I saw it coming. I didn't need to happen in this afternoon to know that there were undercurrents of feeling swirling about. And so the way you feel now is in itself a penalty. If you let Monohan cut any more figure in your thoughts, you'll pay bigger in the end."

"I can't help my thoughts, or I should say my feelings," she said wearily.

"You think you love him," Fyfe made low reply. "As a matter of fact, you love what you think he is. I daresay that he has sworn his affection by all that's good and great. But if you were convinced that he didn't really care, that his flowery protestations had a double end in view, would you still love him?"

"I don't know," she murmured. "But that's beside the point. I do love him. I know it's unwise. It's a feeling that has overwhelmed me in a way that I didn't believe possible, that I had hoped to avoid. But—but I can't pretend, Jack. I don't want you to misunderstand. I don't want this to make us both miserable. I don't want it to generate an atmosphere of suspicion and jealousy. We'd only be fighting about a shadow. I never cheated at anything in my life. You can trust me still, can't you?"

"Absolutely," Fyfe answered without hesitation.

"Then that's all there is to it," she replied, "unless—unless you're ready to give me up as a hopeless case, and let me go away and blunder along the best I can."

He shook his head.

"I haven't even considered that," he said. "Very likely it's unwise of me to say this,—it will probably antagonize you,—but I know Monohan better than you do. I'd go pretty far to keep you two apart—now—for your sake."

"It would be the same if it were any other man," she muttered. "I can understand that feeling in you. It's so—so typically masculine."

"No, you're wrong there, dead wrong," Fyfe frowned. "I'm not a self-sacrificing brute by any means. Still, knowing that you'll only live with me on sufferance, if you were honestly in love with a man that I felt was halfway decent, I'd put my feelings in my pocket and let you go. If you cared enough for him to break every tie, to face the embarrassment of divorce, why, I'd figure you were entitled to your freedom and whatever happiness it might bring. But Monohan—hell, I don't want to talk about him. I trust you, Stella. I'm banking on your own good sense. And along with that good, natural common sense, you've got so many illusions. About life in general, and about men. They seem to have centered about this one particular man. I can't open your eyes or put you on the right track. That's a job for yourself. All I can do is to sit back and wait."

His voice trailed off huskily.

Stella put a hand on his shoulder.

"Do you care so much as all that, Jack?" she whispered. "Even in spite of what you know?"

"For two years now," he answered, "you've been the biggest thing in my life. I don't change easy; I don't want to change. But I'm getting hopeless."

"I'm sorry, Jack," she said. "I can't begin to tell you how sorry I am. I didn't love you to begin with—"

"And you've always resented that," he broke in. "You've hugged that ghost of a loveless marriage to your bosom and sighed for the real romance you'd missed. Well, maybe you did. But you haven't found it yet. I'm very sure of that, although I doubt if I could convince you."

"Let me finish," she pleaded. "You knew I didn't love you—that I was worn out and desperate and clutching at the life line you threw. In spite of that,—well, if I fight down this love, or fascination, or infatuation, or whatever it is,—I'm not sure myself, except that it affects me strongly,—can't we be friends again?"

"Friends! Oh, hell!" Fyfe exploded.

He came up out of his chair with a blaze in his eyes that startled her, caught her by the arm, and thrust her out the door.

"Friends? You and I?" He sank his voice to a harsh whisper. "My God—friends! Go to bed. Good night."

He pushed her into the hall, and the lock clicked between them. For one confused instant Stella stood poised, uncertain. Then she went into her bedroom and sat down, her keenest sensation one of sheer relief. Already in those brief hours emotion had well-nigh exhausted her. To be alone, to lie still and rest, to banish thought,—that was all she desired.

She lay on her bed inert, numbed, all but her mind, and that traversed section by section in swift, consecutive progress all the amazing turns of her life since she first came to Roaring Lake. There was neither method nor inquiry in this back-casting—merely a ceaseless, involuntary activity of the brain.

A little after midnight when all the house was hushed, she went into the adjoining room, cuddled Jack Junior into her arms, and took him to her own bed. With his chubby face nestled against her breast, she lay there fighting against that interminable, maddening buzzing in her brain. She prayed for sleep, her nervous fingers stroking the silky, baby hair.

CHAPTER XVII
IN WHICH THERE IS A FURTHER CLASH

One can only suffer so much. Poignant feeling brings its own anaesthetic. When Stella Fyfe fell into a troubled sleep that night, the storm of her emotions had beaten her sorely. Morning brought its physical reaction. She could see things clearly and calmly enough to perceive that her love for Monohan was fraught with factors that must be taken into account. All the world loves a lover, but her world did not love lovers who kicked over the conventional traces. She had made a niche for herself. There were ties she could not break lightly, and she was not thinking of herself alone when she considered that, but of her husband and Jack Junior, of Linda Abbey and Charlie Benton, of each and every individual whose life touched more or less directly upon her own.

She had known always what a woman should do in such case, what she had been taught a woman should do: grin, as Monohan had said, and take her medicine. For her there was no alternative. Fyfe had made that clear. But her heart cried out in rebellion against the necessity. To her, trying to think logically, the most grievous phase of the doing was the fact that nothing could ever be the same again. She could go on. Oh, yes. She could dam up the wellspring of her impulses, walk steadfast along the accustomed ways. But those ways would not be the old ones. There would always be the skeleton at the feast. She would know it was there, and Jack Fyfe would know, and she dreaded the fruits of that knowledge, the bitterness and smothered resentment it would breed. But it had to be. As she saw it, there was no choice.

She came down to breakfast calmly enough. It was nothing that could be altered by heroics, by tears and wailings. Not that she was much given to either. She had not whined when her brother made things so hard for her that any refuge seemed alluring by comparison. Curiously enough, she did not blame her brother now; neither did she blame Jack Fyfe.

She told herself that in first seeking the line of least resistance she had manifested weakness, that since her present problem was indirectly the outgrowth of that original weakness, she would be weak no more. So she tried to meet her husband as if nothing had happened, in which she succeeded outwardly very well indeed, since Fyfe himself chose to ignore any change in their mutual attitude.

She busied herself about the house that forenoon, seeking deliberately a multitude of little tasks to occupy her hands and her mind.

But when lunch was over, she was at the end of her resources. Jack Junior settled in his crib for a nap. Fyfe went away to that area back of the camp where arose the crash of falling trees and the labored puffing of donkey engines. She could hear faint and far the voices of the falling gangs that cried: "Tim-ber-r-r-r." She could see on the bank, a little beyond the bunkhouse and cook-shack, the big roader spooling up the cable that brought string after string of logs down to the lake. Rain or sun, happiness or sorrow, the work went on. She found it in her heart to envy the sturdy loggers. They could forget their troubles in the strain of action. Keyed as she was to that high pitch, that sense of their unremitting activity, the ravaging of the forest which produced the resources for which she had sold herself irritated her. She was very bitter when she thought that.

She longed for some secluded place to sit and think, or try to stop thinking. And without fully realizing the direction she took, she walked down past the camp, crossed the skid-road, stepping lightly over main line and haul-back at the donkey engineer's warning, and went along the lake shore.

A path wound through the belt of brush and hardwood that fringed the lake. Not until she had followed this up on the neck of a little promontory south of the bay, did she remember with a shock that she was approaching the place where Monohan had begged her to meet him. She looked at her watch. Two-thirty. She sought the shore line for sight of a boat, wondering if he would come in spite of her refusal. But to her great relief she saw no sign of him. Probably he had thought better of it, had seen now as she had seen then that no good and an earnest chance of evil might come of such a clandestine meeting, had taken her stand as final.

She was glad, because she did not want to go back to the house. She did not want to make the effort of wandering away in the other direction to find that restful peace of woods and water. She moved up a little on the point until she found a mossy boulder and sat down on that, resting her chin in her palms, looking out over the placid surface of the lake with somber eyes.

And so Monohan surprised her. The knoll lay thick-carpeted with moss. He was within a few steps of her when a twig cracking underfoot apprised her of some one's approach. She rose, with an impulse to fly, to escape a meeting she had not desired. And as she rose, the breath stopped in her throat.

Twenty feet behind Monohan came Jack Fyfe with his hunter's stride, soundlessly over the moss, a rifle drooping in the crook of his arm. A sunbeam striking obliquely between two firs showed her his face plainly, the faint curl of his upper lip.

Something in her look arrested Monohan. He glanced around, twisted about, froze in his tracks, his back to her. Fyfe came up. Of the three he was the coolest, the most rigorously self-possessed. He glanced from Monohan to his wife, back to Monohan. After that his blue eyes never left the other man's face.

"What did I say to you yesterday?" Fyfe opened his mouth at last. "But then I might have known I was wasting my breath on you!"

"Well," Monohan retorted insolently, "what are you going to do about it? This isn't the Stone Age."

Fyfe laughed unpleasantly.

"Lucky for you. You'd have been eliminated long ago," he said. "No, it takes the present age to produce such rotten specimens as you."

A deep flush rose in Monohan's cheeks. He took a step toward Fyfe, his hands clenched.

"You wouldn't say that if you weren't armed," he taunted hoarsely.

"No?" Fyfe cast the rifle to one side. It fell with a metallic clink against a stone. "I do say it though, you see. You are a sort of a yellow dog, Monohan. You know it, and you know that I know it. That's why it stings you to be told so."

Monohan stepped back and slipped out of his coat. His face was crimson.

"By God, I'll teach you something," he snarled.

He lunged forward as he spoke, shooting a straight-arm blow for Fyfe's face. It swept through empty air, for Fyfe, poised on the balls of his feet, ducked under the driving fist, and slapped Monohan across the mouth with the open palm of his hand.

"Tag," he said sardonically. "You're It."

Monohan pivoted, and rushing, swung right and left, missing by inches. Fyfe's mocking grin seemed to madden him completely. He rushed again, launching another vicious blow that threw him partly off his balance. Before he could recover, Fyfe kicked both feet from under him, sent him sprawling on the moss.

Stella stood like one stricken. The very thing she dreaded had come about. Yet the manner of its unfolding was not as she had visualized it when she saw Fyfe near at hand. She saw now a side of her husband that she had never glimpsed, that she found hard to understand. She could have understood him beating Monohan senseless, if he could. A murderous fury of jealousy would not have surprised her. This did. He had not struck a blow, did not attempt to strike.

She could not guess why, but she saw that he was playing with Monohan, making a fool of him, for all Monohan's advantage of height and reach. Fyfe moved like the light, always beyond Monohan's vengeful blows, slipping under those driving fists to slap his adversary, to trip him, mocking him with the futility of his effort.

She felt herself powerless to stop that sorry exhibition. It was not a fight for her. Dimly she had a feeling that back of her lay something else. An echo of it had been more than once in Fyfe's speech. Here and now, they had forgotten her at the first word. They were engaged in a struggle for mastery, sheer brute determination to hurt each other, which had little or nothing to do with her. She foresaw, watching the odd combat with a feeling akin to fascination, that it was a losing game for Monohan. Fyfe was his master at every move.

Yet he did not once attempt to strike a solid blow, nothing but that humiliating, open-handed slap, that dexterous swing of his foot that plunged Monohan headlong. He grinned steadily, a cold grimace that reflected no mirth, being merely a sneering twist of his features. Stella knew the deadly strength of him. She wondered at his purpose, how it would end.

The elusive light-footedness of the man, the successive stinging of those contemptuous slaps at last maddened Monohan into ignoring the rules by which men fight. He dropped his hands and stood panting with his exertions. Suddenly he kicked, a swift lunge for Fyfe's body.

Fyfe leaped aside. Then he closed. Powerful and weighty a man as Monohan was, Fyfe drove him halfway around with a short-arm blow that landed near his heart, and while he staggered from that, clamped one thick arm about his neck in the strangle-hold. Holding him helpless, bent backwards across his broad chest, Fyfe slowly and systematically choked him; he shut off his breath until Monohan's tongue protruded, and his eyes bulged glassily, and horrible, gurgling noises issued from his gaping mouth.

"Jack, Jack!" Stella found voice to shriek. "You're killing him."

Fyfe lifted his eyes to hers. The horror he saw there may have stirred him. Or he may have considered his object accomplished. Stella could not tell. But he flung Monohan from him with a force that sent him reeling a dozen feet, to collapse on the moss. It took him a full minute to regain his breath, to rise to unsteady feet, to find his voice.

"You can't win all the time," he gasped. "By God, I'll show you that you can't."

With that he turned and went back the way he had come. Fyfe stood silent, hands resting on his hips, watching until Monohan pushed out a slim speed launch from under cover of overhanging alders and set off down the lake.

"Well," he remarked then, in a curiously detached, impersonal tone. "The lightning will begin to play by and by, I suppose."

"What do you mean?" Stella asked breathlessly.

He did not answer. His eyes turned to her slowly. She saw now that his face was white and rigid, that the line of his lips drew harder together as he looked at her; but she was not prepared for the storm that broke. She did not comprehend the tempest that raged within him until he had her by the shoulders, his fingers crushing into her soft flesh like the jaws of a trap, shaking her as a terrier might shake a rat, till the heavy coils of hair cascaded over her shoulders, and for a second fear tugged at her heart. For she thought he meant to kill her.

When he did desist, he released her with a thrust of his arms that sent her staggering against a tree, shaken to the roots of her being, though not with fear. Anger had displaced that. A hot protest against his brute strength, against his passionate outbreak, stirred her. Appearances were against her, she knew. Even so, she revolted against his cave-man roughness. She was amazed to find herself longing for the power to strike him.

She faced him trembling, leaning against the tree trunk, staring at him in impotent rage. And the fire died out of his eyes as she looked. He drew a deep breath or two and turned away to pick up his rifle. When he faced about with that in his hand, the old mask of immobility was in place. He waited while Stella gathered up her scattered hairpins and made shift to coil her hair into a semblance of Order. Then he said gently:

"I won't break out like that again."

"Once is enough."

"More than enough—for me," he answered.

She disdained reply. Striking off along the path that ran to the camp, she walked rapidly, choking a rising flood of desperate thought. With growing coolness paradoxically there burned hotter the flame of an elemental wrath. What right had he to lay hands on her? Her shoulders ached, her flesh was bruised from the terrible grip of his fingers. The very sound of his footsteps behind her was maddening. To be suspected and watched, to be continually the target of jealous fury! No, a thousand times, no. She wheeled on him at last.

"I can't stand this," she cried. "It's beyond endurance. We're like flint and steel to each other now. If to-day's a sample of what we may expect, it's better to make a clean sweep of everything. I've got to get away from here and from you—from everybody."

Fyfe motioned her to a near-by log.

"Sit down," said he. "We may as well have it out here."

For a few seconds he busied himself with a cigar, removing the band with utmost deliberation, biting the end off, applying the match, his brows puckered slightly.

"It's very unwise of you to meet Monohan like that," he uttered finally.

"Oh, I see," she flashed. "Do you suggest that I met him purposely—by appointment? Even if I did—"

"That's for you to say, Stella," he interrupted gravely. "I told you last night that I trusted you absolutely. I do, so far as really vital things are concerned, but I don't always trust your judgment. I merely know that Monohan sneaked along shore, hid his boat, and stole through the timber to where you were sitting. I happened to see him, and I followed him to see what he was up to, why he should take such measures to keep under cover."

"The explanation is simple," she answered stiffly. "You can believe it or not, as you choose. My being there was purely unintentional. If I had seen him before he was close, I should certainly not have been there. I have been at odds with myself all day, and I went for a walk, to find a quiet place where I could sit and think."

"It doesn't matter now," he said. "Only you'd better try to avoid things like that in the future. Would you mind telling me just exactly what you meant a minute ago? Just what you propose to do?"

He asked her that as one might make any commonplace inquiry, but his quietness did not deceive Stella.

"What I said," she began desperately. "Wasn't it plain enough? It seems to me our life is going to be a nightmare from now on if we try to live it together. I—I'm sorry, but you know how I feel. It may be unwise, but these things aren't dictated by reason. You know that. If our emotions were guided by reason and expediency, we'd be altogether different. Last night I was willing to go on and make the best of things. To-day,—especially after this,—it looks impossible. You'll look at me, and guess what I'm thinking, and hate me. And I'll grow to hate you, because you'll be little better than a jailer. Oh, don't you see that the way we'll feel will make us utterly miserable? Why should we stick together when no good can come of it? You've been good to me. I've appreciated that and liked you for it. I'd like to be friends. But I—I'd hate you with a perfectly murderous hatred if you were always on the watch, always suspecting me, if you taunted me as you did a while ago. I'm just as much a savage at heart as you are, Jack Fyfe. I could gladly have killed you when you were jerking me about back yonder."

"I wonder if you are, after all, a little more of a primitive being than I've supposed?"

Fyfe leaned toward her, staring fixedly into her eyes—eyes that were bright with unshed tears.

"And I was holding the devil in me down back there, because I didn't want to horrify you with anything like brutality," he went on thoughtfully. "You think I grinned and made a monkey of *him* because it pleased me to do that? Why, I could have—and ached to—break him into little bits, to smash him up so that no one would ever take pleasure in looking at him again. And I didn't, simply and solely because I didn't want to let you have even a glimpse of what I'm capable of when I get started. I wonder if I made a mistake? It was merely the reaction from letting him go scot-free that made me shake you so. I wonder—well, never mind. Go on."

"I think it's better that I should go away," Stella said. "I want you to agree that I should; then there will be no talk or anything disagreeable from outside sources. I'm strong, I can get on. It'll be a relief to have to work. I won't have to be the kitchen drudge Charlie made of me. I've got my voice. I'm quite sure I can capitalize that. But I've got to go. Anything's better than this; anything that's clean and decent. I'd despise myself if I stayed on as your wife, feeling as I do. It was a mistake in the beginning, our marriage."

"Nevertheless," Fyfe said slowly, "I'm afraid it's a mistake you'll have to abide by—for a time. All that you say may be true, although I don't admit it myself. Offhand, I'd say you were simply trying to welch on a fair bargain. I'm not going to let you do it blindly, all wrought up to a pitch where you can scarcely think coherently. If you are fully determined to break away from me, you owe it to us both to be sure of what you're doing before you act. I'm going to talk plain. You can believe it and disdain it if you please. If you were leaving me for a man, a real man, I think I could bring myself to make it easy for you and wish you luck. But you're not. He's—"

"Can't we leave him out of it?" she demanded. "I want to get away from you both. Can you understand that? It doesn't help you any to pick *him* to pieces."

"No, but it might help you, if I could rip off that swathing of idealization you've wrapped around him," Fyfe observed patiently. "It's not a job I have much stomach for however, even if you were willing to let me try. But to come back. You've got to stick it out with me, Stella. You'll hate me for the constraint, I suppose. But until—until things shape up differently—you'll understand what I'm talking about by and by, I think—you've got to abide by the bargain you made with me. I couldn't force you to stay, I know. But there's one hold you can't break not if I know you at all."

"What is that?" she asked icily.

"The kid's," he murmured.

Stella buried her face in her hands for a minute.

"I'd forgotten—I'd forgotten," she whispered.

"You understand, don't you?" he said hesitatingly. "If you leave—I keep our boy."

"Oh, you're devilish—to use a club like that," she cried. "You know I wouldn't part from my baby—the only thing I've got that's worth having."

"He's worth something to me too," Fyfe muttered. "A lot more than you think, maybe. I'm not trying to club you. There's nothing in it for me. But for him; well, he needs you. It isn't his fault he's here, or that you're unhappy. I've got to protect him, see that he gets a fair shake. I can't see anything to it but for you to go on being Mrs. Jack Fyfe until such time as you get back to a normal poise. Then it will be time enough to try and work out some arrangement that won't be too much of a hardship on him. It's that—or a clean break in which you go your own way, and I try to mother him to the best of my ability. You'll understand sometime why I'm showing my teeth this way."

"You have everything on your side," she admitted dully, after a long interval of silence. "I'm a fool. I admit it. Have things your way. But it won't work, Jack. This flare-up between us will only smoulder. I think you lay a little too much stress on Monohan. It isn't that I love him so much as that I don't love you at all. I can live without him—which I mean to do in any case—far easier than I can live with you. It won't work."

"Don't worry," he replied. "You won't be annoyed by me in person. I'll have my hands full elsewhere."

They rose and walked on to the house. On the porch Jack Junior was being wheeled back and forth in his carriage. He lifted chubby arms to his mother as she came up the steps. Stella carried him inside, hugging the sturdy, blue-eyed mite close to her breast. She did not want to cry, but she could not help it. It was as if she had been threatened with irrevocable loss of that precious bit of her own flesh and blood. She hugged him to her, whispering mother-talk, half-hysterical, wholly tender.

Fyfe stood aside for a minute. Then he came up behind her and stood resting one hand on the back of her chair.

"Stella."

"Yes."

"I got word from my sister and her husband in this morning's mail. They will very likely be here next week for a three days' stay. Brace up. Let's try and keep our skeleton from rattling while they're here. Will you?"

"All right, Jack. I'll try."

He patted her tousled hair lightly and left the room. Stella looked after him with a surge of mixed feeling. She told herself she hated him and his dominant will that always beat her own down; she hated him for his amazing strength and for his unvarying sureness of himself. And in the same breath she found herself wondering if,—with their status reversed,— Walter Monohan would be as patient, as gentle, as self-controlled with a wife who openly acknowledged her affection for another man. And still her heart cried out for Monohan. She flared hot against the disparaging note, the unconcealed contempt Fyfe seemed to have for him.

Yet in spite of her eager defence of him, there was something ugly about that clash with Fyfe in the edge of the woods, something that jarred. It wasn't spontaneous. She could not understand that tigerish onslaught of Monohan's. It was more the action she would have expected from her husband.

It puzzled her, grieved her, added a little to the sorrowful weight that settled upon her. They were turbulent spirits both. The matter might not end there.

In the next ten days three separate incidents, each isolated and relatively unimportant, gave Stella food for much puzzled thought.

The first was a remark of Fyfe's sister in the first hours of their acquaintance. Mrs. Henry Alden could never have denied blood kinship with Jack Fyfe. She had the same wide, good-humored mouth, the blue eyes that always seemed to be on the verge of twinkling, and the same fair, freckled skin. Her characteristics of speech resembled his. She was direct, bluntly so, and she was not much given to small talk. Fyfe and Stella met the Aldens at Roaring Springs with the *Waterbug*. Alden proved a genial sort of man past forty, a big, loose-jointed individual whose outward appearance gave no indication of what he was professionally,—a civil engineer with a reputation that promised to spread beyond his native States.

"You don't look much different, Jack," his sister observed critically, as the *Waterbug* backed away from the wharf in a fine drizzle of rain. "Except that as you grow older, you more and more resemble the pater. Has matrimony toned him down, my dear?" she turned to Stella. "The last time I saw him he had a black eye!"

Fyfe did not give her a chance to answer.

"Be a little more diplomatic, Dolly," he smiled. "Mrs. Jack doesn't realize what a rowdy I used to be. I've reformed."

"Ah," Mrs. Alden chuckled, "I have a vision of you growing meek and mild."

They talked desultorily as the launch thrashed along. Alden's profession took him to all corners of the earth. That was why the winter of Fyfe's honeymoon had not made them acquainted. Alden and his wife were then in South America. This visit was to fill in the time before the departure of a trans-Pacific liner which would land the Aldens at Manila.

Presently the Abbey-Monohan camp and bungalow lay abeam. Stella told Mrs. Alden something of the place.

"That reminds me," Mrs. Alden turned to her brother. "I was quite sure I saw Walter Monohan board a train while we were waiting for the hotel car in Hopyard. I heard that he was in timber out here. Is he this Monohan?"

Fyfe nodded.

"How odd," she remarked, "that you should be in the same region. Do you still maintain the ancient feud?"

Fyfe shot her a queer look.

"We've grown up, Dolly," he said drily. Then: "Do you expect to get back to God's country short of a year, Alden?"

That was all. Neither of them reverted to the subject again. But Stella pondered. An ancient feud? She had not known of that. Neither man had ever dropped a hint.

For the second incident, Paul Abbey dropped in to dinner a few days later and divulged a bit of news.

"There's been a shake-up in our combination," he remarked casually to Fyfe. "Monohan and dad have split over a question of business policy. Walter's taking over all our interests on Roaring Lake. He appears to be going to peel off his coat and become personally active in the logging industry. Funny streak for Monohan to take, isn't it? He never seemed to care a hoot about the working end of the business, so long as it produced dividends."

Lastly, Charlie Benton came over to eat a farewell dinner with the Aldens the night before they left. He followed Stella into the nursery when she went to tuck Jack Junior in his crib.

"Say, Stella" he began, "I have just had a letter from old man Lander; you remember he was dad's legal factotum and executor."

"Of course," she returned.

"Well, do you recall—you were there when the estate was wound up, and I was not—any mention of some worthless oil stock? Some California wildcat stuff the governor got bit on? It was found among his effects."

"I seem to recall something of the sort," she answered. "But I don't remember positively. What about it?"

"Lander writes me that there is a prospect of it being salable. The company is reviving. And he finds himself without legal authority to do business, although the stock certificates are still in his hands. He suggests that we give him a power of attorney to sell this stuff. He's an awfully conservative old chap, so there must be a reasonable prospect of some cash, or he wouldn't bother. My hunch is to give him a power of attorney and let him use his own judgment."

"How much is it worth?" she asked.

"The par value is forty thousand dollars," Benton grinned. "But the governor bought it at ten cents on the dollar. If we get what he paid, we'll be lucky. That'll be two thousand apiece. I brought you a blank form. I'm going down with you on the *Bug* to-morow to send mine. I'd advise you to have yours signed up and witnessed before a notary at Hopyard and send it too."

"Of course I will," she said.

"It isn't much," Benton mused, leaning on the foot of the crib, watching her smooth the covers over little Jack. "But it won't come amiss—to me, at least. I'm going to be married in the spring."

Stella looked up.

"You are?" she murmured. "To Linda Abbey?"

He nodded. A slight flush crept over his tanned face at the steady look she bent on him.

"Hang it, what are you thinking?" he broke out. "I know you've rather looked down on me because I acted like a bounder that winter. But I really took a tumble to myself. You set me thinking when you made that sudden break with Jack. I felt rather guilty about that—until I saw how it turned out. I know I'm not half good enough for Linda. But so long as she thinks I am and I try to live up to that, why we've as good a chance to be happy as anybody. We all make breaks, us fellows that go at everything roughshod. Still, when we pull up and take a new tack, you shouldn't hold grudges. If we could go back to that fall and winter, I'd do things a lot differently."

"If you're both really and truly in love," Stella said quietly, "that's about the only thing that matters. I hope you'll be happy. But you'll have to be a lot different with Linda Abbey than you were with me."

"Ah, Stella, don't harp on that," he said shame-facedly. "I was rotten, it's true. But we're all human. I couldn't see anything then only what I wanted myself. I was like a bull in a china shop. It's different now. I'm on my feet financially, and I've had time to draw my breath and take a squint at myself from a different angle. I did you a good turn, anyway, even if I was the cause of you taking a leap before you looked. You landed right."

Stella mustered a smile that was purely facial. It maddened her to hear his complacent justification of himself. And the most maddening part of it was her knowledge that Benton was right, that in many essential things he had done her a good turn, which her own erratic inclinations bade fair to wholly nullify.

"I wish you all the luck and happiness in the world," she said gently. "And I don't bear a grudge, believe me, Charlie. Now, run along. We'll keep baby awake, talking."

"All right." He turned to go and came back again.

"What I really came in to say, I've hardly got nerve enough for." He sank his voice to a murmur. "Don't fly off at me, Stell. But—you haven't got a trifle interested in Monohan, have you? I mean, you haven't let him think you are?"

Stella's hands tightened on the crib rail. For an instant her heart stood still. A wholly unreasoning blaze of anger seized her. But she controlled that. Pride forbade her betraying herself.

"What a perfectly ridiculous question," she managed to reply.

He looked at her keenly.

"Because, if you have—well, you might be perfectly innocent in the matter and still get in bad," he continued evenly. "I'd like to put a bug in your ear."

She bent over Jack Junior, striving to inject an amused note into her reply.

"Don't be so absurd, Charlie."

"Oh, well, I suppose it is. Only, darn it, I've seen him look at you in a way—Pouf! I was going to tell you something. Maybe Jack has—only he's such a close-mouthed beggar. I'm not very anxious to peddle things." Benton turned again. "I guess you don't need any coaching from me, anyhow."

He walked out. Stella stared after him, her eyes blazing, hands clenched into hard-knuckled little fists. She could have struck him.

And still she wondered over and over again, burning with a consuming fire to know what that "something" was which he had to tell. All the slumbering devils of a stifled passion awoke to rend her, to make her rage against the coil in which she was involved. She despised herself for the weakness of unwise loving, even while she ached to sweep away the barriers that stood between her and love. Mingled with that there whispered an intuition of disaster to come, of destiny shaping to peculiar ends. In Monohan's establishing himself on Roaring Lake she sensed something more than an industrial shift. In his continued presence there she saw incalculable sources of trouble. She stood leaning over the bed rail, staring wistfully at her boy for a few minutes. When she faced the mirror in her room, she was startled at the look in her eyes, the nervous twitch of her lips. There was a physical ache in her breast.

"You're a fool, a fool," she whispered to her image. "Where's your will, Stella Fyfe? Borrow a little of your husband's backbone. Presently— presently it won't matter."

One can club a too assertive ego into insensibility. A man may smile and smile and be a villain still, as the old saying has it, and so may a woman smile and smile when her heart is tortured, when every nerve in her is strained to the snapping point. Stella went back to the living room and sang for them until it was time to go to bed.

The Aldens went first, then Charlie. Stella left her door ajar. An hour afterward, when Fyfe came down the hall, she rose. It had been her purpose to call him in, to ask him to explain that which her brother had hinted he could explain, what prior antagonism lay between him and Monohan, what that "something" about Monohan was which differentiated him from other men where she was concerned. Instead she shut the door, slid the bolt home, and huddled in a chair with her face in her hands.

She could not discuss Monohan with him, with any one. Why should she ask? she told herself. It was a closed book, a balanced account. One does not revive dead issues.

CHAPTER XVIII
THE OPENING GUN

The month of November slid day by day into the limbo of the past. The rains washed the land unceasingly. Gray veilings of mist and cloud draped the mountain slopes. As drab a shade colored Stella Fyfe's daily outlook. She was alone a great deal. Even when they were together, she and her husband, words did not come easily between them. He was away a great deal, seeking, she knew, the old panacea of work, hard, unremitting work, to abate the ills of his spirit. She envied him that outlet. Work for her there was none. The two Chinamen and Martha the nurse left her no tasks. She could not read, for all their great store of books and magazines; the printed page would lie idle in her lap, and her gaze would wander off into vacancy, into that thought-world where her spirit wandered in distress. The Abbeys were long gone; her brother hard at his logging. There were no neighbors and no news. The savor was gone out of everything. The only bright spot in her days was Jack Junior, now toddling precociously on his sturdy legs, a dozen steps at a time, crowing victoriously when he negotiated the passage from chair to chair.

From the broad east windows of their house she saw all the traffic that came and went on the upper reaches of Roaring Lake, Siwashes in dugouts and fishing boats, hunters, prospectors. But more than any other she saw the craft of her husband and Monohan, the powerful, black-hulled *Panther*, the smaller, daintier *Waterbug*.

There was a big gasoline workboat, gray with a yellow funnel, that she knew was Monohan's. And this craft bore past there often, inching its downward way with swifters of logs, driving fast up-lake without a tow. Monohan had abandoned work on the old Abbey-Monohan logging-grounds. The camps and the bungalow lay deserted, given over to a solitary watchman. The lake folk had chattered at this proceeding, and the chatter had come to Stella's ears. He had put in two camps at the lake head, so she heard indirectly: one on the lake shore, one on the Tyee River, a little above the mouth. He had sixty men in each camp, and he was getting the name of a driver. Three miles above his Tyee camp, she knew, lay the camp her husband had put in during the early summer to cut a heavy limit of cedar. Fyfe had only a small crew there.

She wondered a little why he spent so much time there, when he had seventy-odd men working near home. But of course he had an able lieutenant in Lefty Howe. And she could guess why Jack Fyfe kept away. She was sorry for him—and for herself. But being sorry—a mere semi-neutral state of mind—did not help matters, she told herself gloomily.

Lefty Howe's wife was at the camp now, on one of her occasional visits. Howe was going across the lake one afternoon to see a Siwash whom he had engaged to catch and smoke a winter's supply of salmon for the camps. Mrs. Howe told Stella, and on impulse Stella bundled Jack Junior into warm clothing and went with them for the ride.

Halfway across the six mile span she happened to look back, and a new mark upon the western shore caught her eye. She found a glass and leveled it on the spot. Two or three buildings, typical logging-camp shacks of split cedar, rose back from the beach. Behind these again the beginnings of a cut had eaten a hole in the forest,—a slashing different from the ordinary logging slash, for it ran narrowly, straight back through the timber; whereas the first thing a logger does is to cut all the merchantable timber he can reach on his limit without moving his donkey from the water. It was not more than two miles from their house.

"What new camp is that?" she asked Howe.

"Monohan's," he answered casually.

"I thought Jack owned all the shore timber to Medicine Point?" she said.

Howe shook his head.

"Uh-uh. Well, he does too, all but where that camp is. Monohan's got a freak limit in there. It's half a mile wide and two miles straight back from the beach. Lays between our holdin's like the ham in a sandwich. Only," he added thoughtfully, "it's a blame thin piece uh ham. About the poorest timber in a long stretch. I dunno why the Sam Hill he's cuttin' it. But then he's doin' a lot uh things no practical logger would do."

Stella laid down the glasses. It was nothing to her, she told herself. She had seen Monohan only once since the day Fyfe choked him, and then only to exchange the barest civilities—and to feel her heart flutter at the message his eyes telegraphed.

When she returned from the launch trip, Fyfe was home, and Charlie Benton with him. She crossed the heavy rugs on the living room floor noiselessly in her overshoes, carrying Jack Junior asleep in her arms. And so in passing the door of Fyfe's den, she heard her brother say:

"But, good Lord, you don't suppose he'll be sap-head enough to try such fool stunts as that? He couldn't make it stick, and he brings himself within the law first crack; and the most he could do would be to annoy you."

"You underestimate Monohan," Fyfe returned. "He'll play safe, personally, so far as the law goes. He's foxy. I advise you to sell if the offer comes again. If you make any more breaks at him, he'll figure some way to get you. It isn't your fight, you know. You unfortunately happen to be in the road."

"Damned if I do," Benton swore. "I'm all in the clear. There's no way he can get me, and I'll tell him what I think of him again if he gives me half a chance. I never liked him, anyhow. Why should I sell when I'm just getting in real good shape to take that timber out myself? Why, I can make a hundred thousand dollars in the next five years on that block of timber. Besides, without being a sentimental sort of beggar, I don't lose sight of the fact that you helped pull me out of a hole when I sure needed a pull. And I don't like his high-handed style. No, if it comes to a showdown, I'm with you, Jack, as far as I can go. What the hell *can* he do?"

"Nothing—that I can see." Fyfe laughed unpleasantly. "But he'll try. He has dollars to our cents. He could throw everything he's got on Roaring Lake into the discard and still have forty thousand a year fixed income. Sabe? Money does more than talk in this country. I think I'll pull that camp off the Tyee."

"Well, maybe," Benton said. "I'm not sure—"

Stella passed on. She wanted to hear, but it went against her grain to eavesdrop. Her pause had been purely involuntary. When she became conscious that she was eagerly drinking in each word, she hurried by.

Her mind was one urgent question mark while she laid the sleeping youngster in his bed and removed her heavy clothes. What sort of hostilities did Monohan threaten? Had he let a hopeless love turn to the acid of hate for the man who nominally possessed her? Stella could scarcely credit that. It was too much at variance with her idealistic conception of the man. He would never have recourse to such littleness. Still, the biting contempt in Fyfe's voice when he said to Benton: "You underestimate Monohan. He'll play safe ... he's foxy." That stung her to the quick. That was not said for her benefit; it was Fyfe's profound conviction. Based on what? He did not form judgments on momentary impulse. She recalled that only in the most indirect way had he ever passed criticism on Monohan, and then it lay mostly in a tone, suggested more than spoken. Yet he knew Monohan, had known him for years. They had clashed long before she was a factor in their lives.

When she went into the big room, Benton and Fyfe were gone outdoors. She glanced into Fyfe's den. It was empty, but a big blue-print unrolled on the table where the two had been seated caught her eye. She bent over it, drawn by the lettered squares along the wavy shore line and the marked waters of creeks she knew.

She had never before possessed a comprehensive idea of the various timber holdings along the west shore of Roaring Lake, since it had not been a matter of particular interest to her. She was not sure why it now became a matter of interest to her, unless it was an impression that over these squares and oblongs which stood for thousands upon thousands of merchantable logs there was already shaping a struggle, a clash of iron wills and determined purposes directly involving, perhaps arising because of her.

She studied the blue-print closely. Its five feet of length embraced all the west shore of the lake, from the outflowing of Roaring River to the incoming Tyee at the head. Each camp was lettered in with pencil. But her attention focussed chiefly on the timber limits ranging north and south from their home, and she noted two details: that while the limits marked A-M Co. were impartially distributed from Cottonwood north, the squares marked J.H. Fyfe lay in a solid block about Cougar Bay,—save for that long tongue of a limit where she had that day noted the new camp. That thrust like the haft of a spear into the heart of Fyfe's timberland.

There was the Abbey-Monohan cottage, the three limits her brother controlled lying up against Fyfe's southern boundary. Up around the mouth of the Tyee spread the vast checkerboard of Abbey-Monohan limits, and beyond that, on the eastern bank of the river, a single block,—Fyfe's cedar limit,—the camp he thought he would close down.

Why? Immediately the query shaped in her mind. Monohan was concentrating his men and machinery at the lake head. Fyfe proposed to shut down a camp but well-established; established because cedar was climbing in price, an empty market clamoring for cedar logs. Why?

Was there aught of significance in that new camp of Monohan's so near by; that sudden activity on ground that bisected her husband's property? A freak limit of timber so poor that Lefty Howe said it could only be logged at a loss.

She sighed and went out to give dinner orders to Sam Foo. If she could only go to her husband and talk as they had been able to talk things over at first. But there had grown up between them a deadly restraint. She supposed that was inevitable. Both chafed under conditions they could not change or would not for stubbornness and pride.

It made a deep impression on her, all these successive, disassociated finger posts, pointing one and all to things under the surface, to motives and potentialities she had not glimpsed before and could only guess at now.

Fyfe and Benton came to dinner more or less preoccupied, an odd mood for Charlie Benton. Afterwards they went into session behind the closed door of Fyfe's den. An hour or so later Benton went home. While she listened to the soft *chuff-a-chuff-a-chuff* of the *Chickamin* dying away in the distance, Fyfe came in and slumped down in a chair before the fire where a big fir stick crackled. He sat there silent, a half-smoked cigar clamped in one corner of his mouth, the lines of his square jaw in profile, determined, rigid. Stella eyed him covertly. There were times, in those moods of concentration, when sheer brute power seemed his most salient characteristic. Each bulging curve of his thick upper arm, his neck rising like a pillar from massive shoulders, indicated his power. Yet so well-proportioned was he that the size and strength of him was masked by the symmetry of his body, just as the deliberate immobility of his face screened the play of his feelings. Often Stella found herself staring at him, fruitlessly wondering what manner of thought and feeling that repression overlaid. Sometimes a tricksy, half-provoked desire to break through the barricade of his stoicism tempted her. She told herself that she ought to be thankful for his aloofness, his acquiescence in things as they stood. Yet there were times when she would almost have welcomed an outburst, a storm, anything rather than that deadly chill, enduring day after day. He seldom spoke to her now except of most matter-of-fact things. He played his part like a gentleman before others, but alone with her he withdrew into his shell.

Stella was sitting back in the shadow, still studying him, measuring him in spite of herself by the Monohan yardstick. There wasn't much basis for comparison. It wasn't a question of comparison; the two men stood apart, distinctive, in every attribute. The qualities in Fyfe that she understood and appreciated, she beheld glorified in Monohan. Yet it was not, after all, a question of qualities. It was something more subtle, something of the heart which defied logical analysis.

Fyfe had never been able to set her pulse dancing. She had never craved physical nearness to him, so that she ached with the poignancy of that craving. She had been passively contented with him, that was all. And Monohan had swept across her horizon like a flame. Why couldn't Jack Fyfe have inspired in her that headlong sort of passion? She smiled hopelessly. The tears were very close to her eyes. She loved Monohan; Monohan loved her. Fyfe loved her in his deliberate, repressed fashion and possessed her, according to the matrimonial design. And although now his possession was a hollow mockery, he would never give her up—not to Walter Monohan. She had that fatalistic conviction.

How would it end in the long run?

She leaned forward to speak. Words quivered on her lips. But as she struggled to shape them to utterance, the blast of a boat whistle came screaming up from the water, near and shrill and imperative.

Fyfe came out of his chair like a shot. He landed poised on his feet, lips drawn apart, hands clenched. He held that pose for an instant, then relaxed, his breath coming with a quick sigh.

Stella stared at him. Nerves! She knew the symptoms too well. Nerves at terrible tension in that big, splendid body. A slight quiver seemed to run over him. Then he was erect and calmly himself again, standing in a listening attitude.

"That's the *Panther*?" he said. "Pulling in to the *Waterbug's* landing. Did I startle you when I bounced up like a cougar, Stella?" he asked, with a wry smile. "I guess I was half asleep. That whistle jolted me."

Stella glanced out the shaded window.

"Some one's coming up from the float with a lantern," she said. "Is there—is there likely to be anything wrong, Jack?"

"Anything wrong?" He shot a quick glance at her. Then casually: "Not that I know of."

The bobbing lantern came up the path through the lawn. Footsteps crunched on the gravel.

"I'll go see what he wants," Fyfe remarked, "Calked boots won't be good for the porch floor."

She followed him.

"Stay in. It's cold." He stopped in the doorway.

"No. I'm coming," she persisted.

They met the lantern bearer at the foot of the steps.

"Well, Thorsen?" Fyfe shot at him. There was an unusual note of sharpness in his voice, an irritated expectation.

Stella saw that it was the skipper of the *Panther*, a big and burly Dane. He raised the lantern a little. The dim light on his face showed it bruised and swollen. Fyfe grunted.

"Our boom is hung up," he said plaintively. "They've blocked the river. I got licked for arguin' the point."

"How's it blocked?" Fyfe asked.

"Two swifters uh logs strung across the channel. They're drivin' piles in front. An' three donkeys buntin' logs in behind."

"Swift work. There wasn't a sign of a move when I left this morning," Fyfe commented drily. "Well, take the *Panther* around to the inner landing. I'll be there."

"What's struck that feller Monohan?" the Dane sputtered angrily. "Has he got any license to close the Tyee? He says he has—an' backs his argument strong, believe me. Maybe you can handle him. I couldn't. Next time I'll have a cant-hook handy. By jingo, you gimme my pick uh Lefty's crew, Jack, an' I'll bring that cedar out."

"Take the *Panther* 'round," Fyfe replied. "We'll see."

Thorsen turned back down the slope. In a minute the thrum of the boat's exhaust arose as she got under way.

"Come on in. You'll get cold standing here," Fyfe said to Stella.

She followed him back into the living room. He sat on the arm of a big leather chair, rolling the dead cigar thoughtfully between his lips, little creases gathering between his eyes.

"I'm going up the lake," he said at last, getting up abruptly.

"What's the matter, Jack?" she asked. "Why, has trouble started up there?"

"Part of the logging game," he answered indifferently. "Don't amount to much."

"But Thorsen has been fighting. His face was terrible. And I've heard you say he was one of the most peaceable men alive. Is it—is Monohan—"

"We won't discuss Monohan," Fyfe said curtly. "Anyway, there's no danger of *him* getting hurt."

He went into his den and came out with hat and coat on. At the door he paused a moment.

"Don't worry," he said kindly. "Nothing's going to happen."

But she stood looking out the window after he left, uneasy with a prescience of trouble. She watched with a feverish interest the stir that presently arose about the bunkhouses. That summer a wide space had been cleared between bungalow and camp. She could see moving lanterns, and even now and then hear the voices of men calling to each other. Once the *Panther's* dazzling eye of a searchlight swung across the landing, and its beam picked out a file of men carrying their blankets toward the boat. Shortly after that the tender rounded the point. Close behind her went the *Waterbug*, and both boats swarmed with men.

Stella looked and listened until there was but a faint thrum far up the lake. Then she went to bed, but not to sleep. What ugly passions were loosed at the lake head she did not know. But on the face of it she could not avoid wondering if Monohan had deliberately set out to cross and harass Jack Fyfe. Because of her? That was the question which had hovered on her lips that evening, one she had not brought herself to ask. Because of her, or because of some enmity that far preceded her? She had thought him big enough to do as she had done, as Fyfe was tacitly doing,—make the best of a grievous matter.

But if he had allowed his passions to dictate reprisals, she trembled for the outcome. Fyfe was not a man to sit quiet under either affront or injury. He would fight with double rancor if Monohan were his adversary.

"If anything happens up there, I'll hate myself," she whispered, when the ceaseless turning of her mind had become almost unendurable. "I was a silly, weak fool to ever let Walter Monohan know I cared. And I'll hate him too if he makes me a bone of contention. I elected to play the game the only decent way there is to play it. So did he. Why can't he abide by that?"

Noon of the next day saw the *Waterbug* heave to a quarter mile abeam of Cougar Point to let off a lone figure in her dinghy, and then bore on, driving straight and fast for Roaring Springs. Stella flew to the landing. Mother Howe came puffing at her heels.

"Land's sake, I been worried to death," the older woman breathed. "When men git to quarrellin' about timber, you never can tell where they'll stop, Mrs. Jack. I've knowed some wild times in the woods in the past."

The man in the dink was Lefty Howe. He pulled in beside the float. When he stepped up on the planks, he limped perceptibly.

"Land alive, what happened yuh, Lefty?" his wife cried.

"Got a rap on the leg with a peevy," he said. "Nothin' much."

"Why did the *Waterbug* go down the lake?" Stella asked breathlessly. The man's face was serious. "What happened up there?"

"There was a fuss," he answered quietly. "Three or four of the boys got beat up so they need patchin'. Jack's takin' 'em down to the hospital. Damn that yeller-headed Monohan!" his voice lifted suddenly in uncontrollable anger. "Billy Dale was killed this mornin', mother."

Stella felt herself grow sick. Death is a small matter when it strikes afar, among strangers. When it comes to one's door! Billy Dale had piloted the *Waterbug* for a year, a chubby, round-faced boy of twenty, a foster-son, of Mother Howe's before she had children of her own. Stella had asked Jack to put him on the *Waterbug* because he was such a loyal, cheery sort of soul, and Billy had been a part of every expedition they had taken around the lake. She could not think of him as a rigid, lifeless lump of clay. Why, only the day before he had been laughing and chattering aboard the cruiser, going up and down the cabin floor on his hands and knees, Jack Junior perched triumphantly astride his back.

"What happened?" she cried wildly. "Tell me, quick."

"It's quick told," Howe said grimly. "We were ready at daylight. Monohan's got a hard crew, and they jumped us as soon as we started to clear the channel. So we cleared them, first. It didn't take so long. Three of our men was used bad, and there's plenty of sore heads on both sides. But we did the job. After we got them on the run, we blowed up their swifters an' piles with giant. Then we begun to put the cedar through. Billy was on the bank when somebody shot him from across the river. One mercy, he never knew what hit him. An' you'll never come so close bein' a widow again, Mrs. Fyfe, an' not be. That bullet was meant for Jack, I figure. He was sittin' down. Billy was standin' right behind him watchin' the logs go through. Whoever he was, he shot high, that's all. There, mother, don't cry. That don't help none. What's done's done."

Stella turned and walked up to the house, stunned. She could not credit bloodshed, death. Always in her life both had been things remote. And as the real significance of Lefty Howe's story grew on her, she shuddered. It lay at her door, equally with her and Monohan, even if neither of their hands had sped the bullet,—an indirect responsibility but gruesomely real to her.

God only knows to what length she might have gone in reaction. She was quivering under that self-inflicted lash, bordering upon hysteria when she reached the house. She could not shut out a too-vivid picture of Billy Dale lying murdered on the Tyee's bank, of the accusing look with which Fyfe must meet her. Rightly so, she held. She did not try to shirk. She had followed the line of least resistance, lacked the dour courage to pull herself up in the beginning, and it led to this. She felt Billy Dale's blood wet on her soft hands. She walked into her own house panting like a hunted animal.

And she had barely crossed the threshold when back in the rear Jack Junior's baby voice rose in a shrill scream of pain.

Stella scarcely heard her husband and the doctor come in. For a weary age she had been sitting in a low rocker, a pillow across her lap, and on that the little, tortured body swaddled with cotton soaked in olive oil, the only dressing she and Mrs. Howe could devise to ease the pain. All those other things which had so racked her, the fight on the Tyee, the shooting of Billy Dale, they had vanished somehow into thin air before the dread fact that her baby was dying slowly before her anguished eyes. She sat numbed with that deadly assurance, praying without hope for help to come, hopeless that any medical skill would avail when it did come. So many hours had been wasted while a man rowed to Benton's camp, while the *Chickamin* steamed to Roaring Springs, while the *Waterbug* came driving back. Five hours! And the skin, yes, even shreds of flesh, had come away in patches with Jack Junior's clothing when she took it off. She bent over him, fearful that every feeble breath would be his last.

She looked up at the doctor. Fyfe was beside her, his calked boots biting into the oak floor.

"See what you can do, doc," he said huskily. Then to Stella: "How did it happen?"

"He toddled away from Martha," she whispered. "Sam Foo had set a pan of boiling water on the kitchen floor. He fell into it. Oh, my poor little darling."

They watched the doctor bare the terribly scalded body, examine it, listen to the boy's breathing, count his pulse. In the end he re-dressed the tiny body with stuff from the case with which a country physician goes armed against all emergencies. He was very deliberate and thoughtful. Stella looked her appeal when he finished.

"He's a sturdy little chap," he said, "and we'll do our best. A child frequently survives terrific shock. It would be mistaken kindness for me to make light of his condition simply to spare your feelings. He has an even chance. I shall stay until morning. Now, I think it would be best to lay him on a bed. You must relax, Mrs. Fyfe. I can see that the strain is telling on you. You mustn't allow yourself to get in that abnormal condition. The baby is not conscious of pain. He is not suffering half so much in his body as you are in your mind, and you mustn't do that. Be hopeful. We'll need your help. We should have a nurse, but there was no time to get one."

They laid Jack Junior amid downy pillows on Stella's bed. The doctor stood looking at him, then drew a chair beside the bed.

"Go and walk about a little, Mrs. Fyfe," he advised, "and have your dinner. I'll want to watch the boy a while."

But Stella did not want to walk. She did not want to eat. She was scarcely aware that her limbs were cramped and aching from her long vigil in the chair. She was not conscious of herself and her problems, any more. Every shift of her mind turned on her baby, the little mite she had nursed at her breast, the one joy untinctured with bitterness that was left her. The bare chance that those little feet might never patter across the floor again, that little voice never wake her in the morning crying "Mom-mom," drove her distracted.

She went out into the living room, walked to a window, stood there drumming on the pane with nervous fingers. Dusk was falling outside; a dusk was creeping over her. She shuddered.

Fyfe came up behind her, put his hands on her shoulders, and turned her so that she faced him.

"I wish I could help, Stella," he whispered. "I wish I could make you feel less forlorn. Poor little kiddies—both of you."

She shook off his hands, not because she rebelled against his touch, against his sympathy, merely because she had come to that nervous state where she scarce realized what she did.

"Oh," she choked, "I can't bear it. My baby, my little baby boy. The one bright spot that's left, and he has to suffer like that. If he dies, it's the end of everything for me."

Fyfe stared at her. The warm, pitying look on his face ebbed away, hardened into his old, mask-like absence of expression.

"No," he said quietly, "it would only be the beginning. Lord God, but this has been a day."

He whirled about with a quick gesture of his hands, a harsh, raspy laugh that was very near a sob, and left her. Twenty minutes later, when Stella was irresistibly drawn back to the bedroom, she found him sitting sober and silent, looking at his son.

A little past midnight Jack Junior died.

CHAPTER XIX
FREE AS THE WIND

Stella sat watching the gray lines of rain beat down on the asphalt, the muddy rivulets that streamed along the gutter. A forlorn sighing of wind in the bare boughs of a gaunt elm that stood before her window reminded her achingly of the wind drone among the tall firs.

A ghastly two weeks had intervened since Jack Junior's little life blinked out. There had been wild moments when she wished she could keep him company on that journey into the unknown. But grief seldom kills. Sometimes it hardens. Always it works a change, a greater or less revamping of the spirit. It was so with Stella Fyfe, although she was not keenly aware of any forthright metamorphosis. She was, for the present, too actively involved in material changes.

The storm and stress of that period between her yielding to the lure of Monohan's personality and the burial of her boy had sapped her of all emotional reaction. When they had performed the last melancholy service for him and went back to the bungalow at Cougar Point, she was as physically exhausted, as near the limit of numbed endurance in mind and body as it is possible for a young and healthy woman to become. And when a measure of her natural vitality re-asserted itself, she laid her course. She could no more abide the place where she was than a pardoned convict can abide the prison that has restrained him. It was empty now of everything that made life tolerable, the hushed rooms a constant reminder of her loss. She would catch herself listening for that baby voice, for those pattering footsteps, and realize with a sickening pang that she would never hear them again.

The snapping of that last link served to deepen and widen the gulf between her and Fyfe. He went about his business grave and preoccupied. They seldom talked together. She knew that his boy had meant a lot to him; but he had his work. He did not have to sit with folded hands and think until thought drove him into the bogs of melancholy.

And so the break came. With desperate abruptness Stella told him that she could not stay, that feeling as she did, she despised herself for unwilling acceptance of everything where she could give nothing in return, that the original mistake of their marriage would never be rectified by a perpetuation of that mistake.

"What's the use, Jack?" she finished. "You and I are so made that we can't be neutral. We've got to be thoroughly in accord, or we have to part. There's no chance for us to get back to the old way of living. I don't want to; I can't. I could never be complaisant and agreeable again. We might as well come to a full stop, and each go his own way."

She had braced herself for a clash of wills. There was none. Fyfe listened to her, looked at her long and earnestly, and in the end made a quick, impatient gesture with his hands.

"Your life's your own to make what you please of, now that the kid's no longer a factor," he said quietly. "What do you want to do? Have you made any plans?"

"I have to live, naturally," she replied. "Since I've got my voice back, I feel sure I can turn that to account. I should like to go to Seattle first and look around. It can be supposed I have gone visiting, until one or the other of us takes a decisive legal step."

"That's simple enough," he returned, after a minute's reflection. "Well, if it has to be, for God's sake let's get it over with."

And now it was over with. Fyfe remarked once that with them luckily it was not a question of money. But for Stella it was indeed an economic problem. When she left Roaring Lake, her private account contained over two thousand dollars. Her last act in Vancouver was to re-deposit that to her husband's credit. Only so did she feel that she could go free of all obligation, clean-handed, without stultifying herself in her own eyes. She had treasured as a keepsake the only money she had ever earned in her life, her brother's check for two hundred and seventy dollars, the wages of that sordid period in the cookhouse. She had it now. Two hundred and seventy dollars capital. She hadn't sold herself for that. She had given honest value, double and treble, in the sweat of her brow. She was here now, in a five-dollar-a-week housekeeping room, foot-loose, free as the wind. That was Fyfe's last word to her. He had come with her to Seattle and waited patiently at a hotel until she found a place to live. Then he had gone away without protest.

"Well, Stella," he had said, "I guess this is the end of our experiment. In six months,—under the State law,—you can be legally free by a technicality. So far as I'm concerned, you're free as the wind right now. Good luck to you."

He turned away with a smile on his lips, a smile that his eyes belied, and she watched him walk to the corner through the same sort of driving rain that now pelted in gray lines against her window.

She shook herself impatiently out of that retrospect. It was done. Life, as her brother had prophesied, was no kid-glove affair. The future was her chief concern now, not the past. Yet that immediate past, bits of it, would now and then blaze vividly before her mental vision. The only defense against that lay in action, in something to occupy her mind and hands. If that motive, the desire to shun mental reflexes that brought pain, were not sufficient, there was the equally potent necessity to earn her bread. Never again would she be any man's dependent, a pampered doll, a parasite trading on her sex. They were hard names she called herself.

Meantime she had not been idle; neither had she come to Seattle on a blind impulse. She knew of a singing teacher there whose reputation was more than local, a vocal authority whose word carried weight far beyond Puget Sound. First she meant to see him, get an impartial estimate of the value of her voice, of the training she would need. Through him she hoped to get in touch with some outlet for the only talent she possessed. And she had received more encouragement than she dared hope. He listened to her sing, then tested the range and flexibility of her voice.

"Amazing," he said frankly. "You have a rare natural endowment. If you have the determination and the sense of dramatic values that musical discipline will give you, you should go far. You should find your place in opera."

"That's my ambition," Stella answered. "But that requires time and training. And that means money. I have to earn it."

The upshot of that conversation was an appointment to meet the manager of a photoplay house, who wanted a singer. Stella looked at her watch now, and rose to go. Money, always money, if one wanted to get anywhere, she reflected cynically. No wonder men struggled desperately for that token of power.

She reached the Charteris Theater, and a doorman gave her access to the dim interior. There was a light in the operator's cage high at the rear, another shaded glow at the piano, where a young man with hair brushed sleekly back chewed gum incessantly while he practiced picture accompaniments. The place looked desolate, with its empty seats, its bald stage front with the empty picture screen. Stella sat down to wait for the manager. He came in a few minutes; his manner was very curt, business-like. He wanted her to sing a popular song, a bit from a Verdi opera, Gounod's Ave Maria, so that he could get a line on what she could do. He appeared to be a pessimist in regard to singers.

"Take the stage right there," he instructed. "Just as if the spot was on you. Now then."

It wasn't a heartening process to stand there facing the gum-chewing pianist, and the manager's cigar glowing redly five rows back, and the silent emptinesses beyond,—much like singing into the mouth of a gloomy cave. It was more or less a critical moment for Stella. But she was keenly aware that she had to make good in a small way before she could grasp the greater opportunity, so she did her best, and her best was no mediocre performance. She had never sung in a place designed to show off—or to show up—a singer's quality. She was even a bit astonished herself.

She elected to sing the Ave Maria first. Her voice went pealing to the domed ceiling as sweet as a silver bell, resonant as a trumpet. When the last note died away, there was a momentary silence. Then the accompanist looked up at her, frankly admiring.

"You're *some* warbler," he said emphatically, "believe *me*."

Behind him the manager's cigar lost its glow. He remained silent. The pianist struck up "Let's Murder Care," a rollicking trifle from a Broadway hit. Last of all he thumped, more or less successfully, through the accompaniment to an aria that had in it vocal gymnastics as well as melody.

"Come up to the office, Mrs. Fyfe," Howard said, with a singular change from his first manner.

"I can give you an indefinite engagement at thirty a week," he made a blunt offer. "You can sing. You're worth more, but right now I can't pay more. If you pull business,—and I rather think you will,—have to sing twice in the afternoon and twice in the evening."

Stella considered briefly. Thirty dollars a week meant a great deal more than mere living, as she meant to live. And it was a start, a move in the right direction. She accepted; they discussed certain details. She did not care to court publicity under her legal name, so they agreed that she should be billed as Madame Benton,—the Madame being Howard's suggestion,—and she took her leave.

Upon the Monday following Stella stood for the first time in a fierce white glare that dazzled her and so shut off partially her vision of the rows and rows of faces. She went on with a horrible slackness in her knees, a dry feeling in her throat; and she was not sure whether she would sing or fly. When she had finished her first song and bowed herself into the wings, she felt her heart leap and hammer at the hand-clapping that grew and grew till it was like the beat of ocean surf.

Howard came running to meet her.

"You've sure got 'em going," he laughed. "Fine work. Go out and give 'em some more."

In time she grew accustomed to these things, to the applause she never failed to get, to the white beam that beat down from the picture cage, to the eager, upturned faces in the first rows. Her confidence grew; ambition began to glow like a flame within her. She had gone through the primary stages of voice culture, and she was following now a method of practice which produced results. She could see and feel that herself. Sometimes the fear that her voice might go as it had once gone would make her tremble. But that, her teacher assured her, was a remote chance.

So she gained in those weeks something of her old poise. Inevitably, she was very lonely at times. But she fought against that with the most effective weapon she knew,—incessant activity. She was always busy. There was a rented piano now sitting in the opposite corner from the gas stove on which she cooked her meals. Howard kept his word. She "pulled business," and he raised her to forty a week and offered her a contract which she refused, because other avenues, bigger and better than singing in a motion-picture house, were tentatively opening.

December was waning when she came to Seattle. In the following weeks her only contact with the past, beyond the mill of her own thoughts, was an item in the *Seattle Times* touching upon certain litigation in which Fyfe was involved. Briefly, Monohan, under the firm name of the Abbey-Monohan Timber Company, was suing Fyfe for heavy damages for the loss of certain booms of logs blown up and set adrift at the mouth of the Tyee River. There was appended an account of the clash over the closed channel and the killing of Billy Dale. No one had been brought to book for that yet. Any one of sixty men might have fired the shot.

It made Stella wince, for it took her back to that dreadful day. She could not bear to think that Billy Dale's blood lay on her and Monohan, neither could she stifle an uneasy apprehension that something more grievous yet might happen on Roaring Lake. But at least she had done what she could. If she were the flame, she had removed herself from the powder magazine. Fyfe had pulled his cedar crew off the Tyee before she left. If aggression came, it must come from one direction.

They were both abstractions now, she tried to assure herself. The glamour of Monohan was fading, and she could not say why. She did not know if his presence would stir again all that old tumult of feeling, but she did know that she was cleaving to a measure of peace, of serenity of mind, and she did not want him or any other man to disturb it. She told herself that she had never loved Jack Fyfe. She recognized in him a lot that a woman is held to admire, but there were also qualities in him that had often baffled and sometimes frightened her. She wondered sometimes what he really thought of her and her actions, why, when she had been nerved to a desperate struggle for her freedom, if she could gain it no other way, he had let her go so easily?

After all, she reflected cynically, love comes and goes, but one is driven to pursue material advantages while life lasts. And she wondered, even while the thought took form in her mind, how long she would retain that point of view.

CHAPTER XX
ECHOES

In the early days of February Stella had an unexpected visitor. The landlady called her to the common telephone, and when she took up the receiver, Linda Abbey's voice came over the wire.

"When can I see you?" she asked. "I'll only be here to-day and to-morrow."

"Now, if you like," Stella responded. "I'm free until two-thirty."

"I'll be right over," Linda said. "I'm only about ten minutes drive from where you are."

Stella went back to her room both glad and sorry: glad to hear a familiar, friendly voice amid this loneliness which sometimes seemed almost unendurable; sorry because her situation involved some measure of explanation to Linda. That hurt.

But she was not prepared for the complete understanding of the matter Linda Abbey tacitly exhibited before they had exchanged a dozen sentences.

"How did you know?" Stella asked. "Who told you?"

"No one. I drew my own conclusions when I heard you had gone to Seattle," Linda replied. "I saw it coming. My dear, I'm not blind, and I was with you a lot last summer. I knew you too well to believe you'd make a move while you had your baby to think of. When he was gone—well, I looked for anything to happen."

"Still, nothing much has happened," Stella remarked with a touch of bitterness, "except the inevitable break between a man and a woman when there's no longer any common bond between them. It's better so. Jack has a multiplicity of interests. He can devote himself to them without the constant irritation of an unresponsive wife. We've each taken our own road. That's all that has happened."

"So far," Linda murmured. "It's a pity. I liked that big, silent man of yours. I like you both. It seems a shame things have to turn out this way just because—oh, well. Charlie and I used to plan things for the four of us, little family combinations when we settled down on the lake. Honestly, Stella, do you think it's worth while? I never could see you as a sentimental little chump, letting a momentary aberration throw your whole life out of gear."

"How do you know that I have?" Stella asked gravely.

Linda shrugged her shoulders expressively.

"I suppose it looks silly, if not worse, to you," Stella said. "But I can't help what you think. My reason has dictated every step I've taken since last fall. If I'd really given myself up to sentimentalism, the Lord only knows what might have happened."

"Exactly," Linda responded drily. "Now, there's no use beating around the bush. We get so in that habit as a matter of politeness,—our sort of people,—that we seldom say in plain English just what we really mean. Surely, you and I know each other well enough to be frank, even if it's painful. Very likely you'll say I'm a self-centered little beast, but I'm going to marry your brother, my dear, and I'm going to marry him in the face of considerable family opposition. I *am* selfish. Can you show me any one who isn't largely swayed by motives of self-interest, if it comes to that? I want to be happy. I want to be on good terms with my own people, so that Charlie will have some of the opportunities dad can so easily put in his way. Charlie isn't rich. He hasn't done anything, according to the Abbey standard, but make a fair start. Dad's patronizing as sin, and mother merely tolerates the idea because she knows that I'll marry Charlie in any case, opposition or no opposition. I came over expressly to warn you, Stella. Anything like scandal now would be—well, it would upset so many things."

"You needn't be uneasy," Stella answered coldly. "There isn't any foundation for scandal. There won't be."

"I don't know," Linda returned, "Walter Monohan came to Seattle a boat ahead of me. In fact, that's largely why I came."

Stella flushed angrily.

"Well, what of that?" she demanded. "His movements are nothing to me."

"I don't know," Linda rejoined. She had taken off her gloves and was rolling them nervously in a ball. Now she dropped them and impulsively grasped Stella's hands.

"Stella, Stella," she cried. "Don't get that hurt, angry look. I don't like to say these things to you, but I feel that I have to. I'm worried, and I'm afraid for you and your husband, for Charlie and myself, for all of us together. Walter Monohan is as dangerous as any man who's unscrupulous and rich and absolutely self-centered can possibly be. I know the glamour of the man.

I used to feel it myself. It didn't go very far with me, because his attention wandered away from me before my feelings were much involved, and I had a chance to really fathom them and him. He has a queer gift of making women care for him, and he trades on it deliberately. He doesn't play fair; he doesn't mean to. Oh, I know so many cruel things, despicable things, he's done. Don't look at me like that, Stella. I'm not saying this just to wound you. I'm simply putting you on your guard. You can't play with fire and not get burned. If you've been nursing any feeling for Walter Monohan, crush it, cut it out, just as you'd have a surgeon cut out a cancer. Entirely apart from any question of Jack Fyfe, don't let this man play any part whatever in your life. You'll be sorry if you do. There's not a man or woman whose relations with Monohan have been intimate enough to enable them to really know the man and his motives who doesn't either hate or fear or despise him, and sometimes all three."

"That's a sweeping indictment," Stella said stiffly. "And you're very earnest. Yet I can hardly take your word at its face value. If he's so impossible a person, how does it come that you and your people countenanced him socially? Besides, it's all rather unnecessary, Linda. I'm not the least bit likely to do anything that will reflect on your prospective husband, which is what it simmers down to, isn't it? I've been pulled and hauled this way and that ever since I've been on the coast, simply because I was dependent on some one else—first Charlie and then Jack—for the bare necessities of life. When there's mutual affection, companionship, all those intimate interests that marriage is supposed to imply, I daresay a woman gives full measure for all she receives. If she doesn't, she's simply a sponge, clinging to a man for what's in it. I couldn't bear that. You've been rather painfully frank; so will I be. One unhappy marriage is quite enough for me. Looking back, I can see that even if Walter Monohan hadn't stirred a feeling in me which I don't deny,—but which I'm not nearly so sure of as I was some time ago,—I'd have come to just this stage, anyway. I was drifting all the time. My baby and the conventions, that reluctance most women have to make a clean sweep of all the ties they've been schooled to think unbreakable, kept me moving along the old grooves. It would have come about a little more gradually, that's all. But I have broken away, and I'm going to live my own life after a fashion, and I'm going to achieve independence of some sort. I'm never going to be any man's mate again until I'm sure of myself—and of him. There's my philosophy of life, as simply as I can put it. I don't think you need to worry about me. Right now I couldn't muster up the least shred of passion of any sort. I seem to have felt so much since last summer, that I'm like a sponge that's been squeezed dry."

"I don't blame you, dear," Linda said wistfully. "A woman's heart is a queer thing, though. When you compare the two men—Oh, well, I know Walter so thoroughly, and you don't. You couldn't ever have cared much for Jack."

"That hasn't any bearing on it now," Stella answered. "I'm still his wife, and I respect him, and I've got a stubborn sort of pride. There won't be any divorce proceedings or any scandal. I'm free personally to work out my own economic destiny. That, right now, is engrossing enough for me."

Linda sat a minute, thoughtful.

"So you think my word for Walter Monohan's deviltry isn't worth much," she said. "Well, I could furnish plenty of details. But I don't think I shall. Not because you'd be angry, but because I don't think you're quite as blind as I believed. And I'm not a natural gossip. Aside from that, he's quite too busy on Roaring Lake for it to mean any good. He never gets active like that unless he has some personal axe to grind. In this case, I can grasp his motive easily enough. Jack Fyfe may not have said a word to you, but he certainly knows Monohan. They've clashed before, so I've been told. Jack probably saw what was growing on you, and I don't think he'd hesitate to tell Monohan to walk away around. If he did,—or if you definitely turned Monohan down; you see I'm rather in the dark,—he'd go to any length to play even with. Fyfe. When Monohan wants anything, he looks upon it as his own; and when you wound his vanity, you've stabbed him in his most vital part. He never rests then until he's paid the score. Father was always a little afraid of him. I think that's the chief reason for selling out his Roaring Lake interests to Monohan. He didn't want to be involved in whatever Monohan contemplated doing. He has a wholesome respect for your husband's rather volcanic ability. Monohan has, too. But he has always hated Jack Fyfe. To my knowledge for three years,—prior to pulling you out of the water that time,—he never spoke of Jack Fyfe without a sneer. He hates any one who beats him at anything. That ruction on the Tyee is a sample. He'll spend money, risk lives, all but his own, do anything to satisfy a grudge. That's one of the things that worries me. Charlie will be into anything that Fyfe is, for Fyfe's his friend. I admire the spirit of the thing, but I don't want our little applecart upset in the sort of struggle Fyfe and Monohan may stage. I don't even know what form it will ultimately take, except that from certain indications he'll try to make Fyfe spend money faster than he can make it, perhaps in litigation over timber, over anything that offers, by making trouble in his camps, harassing him at every turn. He can, you know. He has immense resources. Oh, well, I'm satisfied, Stella, that you're a much wiser girl than I thought when I knew you'd left Jack Fyfe. I'm quite sure now you aren't the sort of woman Monohan could wind around his little finger. But

I'm sure he'll try. You'll see, and remember what I tell you. There, I think I'd better run along. You're not angry, are you, Stella?"

"You mean well enough, I suppose," Stella answered. "But as a matter of fact, you've made me feel rather nasty, Linda. I don't want to talk or even think of these things. The best thing you and Charlie and Jack Fyfe could do is to forget such a discontented pendulum as I ever existed."

"Oh, bosh!" Linda exclaimed, as she drew on her gloves. "That's sheer nonsense. You're going to be my big sister in three months. Things will work out. If you felt you had to take this step for your own good, no one can blame you. It needn't make any difference in our friendship."

On the threshold she turned on her heel. "Don't forget what I've said," she repeated. "Don't trust Monohan. Not an inch."

Stella flung herself angrily into a chair when the door closed on Linda Abbey. Her eyes snapped. She resented being warned and cautioned, as if she were some moral weakling who could not be trusted to make the most obvious distinctions. Particularly did she resent having Monohan flung in her teeth, when she was in a way to forget him, to thrust the strange charm of the man forever out of her thoughts. Why, she asked bitterly, couldn't other people do as Jack Fyfe had done: cut the Gordian knot at one stroke and let it rest at that?

So Monohan was in Seattle? Would he try to see her?

Stella had not minced matters with herself when she left Roaring Lake. Dazed and shaken by suffering, nevertheless she knew that she would not always suffer, that in time she would get back to that normal state in which the human ego diligently pursues happiness. In time the legal tie between herself and Jack Fyfe would cease to exist. If Monohan cared for her as she thought he cared, a year or two more or less mattered little. They had all their lives before them. In the long run, the errors and mistakes of that upheaval would grow dim, be as nothing. Jack Fyfe would shrug his shoulders and forget, and in due time he would find a fitter mate, one as loyal as he deserved. And why might not she, who had never loved him, whose marriage to him had been only a climbing out of the fire into the frying-pan?

So that with all her determination to make the most of her gift of song, so that she would never again be buffeted by material urgencies in a material world, Stella had nevertheless been listening with the ear of her mind, so to speak, for a word from Monohan to say that he understood, and that all was well.

Paradoxically, she had not expected to hear that word. Once in Seattle, away from it all, there slowly grew upon her the conviction that in Monohan's fine avowal and renunciation he had only followed the cue she had given. In all else he had played his own hand. She couldn't forget Billy Dale. If the motive behind that bloody culmination were thwarted love, it was a thing to shrink from. It seemed to her now, forcing herself to reason with cold-blooded logic, that Monohan desired her less than he hated Fyfe's possession of her; that she was merely an added factor in the breaking out of a struggle for mastery between two diverse and dominant men. Every sign and token went to show that the pot of hate had long been simmering. She had only contributed to its boiling over.

"Oh, well," she sighed, "it's out of my hands altogether now. I'm sorry, but being sorry doesn't make any difference. I'm the least factor, it seems, in the whole muddle. A woman isn't much more than an incident in a man's life, after all."

She dressed to go to the Charteris, for her day's work was about to begin. As so often happens in life's uneasy flow, periods of calm are succeeded by events in close sequence. Howard and his wife insisted that Stella join them at supper after the show. They were decent folk who accorded frank admiration to her voice and her personality. They had been kind to her in many little ways, and she was glad to accept.

At eleven a taxi deposited them at the door of Wain's. The Seattle of yesterday needs no introduction to Wain's, and its counterpart can be found in any cosmopolitan, seaport city. It is a place of subtle distinction, tucked away on one of the lower hill streets, where after-theater parties and nighthawks with an eye for pretty women, an ear for sensuous music, and a taste for good food, go when they have money to spend.

Ensconced behind a potted palm, with a waiter taking Howard's order, Stella let her gaze travel over the diners. She brought up with a repressed start at a table but four removes from her own, her eyes resting upon the unmistakable profile of Walter Monohan. He was dining vis-à-vis with a young woman chiefly remarkable for a profusion of yellow hair and a blazing diamond in the lobe of each ear,—a plump, blond, vivacious person of a type that Stella, even with her limited experience, found herself instantly classifying.

A bottle of wine rested in an iced dish between them. Monohan was toying with the stem of a half-emptied glass, smiling at his companion. The girl leaned toward him, speaking rapidly, pouting. Monohan nodded, drained his glass, signaled a waiter. When she got into an elaborate opera cloak and Monohan into his Inverness, they went out, the plump, jeweled hand resting familiarly on Monohan's arm. Stella breathed a sigh of relief as they passed, looking straight ahead. She watched through the upper half of the café window and saw a machine draw against the curb, saw the be-scarfed yellow head enter and Monohan's silk hat follow. Then she relaxed, but she had little appetite for her food. A hot wave of shamed disgust kept coming over her. She felt sick, physically revolted. Very likely Monohan had put her in *that* class, in his secret thought. She was glad when the evening ended, and the Howards left her at her own doorstep.

On the carpet where it had been thrust by the postman under the door, a white square caught her eye, and she picked it up before she switched on the light. And she got a queer little shock when the light fell on the envelope, for it was addressed in Jack Fyfe's angular handwriting.

She tore it open. It was little enough in the way of a letter, a couple of lines scrawled across a sheet of note-paper.

"*Dear Girl:*

"I was in Seattle a few days ago and heard you sing. Here's hoping
good luck rides with you.

"JACK."

Stella sat down by the window. Outside, the ever-present Puget Sound rain drove against wall and roof and sidewalk, gathered in wet, glistening pools in the street. Through that same window she had watched Jack Fyfe walk out of her life three months ago without a backward look, sturdily, silently, uncomplaining. He hadn't whined, he wasn't whining now,—only flinging a cheerful word out of the blank spaces of his own life into the blank spaces of hers. Stella felt something warm and wet steal down her cheeks.

She crumpled the letter with a sudden, spasmodic clenching of her hand. A lump rose chokingly in her throat. She stabbed at the light switch and threw herself on the bed, sobbing her heart's cry in the dusky quiet. And she could not have told why, except that she had been overcome by a miserably forlorn feeling; all the mental props she relied upon were knocked out from under her. Somehow those few scrawled words had flung swiftly before her, like a picture on a screen, a vision of her baby toddling uncertainly across the porch of the white bungalow. And she could not bear to think of that!

When the elm before her window broke into leaf, and the sodden winter skies were transformed into a warm spring vista of blue, Stella was singing a special engagement in a local vaudeville house that boasted a "big time" bill. She had stepped up. The silvery richness of her voice had carried her name already beyond local boundaries, as the singing master under whom she studied prophesied it would. In proof thereof she received during April a feminine committee of two from Vancouver bearing an offer of three hundred dollars for her appearance in a series of three concerts under the auspices of the Woman's Musical Club, to be given in the ballroom of Vancouver's new million-dollar hostelry, the Granada. The date was mid-July. She took the offer under advisement, promising a decision in ten days.

The money tempted her; that was her greatest need now,—not for her daily bread, but for an accumulated fund that would enable her to reach New York and ultimately Europe, if that seemed the most direct route to her goal. She had no doubts about reaching it now. Confidence came to abide with her. She throve on work; and with increasing salary, her fund grew. Coming from any other source, she would have accepted this further augmentation of it without hesitation, since for a comparative beginner, it was a liberal offer.

But Vancouver was Fyfe's home town; it had been hers. Many people knew her; the local papers would feature her. She did not know how Fyfe would take it; she did not even know if there had been any open talk of their separation. Money, she felt, was a small thing beside opening old sores. For herself, she was tolerably indifferent to Vancouver's social estimate of her or her acts. Nevertheless, so long as she bore Fyfe's name, she did not feel free to make herself a public figure there without his sanction. So she wrote to him in some detail concerning the offer and asked point-blank if it mattered to him.

His answer came with uncanny promptness, as if every mail connection had been made on the minute.

> "If it is to your advantage to sing here," he wrote, "by all means
> accept. Why should it matter to me? I would even be glad to come and
> hear you sing if I could do so without stirring up vain longings and
> useless regrets. As for the other considerations you mention, they
> are of no weight at all. I never wanted to keep you in a glass case.
> Even if all were well between us, I wouldn't have any feeling about
> your singing in public other than pride in your ability to

command
public favor with your voice. It's a wonderful voice, too big and
fine a thing to remain obscure.

"JACK."

He added, evidently as an afterthought, a somewhat lengthy postscript:

"I wish you would do something next month, not as a favor to me
particularly, but to ease things along for Charlie and Linda. They
are genuinely in love with each other. I can see you turning up your
little nose at that. I know you've held a rather biased opinion of
your brother and his works since that unfortunate winter. But it
doesn't do to be too self-righteous. Charlie, then, was very little
different from any rather headlong, self-centered, red-blooded
youngster. I'm afraid I'm expressing myself badly. What I mean is
that while he was drifting then into a piggy muddle, he had the
sense to take a brace before his lapses became vices. Partly
because—I've flattered myself—I talked to him like a Dutch uncle,
and partly because he's cast too much in the same clean-cut mold
that you are, to let his natural passions run clean away with him.
He'll always be more or less a profound egotist. But he'll be a good
deal more of a man than you, perhaps, think.

"I never used to think much of these matters. I suppose my own
failure at a thing in which I was cocksure of success had made me a
bit dubious about anybody I care for starting so serious an
undertaking as marriage under any sort of handicap. I do

like

Charlie Benton and Linda Abbey. They are marrying in the face of her

people's earnest attempt to break it up. The Abbeys are hopelessly

conservative. Anything in the nature of our troubles aired in public

would make it pretty tough sledding for Linda. As it stands, they

are consenting very ungracefully, but as a matter of family pride,

intend to give Linda a big wedding.

"Now, no one outside of you and me and—well you and me—knows that

there is a rift in our lute. I haven't been quizzed—naturally. It

got about that you'd taken up voice culture with an eye to opera as

a counteracting influence to the grief of losing your baby. I fostered that rumor—simply to keep gossip down until things shaped

themselves positively. Once these two are married, they have

started—Abbey *père* and *mère* will then be unable to frown on

Linda's contemplated alliance with a family that's produced a

divorce case.

"I do not suppose you will take any legal steps until after those

concerts. Until then, please keep up the fiction that the house of

Fyfe still stands on a solid foundation—a myth that you've taken no

measures to dispel since you left. When it does come, it will be a

sort of explosion, and I'd rather have it that way—one amazed yelp

from our friends and the newspapers, and it's over.

"Meantime, you will receive an invitation to the wedding. I hope you'll accept. You needn't have any compunctions about playing the

game. You will not encounter me, as I have my hands full here, and

I'm notorious in Vancouver for backing out of functions, anyway. It

is not imperative that you should do this. It's merely a safeguard

against a bomb from the Abbey fortress.

"Linda is troubled by a belief that upon small pretext they would be

very nasty, and she naturally doesn't want any friction with her

folks. They have certain vague but highly material ambitions for her

matrimonially, which she, a very sensible girl, doesn't subscribe

to. She's a very shrewd and practical young person, for all her

whole-hearted passion for your brother. I rather think she pretty

clearly guesses the breach in our rampart—not the original mistake

in our over-hasty plunge—but the wedge that divided us for good. If

she does, and I'm quite sure she does, she is certainly good stuff,

because she is most loyally your champion. I say that because

Charlie had a tendency this spring to carp at your desertion of

Roaring Lake. Things aren't going any too good with us, one way and

another, and of course he, not knowing the real reason of your

absence, couldn't understand why you stay away. I had to squelch

him, and Linda abetted me successfully. However, that's beside the

point. I hope I haven't irritated you. I'm such a dumb sort of brute

generally. I don't know what imp of prolixity got into my pen. I've
got it all off my chest now, or pretty near.

"J.H.F."

Stella sat thoughtfully gazing at the letter for a long time.

"I wonder?" she said aloud, and the sound of her own voice galvanized her into action. She put on a coat and went out into the mellow spring sunshine, and walked till the aimless straying of her feet carried her to a little park that overlooked the far reach of the Sound and gave westward on the snowy Olympics, thrusting hoary and aloof to a perfect sky, like their brother peaks that ringed Roaring Lake. And all the time her mind kept turning on a question whose asking was rooted neither in fact nor necessity, an inquiry born of a sentiment she had never expected to feel.

Should she go back to Jack Fyfe?

She shook her head impatiently when she faced that squarely. Why tread the same bitter road again? But she put that self-interested phase of it aside and asked herself candidly if she *could* go back and take up the old threads where they had been broken off and make life run smoothly along the old, quiet channels? She was as sure as she was sure of the breath she drew that Fyfe wanted her, that he longed for and would welcome her. But she was equally sure that the old illusions would never serve. She couldn't even make him happy, much less herself. Monohan—well, Monohan was a dead issue. He had come to the Charteris to see her, all smiles and eagerness. She had been able to look at him and through him—and cut him dead—and do it without a single flutter of her heart.

That brief and illuminating episode in Wain's had merely confirmed an impression that had slowly grown upon her, and her outburst of feeling that night had only been the overflowing of shamed anger at herself for letting his magnetic personality make so deep an impression on her that she could admit to him that she cared. She felt that she had belittled herself by that. But he was no longer a problem. She wondered now how he ever could have been. She recalled that once Jack Fyfe had soberly told her she would never sense life's real values while she nursed so many illusions. Monohan had been one of them.

"But it wouldn't work," she whispered to herself. "I couldn't do it. He'd know I only did it because I was sorry, because I thought I should, because the old ties, and they seem so many and so strong in spite of everything, were harder to break than the new road is to follow alone. He'd resent anything like pity for his loneliness. And if Monohan has made any real trouble, it began over me, or at least it focussed on me. And he might resent that. He's ten times a better man than I am a woman. He thinks about the other fellow's side of things. I'm just what he said about Charlie, self-centered, a profound egotist. If I really and truly loved Jack Fyfe, I'd be a jealous little fury if he so much as looked at another woman. But I don't, and I don't see why I don't. I want to be loved; I want to love. I've always wanted that so much that I'll never dare trust my instincts about it again. I wonder why people like me exist to go blundering about in the world, playing havoc with themselves and everybody else?"

Before she reached home, that self-sacrificing mood had vanished in the face of sundry twinges of pride. Jack Fyfe hadn't asked her to come back; he never would ask her to come back. Of that she was quite sure. She knew the stony determination of him too well. Neither hope or heaven nor fear of hell would turn him aside when he had made a decision. If he ever had moments of irresolution, he had successfully concealed any such weakness from those who knew him best. No one ever felt called upon to pity Jack Fyfe, and in those rocked-ribbed qualities, Stella had an illuminating flash, perhaps lay the secret of his failure ever to stir in her that yearning tenderness which she knew herself to be capable of lavishing, which her nature impelled her to lavish on some one.

"Ah, well," she sighed, when she came back to her rooms and put Fyfe's letter away in a drawer. "I'll do the decent thing if they ask me. I wonder what Jack would say if he knew what I've been debating with myself this afternoon? I wonder if we were actually divorced and I'd made myself a reputation as a singer, and we happened to meet quite casually sometime, somewhere, just how we'd really feel about each other?"

She was still musing on that, in a detached, impersonal fashion, when she caught a car down to the theater for the matinée.

CHAPTER XXI
AN UNEXPECTED MEETING

The formally worded wedding card arrived in due course. Following close came a letter from Linda Abbey, a missive that radiated friendliness and begged Stella to come a week before the date.

"You're going to be pretty prominent in the public eye when you sing
here," Linda wrote. "People are going to make a to-do over you. Ever
so many have mentioned you since the announcement was made that
you'll sing at the Granada concerts. I'm getting a lot of reflected
glory as the future sister-in-law of a rising singer. So you may as
well come and get your hand into the social game in preparation for
being fussed over in July."

In the same mail was a characteristic note from Charlie which ran:

"*Dear Sis:*

"As the Siwashes say, long time I see you no. I might have dropped a
line before, but you know what a punk correspondent I am. They tell
me you're becoming a real noise musically. How about it?

"Can't you break away from the fame and fortune stuff long enough to
be on hand when Linda and I get married? I wasn't invited to your
wedding, but I'd like to have you at mine. Jack says it's up to you
to represent the Fyfe connection, as he's too busy. I'll come over
to Seattle and get you, if you say so."

She capitulated at that and wrote saying that she would be there, and that she did not mind the trip alone in the least. She did not want Charlie asking pertinent questions about why she lived in such grubby quarters and practiced such strict economy in the matter of living.

Then there was the detail of arranging a break in her engagements, which ran continuously to the end of June. She managed that easily enough, for she was becoming too great a drawing card for managers to curtly override her wishes.

Almost before she realized it, June was at hand. Linda wrote again urgently, and Stella took the night boat for Vancouver a week before the wedding day. Linda met her at the dock with a machine. Mrs. Abbey was the essence of cordiality when she reached the big Abbey house on Vancouver's aristocratic "heights," where the local capitalists, all those fortunate climbers enriched by timber and mineral, grown wealthy in a decade through the great Coast boom, segregated themselves in "Villas" and "Places" and "Views," all painfully new and sometimes garish, striving for an effect in landscape and architecture which the very intensity of the striving defeated. They were well-meaning folk, however, the Abbeys included.

Stella could not deny that she enjoyed the luxury of the Abbey ménage, the little festive round which was shaping about Linda in these last days of her spinsterhood. She relished the change from unremitting work. It amused her to startle little groups with the range and quality of her voice, when they asked her to sing. They made a much ado over that, a genuine admiration that flattered Stella. It was easy for her to fall into the swing of that life; it was only a lapsing back to the old ways.

But she saw it now with a more critical vision. It was soft and satisfying and eminently desirable to have everything one wanted without the effort of striving for it, but a begging wheedling game on the part of these women. They were, she told herself rather harshly, an incompetent, helpless lot, dependent one and all upon some man's favor or affection, just as she herself had been all her life until the past few months. Some man had to work and scheme to pay the bills. She did not know why this line of thought should arise, neither did she so far forget herself as to voice these social heresies. But it helped to reconcile her with her new-found independence, to put a less formidable aspect on the long, hard grind that lay ahead of her before she could revel in equal affluence gained by her own efforts. All that they had she desired,—homes, servants, clothes, social standing,—but she did not want these things bestowed upon her as a favor by some man, the emoluments of sex.

She expected she would have to be on her guard with her brother, even to dissemble a little. But she found him too deeply engrossed in what to him was the most momentous event of his career, impatiently awaiting the day, rather dreading the publicity of it.

"Why in Sam Hill can't a man and a woman get married without all this fuss?" he complained once. "Why should we make our private affairs a spectacle for the whole town?"

"Principally because mamma has her heart set on a spectacle," Linda laughed. "She'd hold up her hands in horror if she heard you. Decorated bridal bower, high church dignitary, bridesmaids, orange blossoms, rice, and all. Mamma likes to show off. Besides, that's the way it's done in society. *And* the honeymoon."

They both giggled, as at some mirthful secret.

"Shall we tell her?" Linda nodded toward Stella.

"Sure," Benton said. "I thought you had."

"The happy couple will spend their honeymoon on a leisurely tour of the Southern and Eastern States, remaining for some weeks in Philadelphia, where the groom has wealthy and influential connections. It's all prepared for the pay-a-purs," Linda whispered with exaggerated secrecy behind her hand.

Benton snorted.

"Can you beat that?" he appealed to Stella.

"And all the time," Linda continued, "the happy couple, unknown to every one, will be spending their days in peace and quietness in their shanty at Halfway Point. My, but mamma would rave if she knew. Don't give us away, Stella. It seems so senseless to squander a lot of money gadding about on trains and living in hotels when we'd much rather be at home by ourselves. My husband's a poor young man, Stella. 'Pore but worthy.' He has to make his fortune before we start in spending it. I'm sick of all this spreading it on because dad has made a pile of money," she broke out impatiently. "Our living used to be simple enough when I was a kid. I think I can relish a little simplicity again for a change. Mamma's been trying for four years to marry me off to her conception of an eligible man. It didn't matter a hang about his essential qualities so long as he had money and an assured social position."

"Forget that," Charlie counseled slangily. "I have all the essential qualities, and I'll have the money and social position too; you watch my smoke."

"Conceited ninny," Linda smiled. But there was no reproof in her tone, only pure comradeship and affection, which Benton returned so openly and unaffectedly that Stella got up and left them with a pang of envy, a dull little ache in her heart. She had missed that. It had passed her by, that clean, spontaneous fusing of two personalities in the biggest passion life holds. Marriage and motherhood she had known, not as the flowering of love, not as an eager fulfilling of her natural destiny, but as something extraneous, an avenue of escape from an irksomeness of living, a weariness with sordid things, which she knew now had obsessed her out of all proportion to their reality. She had never seen that tenderness glow in the eyes of a mating pair that she did not envy them, that she did not feel herself hopelessly defrauded of her woman's heritage.

She went up to her room, moody, full of bitterness, and walked the thick-carpeted floor, the restlessness of her chafing spirit seeking the outlet of action.

"Thank the Lord I've got something to do, something that's worth doing," she whispered savagely. "If I can't have what I want, I can make my life embrace something more than just food and clothes and social trifling. If I had to sit and wait for each day to bring what it would, I believe I'd go clean mad."

A maid interrupted these self-communings to say that some one had called her over the telephone, and Stella went down to the library. She wasn't prepared for the voice that came over the line, but she recognized it instantly as Fyfe's.

"Listen, Stella," he said. "I'm sorry this has happened, but I can't very well avoid it now, without causing comment. I had no choice about coming to Vancouver. It was a business matter I couldn't neglect. And as luck would have it, Abbey ran into me as I got off the train. On account of your being there, of course, he insisted that I come out for dinner. It'll look queer if I don't, as I can't possibly get a return train for the Springs before nine-thirty this evening. I accepted without stuttering rather than leave any chance for the impression that I wanted to avoid you. Now, here's how I propose to fix it. I'll come out about two-thirty and pay a hurry-up five-minute call. Then I'll excuse myself to Mrs. Abbey for inability to join them at dinner—press of important business takes me to Victoria and so forth. That'll satisfy the conventions and let us both out. I called you so you won't be taken by surprise. Do you mind?"

"Of course not," she answered instantly. "Why should I?"

There was a momentary silence.

"Well," he said at last, "I didn't know how you'd feel about it. Anyway, it will only be for a few minutes, and it's unlikely to happen again."

Stella put the receiver back on the hook and looked at her watch. It lacked a quarter of two. In the room adjoining, Charlie and Linda were jubilantly wading through the latest "rag" song in a passable soprano and baritone, with Mrs. Abbey listening in outward resignation. Stella sat soberly for a minute, then joined them.

"Jack's in town," she informed them placidly, when the ragtime spasm ended. "He telephoned that he was going to snatch a few minutes between important business confabs to run out and see me."

"I could have told you that half an hour ago, my dear," Mrs. Abbey responded with playful archness. "Mr. Fyfe will dine with us this evening."

"Oh," Stella feigned surprise. "Why, he spoke of going to Victoria on the afternoon boat. He gave me the impression of mad haste—making a dash out here between breaths, as you might say."

"Oh, I hope he won't be called away on such short notice as that," Mrs. Abbey murmured politely.

She left the room presently. Out of one corner of her eye Stella saw Linda looking at her queerly. Charlie had turned to the window, staring at the blue blur of the Lions across the Inlet.

"It's a wonder Jack would leave the lake," he said suddenly, "with things the way they are. I've been hoping for rain ever since I've been down. I'll be glad when we're on the spot again, Linda."

"Wishing for rain?" Stella echoed. "Why?"

"Fire," he said shortly. "I don't suppose you realize it, but there's been practically no rain for two months. It's getting hot. A few weeks of dry, warm weather, and this whole country is ready to blow away. The woods are like a pile of shavings. That would be a fine wedding present—to be cleaned out by fire. Every dollar I've got's in timber."

"Don't be a pessimist," Linda said sharply.

"What makes you so uneasy now?" Stella asked thoughtfully. "There's always the fire danger in the dry months. That's been a bugaboo ever since I came to the lake."

"Yes, but never like it is this summer," Benton frowned. "Oh, well, no use borrowing trouble, I suppose."

Stella rose.

"When Jack comes, I'll be in the library," she said. "I'm going to read a while."

But the book she took up lay idle in her lap. She looked forward to that meeting with a curious mixture of reluctance and regret. She could not face it unmoved. No woman who has ever lain passive in a man's arms can ever again look into that man's eyes with genuine indifference. She may hate him or love him with a degree of intensity according to her nature, be merely friendly, or nurse a slow resentment. But there is always that intangible something which differentiates him from other men. Stella felt now a shyness of him, a little dread of him, less sureness of herself, as he swung out of the machine and took the house steps with that effortless lightness on his feet that she remembered so well.

She heard him in the hall, his deep voice mingling with the thin, penetrating tones of Mrs. Abbey. And then the library door opened, and he came in. Stella had risen, and stood uncertainly at one corner of a big reading table, repressing an impulse to fly, finding herself stricken with a strange recurrence of the feeling she had first disliked him for arousing in her,—a sense of needing to be on her guard, of impending assertion of a will infinitely more powerful than her own.

But that was, she told herself, only a state of mind, and Fyfe put her quickly at her ease. He came up to the table and seated himself on the edge of it an arm's length from her, swinging one foot free. He looked at her intently. There was no shadow of expression on his face, only in his clear eyes lurked a gleam of feeling.

"Well, lady," he said at length, "you're looking fine. How goes everything?"

"Fairly well," she answered.

"Seems odd, doesn't it, to meet like this?" he ventured. "I'd have dodged it, if it had been politic. As it is, there's no harm done, I imagine. Mrs. Abbey assured me we'd be free from interruption. If the exceedingly cordial dame had an inkling of how things stand between us, I daresay she'd be holding her breath about now."

"Why do you talk like that, Jack?" Stella protested nervously.

"Well, I have to say something," he remarked, after a moment's reflection. "I can't sit here and just look at you. That would be rude, not to say embarrassing."

Stella bit her lip.

"I don't see why we can't talk like any other man and woman for a few minutes," she observed.

"I do," he said quietly. "You know why, too, if you stop to think. I'm the same old Jack Fyfe, Stella. I don't think much where you are concerned; I just feel. And that doesn't lend itself readily to impersonal chatter."

"How do you feel?" she asked, meeting his gaze squarely. "If you don't hate me, you must at least rather despise me."

"Neither," he said slowly. "I admire your grit, lady. You broke away from everything and made a fresh start. You asserted your own individuality in a fashion that rather surprised me. Maybe the incentive wasn't what it might have been, but the result is, or promises to be. I was only a milestone. Why should I hate or despise you because you recognized that and passed on? I had no business setting myself up for the end of your road instead of the beginning. I meant to have it that way until the kid—well, Fate took a hand there. Pshaw," he broke off with a quick gesture, "let's talk about something else."

Stella laid one hand on his knee. Unbidden tears were crowding up in her gray eyes.

"You were good to me," she whispered. "But just being good wasn't enough for a perverse creature like me. I couldn't be a sleek pussy-cat, comfortable beside your fire. I'm full of queer longings. I want wings. I must be a variation from the normal type of woman. Our marriage didn't touch the real me at all, Jack. It only scratched the surface. And sometimes I'm afraid to look deep, for fear of what I'll see. Even if another man hadn't come along and stirred up a temporary tumult in me, I couldn't have gone on forever."

"A temporary tumult," Fyfe mused. "Have you thoroughly chucked that illusion? I knew you would, of course, but I had no idea how long it would take you."

"Long ago," she answered. "Even before I left you, I was shaky about that. There were things I couldn't reconcile. But pride wouldn't let me admit it. I can't even explain it to myself."

"I can," he said, a little sadly. "You've never poured out that big, warm heart of yours on a man. It's there, always has been there, those concentrated essences of passion. Every unattached man's a possible factor, a potential lover. Nature has her own devices to gain her end. I couldn't be the one. We started wrong. I saw the mistake of that when it was too late, Monohan, a highly magnetic animal, came along at a time when you were peculiarly and rather blindly receptive. That's all. Sex—you have it in a word. It couldn't stand any stress, that sort of attraction. I knew it would only last until you got one illuminating glimpse of the real man of him. But I don't want to talk about him. He'll keep. Sometime you'll really love a *man*, Stella, and he'll be a very lucky mortal. There's an erratic streak in you, lady, but there's a bigger streak that's fine and good and true. You'd have gone through with it to the bitter end, if Jack Junior hadn't died. The weaklings don't do that. Neither do they cut loose as you did, burning all their economic bridges behind them. Do you know that it was over a month before I found out that you'd turned your private balance back into my account? I suppose there was a keen personal satisfaction in going on your own and making good from the start. Only I couldn't rest until—until—"

His voice trailed huskily off into silence. The gloves in his left hand were doubled and twisted in his uneasy fingers. Stella's eyes were blurred.

"Well, I'm going," he said shortly. "Be good."

He slipped off the table and stood erect, a wide, deep-chested man, tanned brown, his fair hair with its bronze tinge lying back in a smooth wave from his forehead, blue eyes bent on her, hot with a slumbering fire.

Without warning, he caught her close in his arms so that she could feel the pounding of his heart against her breast, kissed her cheeks, her hair, the round, firm white neck of her, with lips that burned. Then he held her off at arm's length.

"That's how *I* care," he said defiantly. "That's how I want you. No other way. I'm a one-woman man. Some time you may love like that, and if you do, you'll know how I feel. I've watched you sleeping beside me and ached because I couldn't kindle the faintest glow of the real thing in you. I'm sick with a miserable sense of failure, the only thing I've ever failed at, and the biggest, most complete failure I can conceive of,—to love a woman in every way desirable; to have her and yet never have her."

He caught up his hat, and the door clicked shut behind him. A minute later Stella saw him step into the tonneau of the car. He never looked back.

And she fled to her own room, stunned, half-frightened, wholly amazed at this outburst. Her face was damp with his lip-pressure, damp and warm. Her arms tingled with the grip of his. The blood stood in her cheeks like a danger signal, flooding in hot, successive waves to the roots of her thick, brown hair.

"If I thought—I could," she whispered into her pillow, "I'd try. But I daren't. I'm afraid. It's just a mood, I know it is. I've had it before. A— ah! I'm a spineless jellyfish, a weathercock that whirls to every emotional breeze. And I won't be. I'll stand on my own feet if I can—so help me God, I will!"

CHAPTER XXII
THE FIRE BEHIND THE SMOKE

This is no intimate chronicle of Charlie Benton and Linda Abbey, save in so far as they naturally furnish a logical sequence in what transpired. Therefore the details of their nuptials is of no particular concern. They were wedded, ceremonially dined as befitted the occasion, and departed upon their hypothetical honeymoon, surreptitiously abbreviated from an extravagant swing over half of North America to seventy miles by rail and twenty by water,—and a month of blissful seclusion, which suited those two far better than any amount of Pullman touring, besides leaving them money in pocket.

When they were gone, Stella caught the next boat for Seattle. She had drawn fresh breath in the meantime, and while she felt tenderly, almost maternally, sorry for Jack Fyfe, she swung back to the old attitude. Even granting, she argued, that she could muster courage to take up the mantle of wifehood where she laid it off, there was no surety that they could do more than compromise. There was the stubborn fact that she had openly declared her love for another man, that by her act she had plunged her husband into far-reaching conflict. Such a conflict existed. She could put her finger on no concrete facts, but it was in the air. She heard whispers of a battle between giants—a financial duel to the death—with all the odds against Jack Fyfe.

Win or lose, there would be scars. And the struggle, if not of and by her deed, had at least sprung into malevolent activity through her. Men, she told herself, do not forget these things; they rankle. Jack Fyfe was only human. No, Stella felt that they could only come safe to the old port by virtue of a passion that could match Fyfe's own. And she put that rather sadly beyond her, beyond the possibilities. She had felt stirrings of it, but not to endure. She was proud and sensitive and growing wise with bitterly accumulated experience. It had to be all or nothing with them, a cleaving together complete enough to erase and forever obliterate all that had gone before. And since she could not see that as a possibility, there was nothing to do but play the game according to the cards she held. Of these the trump was work, the inner glow that comes of something worth while done toward a definite, purposeful end. She took up her singing again with a distinct relief.

Time passed quickly and uneventfully enough between the wedding day and the date of her Granada engagement. It seemed a mere breathing space before the middle of July rolled around, and she was once more aboard a Vancouver boat. In the interim, she had received a letter from the attorney who had wound up her father's estate, intimating that there was now a market demand for that oil stock, and asking if he should sell or hold for a rise in price which seemed reasonably sure? Stella telegraphed her answer. If that left-over of a speculative period would bring a few hundred dollars, it would never be of greater service to her than now.

All the upper reach of Puget Sound basked in its normal midsummer haze, the day Stella started for Vancouver. That great region of island-dotted sea spread between the rugged Olympics and the foot of the Coast range lay bathed in summer sun, untroubled, somnolent. But nearing the international boundary, the *Charlotte* drove her twenty-knot way into a thickening atmosphere. Northward from Victoria, the rugged shores that line those inland waterways began to appear blurred. Just north of Active Pass, where the steamers take to the open gulf again, a vast bank of smoke flung up blue and gray, a rolling mass. The air was pungent, oppressive. When the *Charlotte* spanned the thirty-mile gap between Vancouver Island and the mainland shore, she nosed into the Lion's Gate under a slow bell, through a smoke pall thick as Bering fog. Stella's recollection swung back to Charlie's uneasy growl of a month earlier. Fire! Throughout the midsummer season there was always the danger of fire breaking out in the woods. Not all the fire-ranger patrols could guard against the carelessness of fishermen and campers.

"It's a tough Summer over here for the timber owners," she heard a man remark. "I've been twenty years on the coast and never saw the woods so dry."

"Dry's no name," his neighbor responded. "It's like tinder. A cigarette stub'll start a blaze forty men couldn't put out. It's me that knows it. I've got four limits on the North Arm, and there's fire on two sides of me. You bet I'm praying for rain."

"They say the country between Chehalis and Roaring Lake is one big blaze," the first man observed.

"So?" the other replied. "Pity, too. Fine timber in there. I came near buying some timber on the lake this spring. Some stuff that was on the market as a result of that Abbey-Monohan split. Glad I didn't now. I'd just as soon have *all* my money out of timber this season."

They moved away in the press of disembarking, and Stella heard no more of their talk. She took a taxi to the Granada, and she bought a paper in the foyer before she followed the bell boy to her room. She had scarcely taken off her hat and settled down to read when the telephone rang. Linda's voice greeted her when she answered.

"I called on the chance that you took the morning boat," Linda said. "Can I run in? I'm just down for the day. I won't be able to hear you sing, but I'd like to see you, dear."

"Can you come right now?" Stella asked. "Come up, and we'll have something served up here. I don't feel like running the gauntlet of the dining room just now."

"I'll be there in a few minutes," Linda answered.

Stella went back to her paper. She hadn't noticed any particular stress laid on forest fires in the Seattle dailies, but she could not say that of this Vancouver sheet. The front page reeked of smoke and fire. She glanced through the various items for news of Roaring Lake, but found only a brief mention. It was "reported" and "asserted" and "rumored" that fire was raging at one or two points there, statements that were overshadowed by positive knowledge of greater areas nearer at hand burning with a fierceness that could be seen and smelled. The local papers had enough feature stuff in fires that threatened the very suburbs of Vancouver without going so far afield as Roaring Lake.

Linda's entrance put a stop to her reading, without, however, changing the direction of her thought. For after an exchange of greetings, Linda divulged the source of her worried expression, which Stella had immediately remarked.

"Who wouldn't be worried," Linda said, "with the whole country on fire, and no telling when it may break out in some unexpected place and wipe one out of house and home."

"Is it so bad as that at the lake?" Stella asked uneasily. "There's not much in the paper. I was looking."

"It's so bad," Linda returned, with a touch of bitterness, "that I've been driven to the Springs for safety; that every able-bodied man on the lake who can be spared is fighting fire. There has been one man killed, and there's half a dozen loggers in the hospital, suffering from burns and other hurts. Nobody knows where it will stop. Charlie's limits have barely been scorched, but there's fire all along one side of them. A change of wind—and there you are. Jack Fyfe's timber is burning in a dozen places. We've been praying for rain and choking in the smoke for a week."

Stella looked out the north window. From the ten-story height she could see ships lying in the stream, vague hulks in the smoky pall that shrouded the harbor.

"I'm sorry," she whispered.

"It's devilish," Linda went on. "Like groping in the dark and being afraid—for me. I've been married a month, and for ten days I've only seen my husband at brief intervals when he comes down in the launch for supplies, or to bring an injured man. And he doesn't tell me anything except that we stand a fat chance of losing everything. I sit there at the Springs, and look at that smoke wall hanging over the water, and wonder what goes on up there. And at night there's the red glow, very faint and far. That's all. I've been doing nursing at the hospital to help out and to keep from brooding. I wouldn't be down here now, only for a list of things the doctor needs, which he thought could be obtained quicker if some one attended to it personally. I'm taking the evening train back."

"I'm sorry," Stella repeated.

She said it rather mechanically. Her mind was spinning a thread, upon which, strung like beads, slid all the manifold succession of things that had happened since she came first to Roaring Lake. Linda's voice, continuing, broke into her thoughts.

"I suppose I shouldn't be croaking into your ear like a bird of ill omen, when you have to throw yourself heart and soul into that concert to-morrow," she said contritely. "I wonder why that Ancient Mariner way of seeking relief from one's troubles by pouring them into another ear is such a universal trait? You aren't vitally concerned, after all, and I am. Let's have that tea, dear, and talk about less grievous things. I still have one or two trifles to get in the shops too."

After they had finished the food that Stella ordered sent up, they went out together. Later Stella saw her off on the train.

"Good-by, dear," Linda said from the coach window. "I'm just selfish enough to wish you were going back with me; I wish you could sit with me on the bank of the lake, aching and longing for your man up there in the smoke as I ache and long for mine. Misery loves company."

Stella's eyes were clouded as the train pulled out. Something in Linda Benton's parting words made her acutely lonely, dispirited, out of joint with the world she was deliberately fashioning for herself. Into Linda's life something big and elemental had come. The butterfly of yesterday had become the strong man's mate of to-day. Linda's heart was unequivocally up there in the smoke and flame with her man, fighting for their mutual possessions, hoping with him, fearing for him, longing for him, secure in the knowledge that if nothing else was left them, they had each other. It was a rare and beautiful thing to feel like that. And beyond that sorrowful vision of what she lacked to achieve any real and enduring happiness, there loomed also a self-torturing conviction that she herself had set in motion those forces which now threatened ruin for her brother and Jack Fyfe.

There was no logical proof of this. Only intuitive, subtle suggestions gleaned here and there, shadowy finger-posts which pointed to Monohan as a deadly hater and with a score chalked up against Fyfe to which she had unconsciously added. He had desired her, and twice Fyfe had treated him like an urchin caught in mischief. She recalled how Monohan sprang at him like a tiger that day on the lake shore. She realized how bitter a humiliation it must have been to suffer that sardonic cuffing at Fyfe's hands. Monohan wasn't the type of man who would ever forget or forgive either that or the terrible grip on his throat.

Even at the time she had sensed this and dreaded what it might ultimately lead to. Even while her being answered eagerly to the physical charm of him, she had fought against admitting to herself what desperate intent might have lain back of the killing of Billy Dale,—a shot that Lefty Howe declared was meant for Fyfe. She had long outgrown Monohan's lure, but if he had come to her or written to make out a case for himself when she first went to Seattle, she would have accepted his word against anything. Her heart would have fought for him against the logic of her brain.

But—she had had a long time to think, to compare, to digest all that she knew of him, much that was subconscious impression rising late to the surface, a little that she heard from various sources. The sum total gave her a man of rank passions, of rare and merciless finesse where his desires figured, a man who got what he wanted by whatever means most fitly served his need. Greater than any craving to possess a woman would be the measure of his rancor against a man who humiliated him, thwarted him. She could understand how a man like Monohan would hate a man like Jack Fyfe, would nurse and feed on the venom of his hate until setting a torch to Fyfe's timber would be a likely enough counterstroke.

She shrank from the thought. Yet it lingered until she felt guilty. Though it made no material difference to her that Fyfe might or might not face ruin, she could not, before her own conscience, evade responsibility. The powder might have been laid, but her folly had touched spark to the fuse, as she saw it. That seared her like a pain far into the night. For every crime a punishment; for every sin a penance. Her world had taught her that. She had never danced; she had only listened to the piper and longed to dance, as nature had fashioned her to do. But the piper was sending his bill. She surveyed it wearily, emotionally bankrupt, wondering in what coin of the soul she would have to pay.

CHAPTER XXIII
A RIDE BY NIGHT

Stella sang in the gilt ballroom of the Granada next afternoon, behind the footlights of a miniature stage, with the blinds drawn and a few hundred of Vancouver's social elect critically, expectantly listening. She sang her way straight into the heart of that audience with her opening number. This was on Wednesday. Friday she sang again, and Saturday afternoon.

When she came back to her room after that last concert, wearied with the effort of listening to chattering women and playing the gracious lady to an admiring contingent which insisted upon making her last appearance a social triumph, she found a letter forwarded from Seattle. She slit the envelope. A typewritten sheet enfolded a green slip,—a check. She looked at the figures, scarcely comprehending until she read the letter.

"We take pleasure in handing you herewith," Mr. Lander
wrote for the
firm, "our check for nineteen thousand five hundred
dollars,
proceeds of oil stock sold as per your telegraphed
instructions,
less brokerage charges. We sold same at par, and trust this
will be
satisfactory."

She looked at the check again. Nineteen thousand, five hundred— payable to her order. Two years ago such a sum would have lifted her to plutocratic heights, filled her with pleasurable excitement, innumerable anticipations. Now it stirred her less than the three hundred dollars she had just received from the Granada Concert committee. She had earned that, had given for it due measure of herself. This other had come without effort, without expectation. And less than she had ever needed money before did she now require such a sum.

Yet she was sensibly aware that this windfall meant a short cut to things which she had only looked to attain by plodding over economic hills. She could say good-by to singing in photoplay houses, to vaudeville engagements, to concert work in provincial towns. She could hitch her wagon to a star and go straight up the avenue that led to a career, if it were in her to achieve greatness. Pleasant dreams in which the buoyant ego soared, until the logical interpretation of her ambitions brought her to a more practical consideration of ways and means, and that in turn confronted her with the fact that she could leave the Pacific coast to-morrow morning if she so chose.

Why should she not so choose?

She was her own mistress, free as the wind. Fyfe had said that. She looked out into the smoky veil that shrouded the water front and the hills across the Inlet, that swirled and eddied above the giant fir in Stanley Park, and her mind flicked back to Roaring Lake where the Red Flower of Kipling's *Jungle Book* bloomed to her husband's ruin. Did it? She wondered. She could not think of him as beaten, bested in any undertaking. She had never been able to think of him in those terms. Always to her he had conveyed the impression of a superman. Always she had been a little in awe of him, of his strength, his patient, inflexible determination, glimpsing under his habitual repression certain tremendous forces. She could not conceive him as a broken man.

Staring out into the smoky air, she wondered if the fires at Roaring Lake still ravaged that noble forest; if Fyfe's resources, like her brother's, were wholly involved in standing timber, and if that timber were doomed? She craved to know. Secured herself by that green slip in her hand against every possible need, she wondered if it were ordained that the two men whose possession of material resources had molded her into what she was to-day should lose all, be reduced to the same stress that had made her an unwilling drudge in her brother's kitchen. Then she recalled that for Charlie there was an equivalent sum due,—a share like her own. At the worst, he had the nucleus of another fortune.

Curled among the pillows of her bed that night, she looked over the evening papers, read with a swift heart-sinking that the Roaring Lake fire was assuming terrific proportions, that nothing but a deluge of rain would stay it now. And more significantly, except for a minor blaze or two, the fire raged almost wholly upon and around the Fyfe block of limits. She laid aside the papers, switched off the lights, and lay staring wide-eyed at the dusky ceiling.

At twenty minutes of midnight she was called to the door of her room to receive a telegram. It was from Linda, and it read:

"Charlie badly hurt. Can you come?"

Stella reached for the telephone receiver. The night clerk at the C.P.R. depot told her the first train she could take left at six in the morning. That meant reaching the Springs at nine-thirty. Nine and a half hours to sit with idle hands, in suspense. She did not knew what tragic dénouement awaited there, what she could do once she reached there. She knew only that a fever of impatience burned in her. The message had strung her suddenly taut, as if a crisis had arisen in which willy-nilly she must take a hand.

So, groping for the relief of action, some method of spanning that nine hours' wait, her eye fell upon a card tucked beside the telephone case. She held it between, finger and thumb, her brows puckered.

TAXIS AND TOURING CARS
Anywhere . . . Anytime

She took down the receiver again and asked for Seymour 9X

"Western Taxi," a man's voice drawled.

"I want to reach Roaring Hot Springs in the shortest time possible," she told him rather breathlessly. "Can you furnish me a machine and a reliable chauffeur?"

"Roaring Springs?" he repeated. "How many passengers?"

"One. Myself."

"Just a minute."

She heard a faint burble of talk away at the other end of the wire. Then the same voice speaking crisply.

"We gotta big six roadster, and a first-class driver. It'll cost you seventy-five dollars—in advance."

"Your money will be waiting for you here," she answered calmly. "How soon can you bring the car around to the Hotel Granada?"

"In ten minutes, if you say so."

"Say twenty minutes, then."

"All right."

She dressed herself, took the elevator down to the lobby, instructed the night clerk to have a maid pack her trunk and send it by express to Hopyard, care of St. Allwoods Hotel on the lake. Then she walked out to the broad-stepped carriage entrance.

A low-hung long-hooded, yellow car stood there, exhaust purring faintly. She paid the driver, sank into the soft upholstering beside him, and the big six slid out into the street. There was no traffic. In a few minutes they were on the outskirts of the city, the long asphalt ribbon of King's Way lying like a silver band between green, bushy walls. They crossed the last car track. The driver spoke to her out of one corner of his mouth.

"Wanna make time, huh?"

"I want to get to Roaring Lake as quickly as you can drive, without taking chances."

"I know the road pretty well," he assured her. "Drove a party clear to Rosebud day before yesterday. I'll do the best I can. Can't drive too fast at night. Too smoky."

She could not gage his conception of real speed if the gait he struck was not "too fast." They were through New Westminster and rolling across the Fraser bridge before she was well settled in the seat, breasting the road with a lurch and a swing at the curves, a noise under that long hood like giant bees in an empty barrel.

Ninety miles of road good, bad and indifferent, forest and farm and rolling hill, and the swamps of Sumas Prairie, lies between Vancouver and Roaring Lake. At four in the morning, with dawn an hour old, they woke the Rosebud ferryman to cross the river. Twenty minutes after that Stella was stepping stiffly out of the machine before Roaring Springs hospital. The doctor's Chinaman was abroad in the garden. She beckoned him.

"You sabe Mr. Benton—Charlie Benton?" she asked. "He in doctor's house?"

The Chinaman pointed across the road. "Mist Bentle obah dah," he said. "Velly much sick. Missa Bentle lib dah, all same gleen house."

Stella ran across the way. The front door of the green cottage stood wide. An electric drop light burned in the front room, though it was broad day. When she crossed the threshold, she saw Linda sitting in a chair, her arms folded on the table-edge, her head resting on her hands. She was asleep, and she did not raise her head till Stella shook her shoulder.

Linda Abbey had been a pretty girl, very fair, with apple-blossom skin and a wonderfully expressive face. It gave Stella a shock to see her now, to gage her suffering by the havoc it had wrought. Linda looked old, haggard, drawn. There was a weary droop to her mouth, her eyes were dull, lifeless, just as one might look who is utterly exhausted in mind and body. Oddly enough, she spoke first of something irrelevant, inconsequential.

"I fell asleep," she said heavily. "What time is it?"

Stella looked at her watch.

"Half-past four," she answered. "How is Charlie? What happened to him?"

"Monohan shot him."

Stella caught her breath. She hadn't been prepared for that.

"Is he—is he—" she could not utter the words.

"He'll get better. Wait." Linda rose stiffly from her seat. A door in one side of the room stood ajar. She opened it, and Stella, looking over her shoulder, saw her brother's tousled head on a pillow. A nurse in uniform sat beside his bed. Linda closed the door silently.

"Come into the kitchen where we won't make a noise," she whispered.

A fire burned in the kitchen stove. Linda sank into a willow rocker.

"I'm weary as Atlas," she said. "I've been fretting for so long. Then late yesterday afternoon they brought him home to me—like that. The doctor was probing for the bullet when I wired you. I was in a panic then, I think. Half-past four! How did you get here so soon? How could you? There's no train."

Stella told her.

"Why should Monohan shoot him?" she broke out. "For God's sake, talk, Linda!"

There was a curious impersonality in Linda's manner, as if she stood aloof from it all, as if the fire of her vitality had burned out. She lay back in her chair with eyelids drooping, speaking in dull, lifeless tones.

"Monohan shot him because Charlie came on him in the woods setting a fresh fire. They've suspected him, or some one in his pay, of that, and they've been watching. There were two other men with Charlie, so there is no mistake. Monohan got away. That's all I know. Oh, but I'm tired. I've been hanging on to myself for so long. About daylight, after we knew for sure that Charlie was over the hill, something seemed to let go in me. I'm awful glad you came, Stella. Can you make a cup of tea?"

Stella could and did, but she drank none of it herself. A dead weight of apprehension lay like lead in her breast. Her conscience pointed a deadly finger. First Billy Dale, now her brother, and, sandwiched in between, the loosed fire furies which were taking toll in bodily injury and ruinous loss.

Yet she was helpless. The matter was wholly out of her hands, and she stood aghast before it, much as the small child stands aghast before the burning house he has fired by accident.

Fyfe next. That was the ultimate, the culmination, which would leave her forever transfixed with remorseful horror. The fact that already the machinery of the law which would eventually bring Monohan to book for the double lawlessness of arson and attempted homicide must be in motion, that the Provincial police would be hard on his trail, did not occur to her. She could only visualize him progressing step by step from one lawless deed to another. And in her mind every step led to Jack Fyfe, who had made a mock of him. She found her hands clenching till the nails dug deep.

Linda's head drooped over the teacup. Her eyelids blinked.

"Dear," Stella said tenderly, "come and lie down. You're worn out."

"Perhaps I'd better," Linda muttered. "There's another room in there."

Stella tucked the weary girl into the bed, and went back to the kitchen, and sat down in the willow rocker. After another hour the nurse came out and prepared her own breakfast. Benton was still sleeping. He was in no danger, the nurse told Stella. The bullet had driven cleanly through his body, missing as by a miracle any vital part, and lodged in the muscles of his back, whence the surgeon had removed it. Though weak from shock, loss of blood, excitement, he had rallied splendidly, and fallen into a normal sleep.

Later the doctor confirmed this. He made light of the wound. One couldn't kill a young man as full of vitality as Charlie Benton with an axe, he informed Stella with an optimistic smile. Which lifted one burden from her mind.

The night nurse went away, and another from the hospital took her place. Benton slept; Linda slept. The house was very quiet. To Stella, brooding in that kitchen chair, it became oppressive, that funeral hush. When it was drawing near ten o'clock, she walked up the road past the corner store and post-office, and so out to the end of the wharf.

The air was hot and heavy, pungent, gray with the smoke. Farther along, St. Allwoods bulked mistily amid its grounds. The crescent of shore line half a mile distant was wholly obscured. Up over the eastern mountain range the sun, high above the murk, hung like a bloody orange, rayless and round. No hotel guests strolled by pairs and groups along the bank. She could understand that no one would come for pleasure into that suffocating atmosphere. Caught in that great bowl of which the lake formed the watery bottom, the smoke eddied and rolled like a cloud of mist.

She stood a while gazing at the glassy surface of the lake where it spread to her vision a little way beyond the piles. Then she went back to the green cottage.

Benton lifted alert, recognizing eyes when she peeped in the bedroom door.

"Hello, Sis," he greeted in strangely subdued tones. "When did you blow in? I thought you'd deserted the sinking ship completely. Come on in."

She winced inwardly at his words, but made no outward sign, as she came up to his bedside. The nurse went out.

"Perhaps you'd better not talk?" she said.

"Oh, nonsense," he retorted feebly. "I'm all right. Sore as the mischief and weak. But I don't feel as bad as I might. Linda still asleep?"

"I think so," Stella answered.

"Poor kid," he breathed; "it's been tough on her. Well, I guess it's been tough on everybody. He turned out to be some bad actor, this Monohan party. I never did like the beggar. He was a little too high-handed in his smooth, kid-glove way. But I didn't suppose he'd try to burn up a million dollars' worth of timber to satisfy a grudge. Well, he put his foot in it proper at last. He'll get a good long jolt in the pen, if the boys don't beat the constables to him and take him to pieces."

"He did start the fire then?" Stella muttered.

"I guess so," Benton replied. "At any rate, he kept it going. Did it by his lonesome, too. Jack suspected that. We were watching for him as well as fighting fire. He'd come down from the head of the lake in that speed boat of his, and this time daylight caught him before he could get back to where he had her cached, after starting a string of little fires in the edge of my north limit. He had it in for me, too, you know; I batted him over the head with a pike-pole here at the wharf one day this spring, so he plunked me as soon as I hollered at him. I wish he'd done it earlier in the game. We might have saved a lot of good timber. As it was, we couldn't do much. Every time the wind changed, it would break out in a new place—too often to be accidental. Damn him!"

"How is it going to end, the fire?" Stella forced herself to ask. "Will you and Jack be able to save any timber?"

"If it should rain hard, and if in the meantime the boys keep it from jumping the fire-trails we've cut, I'll get by with most of mine," he said. "But Jack's done for. He won't have anything but his donkeys and gear and part of a cedar limit on the Tyee which isn't paid for. He had practically everything tied up in that big block of timber around the Point. Monohan made him spend money like water to hold his own. Jack's broke."

Stella's head drooped. Benton reached out an axe-calloused hand, all grimy and browned from the stress of fire fighting, and covered her soft fingers that rested on his bed.

"It's a pity everything's gone to pot like that, Stell," he said softly. "I've grown a lot wiser in human ways the last two years. You taught me a lot, and Jack a lot, and Linda the rest. It seems a blamed shame you and Jack came to a fork in the road. Oh, he never chirped. I've just guessed it the last few weeks. I owe him a lot that he'll never let me pay back in anything but good will. I hate to see him get the worst of it from every direction. He grins and doesn't say anything. But I know it hurts. There can't be anything much wrong between you two. Why don't you forget your petty larceny troubles and start all over again?"

"I can't," she whispered. "It wouldn't work. There's too many scars. Too much that's hard to forget."

"Well, you know about that better than I do," Benton said thoughtfully. "It all depends on how you *feel*."

The poignant truth of that struck miserably home to her. It was not a matter of reason or logic, of her making any sacrifice for her conscience sake. It depended solely upon the existence of an emotion she could not definitely invoke. She was torn by so many emotions, not one of which she could be sure was the vital, the necessary one. Her heart did not cry out for Jack Fyfe, except in a pitying tenderness, as she used to feel for Jack Junior when he bumped and bruised himself. She had felt that before and held it too weak a crutch to lean upon.

The nurse came in with a cup of broth for Benton, and Stella went away with a dumb ache in her breast, a leaden sinking of her spirits, and went out to sit on the porch steps. The minutes piled into hours, and noon came, when Linda wakened. Stella forced herself to swallow a cup of tea, to eat food; then she left Linda sitting with her husband and went back to the porch steps again.

As she sat there, a man dressed in the blue shirt and mackinaw trousers and high, calked boots of the logger turned in off the road, a burly woodsman that she recognized as one of Jack Fyfe's crew.

"Well," said he, "if it ain't Mrs. Jack. Say—ah—"

He broke off suddenly, a perplexed look on his face, an uneasiness, a hesitation in his manner.

"What is it, Barlow?" Stella asked kindly. "How is everything up the lake?"

It was common enough in her experience, that temporary embarrassment of a logger before her. She knew them for men with boyish souls, boyish instincts, rude simplicities of heart. Long ago she had revised those first superficial estimates of them as gross, hulking brutes who worked hard and drank harder, coarsened and calloused by their occupation. They had their weaknesses, but their virtues of abiding loyalty, their reckless generosity, their simple directness, were great indeed. They took their lives in their hands on skid-road and spring-board, that such as she might flourish. They did not understand that, but she did.

"What is it, Barlow?" she repeated. "Have you just come down the lake?"

"Yes'm," he answered. "Say, Jack don't happen to be here, does he?"

"No, he hasn't been here," she told him.

The man's face fell.

"What's wrong?" Stella demanded. She had a swift divination that something was wrong.

"Oh, I dunno's anythin's wrong, particular," Barlow replied. "Only— well, Lefty he sent me down to see if Jack was at the Springs. We ain't seen him for a couple uh days."

Her pulse quickened.

"And he has not come down the lake?"

"I guess not," the logger said. "Oh, I guess it's all right. Jack's pretty *skookum* in the woods. Only Lefty got uneasy. It's desperate hot and smoky up there."

"How did you come down? Are you going back soon?" she asked abruptly.

"I got the *Waterbug*," Barlow told her. "I'm goin' right straight back."

Stella looked out over the smoky lake and back at the logger again, a sudden resolution born of intolerable uncertainty, of a feeling that she could only characterize as fear, sprang full-fledged into her mind. "Wait for me," she said. "I'm going with you."

CHAPTER XXIV
"OUT OF THE NIGHT THAT COVERS ME"

The *Waterbug* limped. Her engine misfired continuously, and Barlow lacked the mechanical knowledge to remedy its ailment. He was satisfied to let it pound away, so long as it would revolve at all. So the boat moved slowly through that encompassing smoke at less than half speed. Outwardly the once spick and span cruiser bore every mark of hard usage. Her topsides were foul, her decks splintered by the tramping of calked boots, grimy with soot and cinders. It seemed to Stella that everything and every one on and about Roaring Lake bore some mark of that holocaust raging in the timber, as if the fire were some malignant disease menacing and marring all that it affected, and affecting all that trafficked within its smoky radius.

But of the fire itself she could see nothing, even when late in the afternoon they drew in to the bay before her brother's camp. A heavier smoke cloud, more pungent of burning pitch, blanketed the shores, lifted in blue, rolling masses farther back. A greater heat made the air stifling, causing the eyes to smart and grow watery. That was the only difference.

Barlow laid the *Waterbug* alongside the float. He had already told her that Lefty Howe, with the greater part of Fyfe's crew, was extending and guarding Benton's fire-trail, and he half expected that Fyfe might have turned up there. Away back in the smoke arose spasmodic coughing of donkey engines, dull resounding of axe-blades. Barlow led the way. They traversed a few hundred yards of path through brush, broken tops, and stumps, coming at last into a fairway cut through virgin timber, a sixty-foot strip denuded of every growth, great firs felled and drawn far aside, brush piled and burned. A breastwork from which to fight advancing fire, it ran away into the heart of a smoky forest. Here and there blackened, fire-scorched patches abutted upon its northern flank, stumps of great trees smoldering, crackling yet. At the first such place, half a dozen men were busy with shovels blotting out streaks of fire that crept along in the dry leaf mold. No, they had not seen Fyfe. But they had been blamed busy. He might be up above.

Half a mile beyond that, beside the first donkey shuddering on its anchored skids as it tore an eighteen-inch cedar out by the roots, they came on Lefty Howe. He shook his head when Stella asked for Fyfe.

"He took twenty men around to the main camp day before yesterday," said Lefty. "There was a piece uh timber beyond that he thought he could save. I—well, I took a shoot around there yesterday, after your brother got hurt. Jack wasn't there. Most of the boys was at camp loadin' gear on the scows. They said Jack's gone around to Tumblin' Creek with one man. He wasn't back this mornin'. So I thought maybe he'd gone to the Springs. I dunno's there's any occasion to worry. He might 'a' gone to the head uh the lake with them constables that went up last night. How's Charlie Benton?"

She told him briefly.

"That's good," said Lefty. "Now, I'd go around to Cougar Bay, if I was you, Mrs. Jack. He's liable to come in there, any time. You could stay at the house to-night. Everything around there, shacks 'n' all, was burned days ago, so the fire can't touch the house. The crew there has grub an' a cook. I kinda expect Jack'll be there, unless he fell in with them constables."

She trudged silently back to the *Waterbug*. Barlow started the engine, and the boat took up her slow way. As they skirted the shore, Stella began to see here and there the fierce havoc of the fire. Black trunks of fir reared nakedly to the smoky sky, lay crisscross on bank and beach. Nowhere was there a green blade, a living bush. Nothing but charred black, a melancholy waste of smoking litter, with here and there a pitch-soaked stub still waving its banner of flame, or glowing redly. Back of those seared skeletons a shifting cloud of smoke obscured everything.

Presently they drew in to Cougar Bay. Men moved about on the beach; two bulky scows stood nose-on to the shore. Upon them rested half a dozen donkey engines, thick-bellied, upright machines, blown down, dead on their skids. About these in great coils lay piled the gear of logging, miles of steel cable, blocks, the varied tools of the logger's trade. The *Panther* lay between the scows, with lines from each passed over her towing bitts.

Stella could see the outline of the white bungalow on its grassy knoll. They had saved only that, of all the camp, by a fight that sent three men to the hospital, on a day when the wind shifted into the northwest and sent a sheet of flame rolling through the timber and down on Cougar Bay like a tidal wave. So Barlow told her. He cupped his hands now and called to his fellows on the beach.

No, Fyfe had not come back yet.

"Go up to the mouth of Tumbling Creek," Stella ordered.

Barlow swung the *Waterbug* about, cleared the point, and stood up along the shore. Stella sat on a cushioned seat at the back of the pilot house, hard-eyed, struggling against that dead weight that seemed, to grow and grow in her breast. That elemental fury raging in the woods made her shrink. Her own hand had helped to loose it, but her hands were powerless to stay it; she could only sit and watch and wait, eaten up with misery of her own making. She was horribly afraid, with a fear she would not name to herself.

Behind that density of atmosphere, the sun had gone to rest. The first shadows of dusk were closing in, betokened by a thickening of the smoke-fog into which the *Waterbug* slowly plowed. To port a dimming shore line; to starboard, aft, and dead ahead, water and air merged in two boat lengths. Barlow leaned through the pilot-house window, one hand on the wheel, straining his eyes on their course. Suddenly he threw out the clutch, shut down his throttle control with one hand, and yanked with the other at the cord which loosed the *Waterbug's* shrill whistle.

Dead ahead, almost upon them, came an answering toot.

"I thought I heard a gas-boat," Barlow exclaimed. "Sufferin' Jerusalem! Hi, there!"

He threw his weight on the wheel, sending it hard over. The cruiser still had way on; the momentum of her ten-ton weight scarcely had slackened, and she answered the helm. Out of the deceptive thickness ahead loomed the sharp, flaring bow of another forty-footer, sheering quickly, as her pilot sighted them. She was upon them, and abreast, and gone, with a watery purl of her bow wave, a subdued mutter of exhaust, passing so near than an active man could have leaped the space between.

"Sufferin' Jerusalem!" Barlow repeated, turning to Stella. "Did you see that, Mrs. Jack? They got him."

She, too, had seen Monohan seated on the after deck.
FRONTISPIECE.

Big Timber | 197

Stella nodded. She too had seen Monohan seated on the after deck, his head sunk on his breast, irons on his wrists. A glimpse, no more.

"That'll help some," Barlow grunted. "Quick work. But they come blame near cuttin' us down, beltin' along at ten knots when you can't see forty feet ahead."

An empty beach greeted them at Tumbling Creek. Reluctantly Stella bade Barlow turn back. It would soon be dark, and Barlow said he would be taking chances of piling on the shore before he could see it, or getting lost in the profound black that would shut down on the water with daylight's end.

Less than a mile from Cougar Bay, the *Waterbug's* engine gave a few premonitory gasps and died. Barlow descended to the engine room, hooked up the trouble lamp, and sought for the cause. He could not find it. Stella could hear him muttering profanity, turning the flywheel over, getting an occasional explosion.

An hour passed. Dark of the Pit descended, shrouding the lake with a sable curtain, close-folded, impenetrable. The dead stillness of the day vanished before a hot land breeze, and Stella, as she felt the launch drift, knew by her experience on the lake that they were moving offshore. Presently this was confirmed, for out of the black wall on the west, from which the night wind brought stifling puffs of smoke, there lifted a yellow effulgence that grew to a red glare as the boat drifted out. Soon that red glare was a glowing line that rose and fell, dipping and rising and wavering along a two-mile stretch, a fiery surf beating against the forest.

Down in the engine room Barlow finally located the trouble, and the motor took up its labors, spinning with a rhythmic chatter of valves. The man came up into the pilot house, wiping the sweat from his grimy face.

"Gee, I'm sorry, Mrs. Fyfe," he said. "A gas-engine man would 'a' fixed that in five minutes. Took me two hours to find out what was wrong. It'll be a heck of a job to fetch Cougar Bay now."

But by luck Barlow made his way back, blundering fairly into the landing at the foot of the path that led to the bungalow, as if the cruiser knew the way to her old berth. And as he reached the float, the front windows on the hillock broke out yellow, pale blurs in the smoky night.

"Well, say," Barlow pointed. "I bet a nickel Jack's home. See? Nobody but him would be in the house."

"I'll go up," Stella said.

"All right, I guess you know the path better'n I do," Barlow said. "I'll take the *Bug* around into the bay."

Stella ran up the path. She halted halfway up the steps and leaned against the rail to catch her breath. Then she went on. Her step was noiseless, for tucked in behind a cushion aboard the *Waterbug* she had found an old pair of her own shoes, rubber-soled, and she had put them on to ease the ache in her feet born of thirty-six hours' encasement in leather. She gained the door without a sound. It was wide open, and in the middle of the big room Jack Fyfe stood with hands thrust deep in his pockets, staring absently at the floor.

She took a step or two inside. Fyfe did not hear her; he did not look up.

"Jack."

He gave ever so slight a start, glanced up, stood with head thrown back a little. But he did not move, or answer, and Stella, looking at him, seeing the flame that glowed in his eyes, could not speak. Something seemed to choke her, something that was a strange compound of relief and bewilderment and a slow wonder at herself,—at the queer, unsteady pounding of her heart.

"How did you get way up here?" he asked at last.

"Linda wired last night that Charlie was hurt. I got a machine to the Springs. Then Barlow came down this afternoon looking for you. He said you'd been missing for two days. So I—I—"

She broke off. Fyfe was walking toward her with that peculiar, lightfooted step of his, a queer, tense look on his face.

"Nero fiddled when Rome was burning," he said harshly. "Did you come to sing while *my* Rome goes up in smoke?"

A little, half-strangled sob escaped her. She turned to go. But he caught her by the arm.

"There, lady," he said, with a swift change of tone, "I didn't mean to slash at you. I suppose you mean all right. But just now, with everything gone to the devil, to look up and see you here—I've really got an ugly temper, Stella, and it's pretty near the surface these days. I don't want to be pitied and sympathized with. I want to fight. I want to hurt somebody."

"Hurt me then," she cried.

He shook his head sadly.

"I couldn't do that," he said. "No, I can't imagine myself ever doing that."

"Why?" she asked, knowing why, but wishful to hear in words what his eyes shouted.

"Because I love you," he said. "You know well enough why."

She lifted her one free hand to his shoulder. Her face turned up to his. A warm wave of blood dyed the round, white neck, shot up into her cheeks. Her eyes were suddenly aglow, lips tremulous.

"Kiss me, then," she whispered. "That's what I came for. Kiss me, Jack."

If she had doubted, if she had ever in the last few hours looked with misgiving upon what she felt herself impelled to do, the pressure of Jack Fyfe's lips on hers left no room for anything but an amazing thrill of pure gladness. She was happy in his arms, content to rest there, to feel his heart beating against hers, to be quit of all the uncertainties, all the useless regrets. By a roundabout way she had come to her own, and it thrilled her to her finger tips. She could not quite comprehend it, or herself. But she was glad, weeping with gladness, straining her man to her, kissing his face, murmuring incoherent words against his breast.

"And so—and so, after all, you do care." Fyfe held her off a little from him, his sinewy fingers gripping gently the soft flesh of her arms. "And you were big enough to come back. Oh, my dear, you don't know what that means to me. I'm broke, and I'd just about reached the point where I didn't give a damn. This fire has cleaned me out. I've—"

"I know," Stella interrupted. "That's why I came back. I wouldn't have come otherwise, at least not for a long time—perhaps never. It seemed as if I ought to—as if it were the least I could do. Of course, it looks altogether different, now that I know I really want to. But you see I didn't know that for sure until I saw you standing here. Oh, Jack, there's such a lot I wish I could wipe out."

"It's wiped out," he said happily. "The slate's clean. Fair weather didn't get us anywhere. It took a storm. Well, the storm's over."

She stirred uneasily in his arms.

"Haven't you got the least bit of resentment, Jack, for all this trouble I've helped to bring about?" she faltered.

"Why, no" he said thoughtfully. "All you did was to touch the fireworks off. And they might have started over anything. Lord no! put that idea out of your head."

"I don't understand," she murmured. "I never have quite understood why Monohan should attack you with such savage bitterness. That trouble he started on the Tyee, then this criminal firing of the woods. I've had hints, first from your sister, then from Linda. I didn't know you'd clashed before. I'm not very clear on that yet. But you knew all the time what he was. Why didn't you tell me, Jack?"

"Well, maybe I should have," Fyfe admitted. "But I couldn't very well. Don't you see? He wasn't even an incident, until he bobbed up and rescued you that day. I couldn't, after that, start in picking his character to pieces as a mater of precaution. We had a sort of an armed truce. He left me strictly alone. I'd trimmed his claws once or twice already. I suppose he was acute enough to see an opportunity to get a whack at me through you. You were just living from day to day, creating a world of illusions for yourself, nourishing yourself with dreams, smarting under a stifled regret for a lot you thought you'd passed up for good. *He* wasn't a factor, at first. When he did finally stir in you an emotion I had failed to stir, it was too late for me to do or say anything. If I'd tried, at that stage of the game, to show you your idol's clay feet, you'd have despised me, as well as refused to believe. I couldn't do anything but stand back and trust the real woman of you to find out what a quicksand you were building your castle on. I purposely refused to let you to, when you wanted to go away the first time,—partly on the kid's account, partly because I could hardly bear to let you go. Mostly because I wanted to make him boil over and show his teeth, on the chance that you'd be able to size him up.

"You see, I knew him from the ground up. I knew that nothing would afford him a keener pleasure than to take away from me a woman I cared for, and that nothing would make him squirm more than for me to checkmate him. That day I cuffed him and choked him on the Point really started him properly. After that, you—as something to be desired and possessed— ran second to his feeling against me. He was bound to try and play even, regardless of you. When he precipitated that row on the Tyee, I knew it was going to be a fight for my financial life—for my own life, if he ever got me foul. And it was not a thing I could talk about to you, in your state of mind, then. You were through with me. Regardless of him, you were getting farther and farther away from me. I had a long time to realize that fully. You had a grudge against life, and it was sort of crystallizing on me. You never kissed me once in all those two years like you kissed me just now."

She pulled his head down and kissed him again.

"So that I wasn't restraining you with any hope for my own advantage," he went on. "There was the kid, and there was you. I wanted to put a brake on you, to make you go slow. You're a complex individual, Stella. Along with certain fixed, fundamental principles, you've got a streak of divine madness in you, a capacity for reckless undertakings. You'd never have married me if you hadn't. I trusted you absolutely. But, I was afraid in spite of my faith. You had draped such an idealistic mantle around Monohan. I wanted to rend that before it came to a final separation between us. It worked out, because he couldn't resist trying to take a crack at me when the notion seized him.

"So," he continued, after a pause, "you aren't responsible, and I've never considered you responsible for any of this. It's between him and me, and it's been shaping for years. Whenever our trails crossed there was bound to be a clash. There's always been a natural personal antagonism between us. It began to show when we were kids, you might say. Monohan's nature is such that he can't acknowledge defeat, he can't deny himself a gratification. He's a supreme egotist. He's always had plenty of money, he's always had whatever he wanted, and it never mattered to him how he gratified his desires.

"The first time we locked horns was in my last year at high school. Monohan was a star athlete. I beat him in a pole vault. That irked him so that he sulked and sneered, and generally made himself so insulting that I slapped him. We fought, and I whipped him. I had a temper that I hadn't learned to keep in hand those days, and I nearly killed him. I had nothing but contempt for him, anyway, because even then, when he wasn't quite twenty, he was a woman hunter, preying on silly girls. I don't know what his magic with women is, but it works, until they find him out. He was playing off two or three fool girls that I knew and at the same time keeping a woman in apartments down-town,—a girl he'd picked up on a trip to Georgia,—like any confirmed rounder.

"Well, from that time on, he hated me, always laid for a chance to sting me. We went to Princeton the same year. We collided there, so hard that when word of it got to my father's ears, he called me home and read the riot act so strong that I flared up and left. Then I came to the coast here and got a job in the woods, got to be a logging boss, and went into business on my own hook eventually. I'd just got nicely started when I ran into Monohan again. He'd got into timber himself. I was hand logging up the coast, and I'd hate to tell you the tricks he tried. He kept it up until I got too big to be harassed in a petty way. Then he left me alone. But he never forgot his grudge. The stage was all set for this act long before you gave him his cue, Stella. You weren't to blame for that, or if you were in part, it doesn't matter now. I'm satisfied. Paradoxically I feel rich, even though it's a long shot that I'm broke flat. I've got something money doesn't buy. And he has overreached himself at last. All his money and pull won't help him out of this jack pot. Arson and attempted murder is serious business."

"They caught him," Stella said. "The constables took him down the lake to-night. I saw him on their launch as they passed the *Waterbug*."

"Yes?" Fyfe said. "Quick work. I didn't even know about the shooting till I came in here to-night about dark. Well," he snapped his fingers, "exit Monohan. He's a dead issue, far as we're concerned. Wouldn't you like something to eat, Stella? I'm hungry, and I was dog-tired when I landed here. Say, you can't guess what I was thinking about, lady, standing there when you came in."

She shook her head.

"I had a crazy notion of touching a match to the house," he said soberly, "letting it go up in smoke with the rest. Yes, that's what I was thinking I would do. Then I'd take the *Panther* and what gear I have on the scows and pull off Roaring Lake. It didn't seem as if I could stay. I'd laid the foundation of a fortune here and tried to make a home—and lost it all, everything that was worth having. And then all at once there you were, like a vision in the door. Miracles *do* happen!"

Her arms tightened involuntarily about him.

"Oh," she cried breathlessly. "Our little, white house!"

"Without you," he replied softly, "it was just an empty shell of boards and plaster, something to make me ache with loneliness."

"But not now," she murmured. "It's home, now."

"Yes," he agreed, smiling.

"Ah, but it isn't quite." She choked down a lump in her throat. "Not when I think of those little feet that used to patter on the floor. Oh, Jack— when I think of my baby boy! My dear, my dear, why did all this have to be, I wonder?"

Fyfe stroked her glossy coils of hair.

"We get nothing of value without a price," he said quietly. "Except by rare accident, nothing that's worth having comes cheap and easy. We've paid the price, and we're square with the world and with each other. That's everything."

"Are you completely ruined, Jack?" she asked after an interval. "Charlie said you were."

"Well," he answered reflectively, "I haven't had time to balance accounts, but I guess I will be. The timber's gone. I've saved most of the logging gear. But if I realized on everything that's left, and squared up everything, I guess I'd be pretty near strapped."

"Will you take me in as a business partner, Jack?" she asked eagerly. "That's what I had in mind when I came up here. I made up my mind to propose that, after I'd heard you were ruined. Oh, it seems silly now, but I wanted to make amends that way; at least, I tried to tell myself that. Listen. When my father died, he left some supposedly worthless oil stock. But it proved to have a market value. I got my share of it the other day. It'll help us to make a fresh start—together."

She had the envelope and the check tucked inside her waist. She took it out now and pressed the green slip into his hand.

Fyfe looked at it and at her, a little chuckle deep in his throat.

"Nineteen thousand, five hundred," he laughed. "Well, that's quite a stake for you. But if you go partners with me, what about your singing?"

"I don't see how I can have my cake and eat it, too," she said lightly. "I don't feel quite so eager for a career as I did."

"Well, we'll see," he said. "That light of yours shouldn't be hidden under a bushel. And still, I don't like the idea of you being away from me, which a career implies."

He put the check back in the envelope, smiling oddly to himself, and tucked it back in her bosom. She caught and pressed his hand there, against the soft flesh.

"Won't you use it, Jack?" she pleaded. "Won't it help? Don't let any silly pride influence you. There mustn't ever be anything like that between us again."

"There won't be," he smiled. "Frankly, if I need it, I'll use it. But that's a matter there's plenty of time to decide. You see, although technically I may be broke, I'm a long way from the end of my tether. I think I'll have my working outfit clear, and the country's full of timber. I've got a standing in the business that neither fire nor anything else can destroy. No, I haven't any false pride about the money, dear. But the money part of our future is a detail. With the incentive I've got now to work and plan, it won't take me five years to be a bigger toad in the timber puddle than I ever was. You don't know what a dynamo I am when I get going."

"I don't doubt that," she said proudly. "But the money's yours, if you need it."

"I need something else a good deal more right now," he laughed. "That's something to eat. Aren't you hungry, Stella? Wouldn't you like a cup of coffee?"

"I'm famished," she admitted—the literal truth. The vaulting uplift of spirit, that glad little song that kept lilting in her heart, filled her with peace and contentment, but physically she was beginning to experience acute hunger. She recalled that she had eaten scarcely anything that day.

"We'll go down to the camp," Fyfe suggested. "The cook will have something left. We're camping like pioneers down there. The shacks were all burned, and somebody sank the cookhouse scow."

They went down the path to the bay, hand in hand, feeling their way through that fire-blackened area, under a black sky.

A red eye glowed ahead of them, a fire on the beach around which men squatted on their haunches or lay stretched on their blankets, sooty-faced fire fighters, a weary group. The air was rank with smoke wafted from the burning woods.

The cook's fire was dead, and that worthy was humped on his bed-roll smoking a pipe. But he had cold meat and bread, and he brewed a pot of coffee on the big fire for them, and Stella ate the plain fare, sitting in the circle of tired loggers.

"Poor fellows, they look worn out," she said, when they were again traversing that black road to the bungalow.

"We've slept standing up for three weeks," Fyfe said simply. "They've done everything they could. And we're not through yet. A north wind might set Charlie's timber afire in a dozen places."

"Oh, for a rain," she sighed.

"If wishing for rain brought it," he laughed, "we'd have had a second flood. We've got to keep pegging away till it does rain, that's all. We can't do much, but we have to keep doing it. You'll have to go back to the Springs to-morrow, I'm afraid, Stella. I'll have to stay on the firing line, literally."

"I don't want to," she cried rebelliously. "I want to stay up here with you. I'm not wax. I won't melt."

She continued that argument into the house, until Fyfe laughingly smothered her speech with kisses.

An oddly familiar sound murmuring in Stella's ear wakened her. At first she thought she must be dreaming. It was still inky dark, but the air that blew in at the open window was sweet and cool, filtered of that choking smoke. She lifted herself warily, looked out, reached a hand through the lifted sash. Wet drops spattered it. The sound she heard was the drip of eaves, the beat of rain on the charred timber, upon the dried grass of the lawn.

Beside her Fyfe was a dim bulk, sleeping the dead slumber of utter weariness. She hesitated a minute, then shook him.

"Listen, Jack," she said.

He lifted his head.

"Rain!" he whispered. "Good night, Mister Fire. Hooray!"

"I brought it," Stella murmured sleepily. "I wished it on Roaring Lake to-night."

Then she slipped her arm about his neck, and drew his face down to her breast with a tender fierceness, and closed her eyes with a contented sigh.